If you want to know where your heart is,
look where your mind goes when it wanders.

-Unknown

CHAPTER
1

Reese

What a waste of smooth, shaven legs.

"Jules? It's Reese. Where the hell are you? I *need* you. This is the *worst* date I've ever been on. I'm literally falling asleep. I've considered smashing my head on the table a few times to keep awake. Unless you want me bloodied and bruised, I need you to call with a fake emergency. Call me back. *Please*." Pressing end call, I blew out a frustrated breath as I stood outside the ladies' room in the dark hallway at the back of the restaurant.

A deep voice from behind me caught me off guard. "Unless he's also an idiot—in addition to being boring—he's going to know."

"Excuse me?" I turned to find a man leaning against the wall, his eyes pointed down as he texted away on his phone. He continued without looking up.

"It's the oldest trick in the book...the emergency phone call. The least you can do is put in a little more effort. It takes two months to get a reservation at this place, and it's not cheap, sweetheart."

"Maybe *he* should be the one to put in more effort. His

sports jacket has a giant hole under the arm, and he's done nothing but talk about his mother all night."

"Ever consider that your snobby attitude makes him nervous?"

My eyes nearly bulged out of my head. "You want to talk about snobby? You eavesdrop on my call and give me your *unwelcome* opinions, all while staring down at your phone. You haven't even made eye contact with me while you're speaking."

The jerk's fingers froze mid text. Then I watched as his head rose, eyes following a leisurely path starting at my ankles, up over my bare legs, and lingering at the hemline of my skirt before continuing to trace their way over my hips, coming to rest briefly on my breasts before finally settling on my face.

"Yes, that's right. Up here. These are my eyes."

He pushed off the wall and stood tall, catching the lone ray that had been lighting the hallway. The streak illuminated his face, and I could see him clearly for the first time.

Really? Not what I was expecting. With that deep, raspy voice and attitude, I assumed I'd find someone older, probably dressed in a stuffy suit. But this guy was gorgeous. *Young and gorgeous.* Dressed entirely in black—simple and sleek, yet there was an edge to the way he looked. Golden brown hair tousled in that sexy *I don't give a shit* way, but still looked perfect. Strong, masculine features—a square, rugged jaw coated with day-old stubble on sunkissed skin, a straight, prominent nose, and big, sexy, sleepy eyes the color of chocolate. Those were now staring intently at me.

Without dropping my gaze, he lifted his arms from his sides, holding them up over his head. "You want to check me for rips before you decide if I'm worthy of speaking to?"

He was gorgeous all right, but definitely an asshole. "That's not necessary. Your attitude has already decided that for me, and you're not."

Lowering his arms, he chuckled. "Suit yourself. Try to enjoy the rest of your evening, sweetheart."

I huffed, but stole one last fleeting look at the beautiful jerk before I walked back to my date.

Martin was sitting with his hands folded when I returned to my seat at the table.

"Sorry," I told him. "There was a line."

"That reminds me of a funny story. This one time, I was at a restaurant with my mother, and when she went to use the ladies' room..."

His voice faded away while I stared at my phone, willing it to ring. *Damn you, Jules. Where are you when I really need you?* Around the middle of the story—at least I think it was the middle—I noticed the jerk from the bathroom walking past our table. He smirked at me after taking a look at my rambling date and my disinterested face. Curious, I followed his path to get a look at who he was here with.

Figures.

Dyed blonde, pretty in a slutty sort of way, with a heaping amount of boobage falling out of her low-cut dress. She made googly eyes at her date as he returned; I rolled mine. Yet...I couldn't help but glance over at their table from time to time.

When our salads arrived, Martin was talking about his mother's recent appendectomy, and I grew particularly bored. My eyes must have lingered a minute too long, because the guy from the bathroom caught me staring at him. Across the restaurant, he winked, arched an eyebrow, and tipped his glass in my direction.

Jerk.

Since I'd been caught, why bother to hide my watching him? He was certainly more interesting than my date. And he wasn't shy about looking my way either. When a waiter stopped by his table, I watched as beautiful bathroom guy pointed in my direction and spoke. Martin was still telling some mommy-dearest story as I glanced behind me to see what the attractive jerk across the room could've been pointing to. When I turned back, the jerk and his date were standing. Reading his lips, I could make out some of what he was saying...something about joining an old friend, I thought. Then suddenly, they were walking right toward our table.

Is he going to say something to Martin about what he overheard?

"Reese. Is that you?"

What in the hell?

"Umm...yes."

"Wow. It's been a long time." He patted his hand on his chest. "It's me, Chase." Before I knew what was happening, the jerk (who was apparently named Chase) reached down and gripped me in a bear hug. While I was in his arms, he whispered, "Play along. Let's make your night more exciting, sweetheart."

Dumbfounded, I could only stare as he turned his attention to Martin, extending his hand.

"I'm Chase Parker. Reese and I go way back."

"Martin Ward." My date nodded.

"Martin, mind if we join you? It's been years since Buttercup and I have seen each other. I'd love to catch up. You don't mind, do you?"

Although he'd asked a question, Chase definitely didn't wait for a response. Instead, he pulled out a chair for his date and introduced her.

"This is Bridget..." He looked to her for help, and she filled in the blank.

"McDermott. Bridget McDermott." She smiled, undaunted by our new double date or Chase's obvious inability to remember her last name.

Martin, on the other hand, looked disappointed that our twosome was now a foursome, although I was certain he would never voice it.

He looked to Chase as he sat. "Buttercup?"

"That's what we used to call her. Reese's Peanut *Butter Cup*. My favorite candy."

Once Chase and Bridget were seated, there was a moment of awkwardness. Surprisingly, it was Martin who broke it. "So, how do you two know each other?"

Even though Martin asked the question looking at both of us, I wanted to make it clear to Chase that *he* was the one on the hot seat. This was his little game.

"I'll let Chase tell you about the first time we met. It's really a funny story, actually." I propped my elbows on the table and rested my head on my folded hands, turning my full attention to Chase while batting my eyelashes with a sly grin.

He didn't flinch, nor did he take more than a few seconds to come up with a story. "Well, it wasn't really the first time we met that's the funny story—more like what happened after we met. My parents split up when I was in eighth grade, and I had to transfer to a new school. I was pretty miserable until I met Reese here on the bus the first week. She was the off-limits pretty girl, but I figured I had no friends to bust my balls if I asked her on a date and she turned me down. So, even though she's a year older than me, I asked her to the eighth-grade dance. Surprised the shit out of me when she agreed to go.

"Anyway, I was young, with a healthy dose of testosterone, and I got it into my head that she was going to be my first kiss. All of my buddies back at my old school had already gotten theirs, and I figured it was my time. So, when the dance was coming to an end, I tugged Buttercup out of the crappy crepe-paper-and-balloon-decorated gymnasium and into the hall for some privacy. Of course, since it was my first time, I had no idea what to expect. But I went for it—got right in there and started to suck her face."

Chase paused and winked at me. "It was all good up until then, wasn't it, Buttercup?"

I couldn't even respond. I was so floored listening to his story. But again, my lack of response didn't seem to bother him because he went right along, weaving his tall tale.

"Anyway, this is where the story gets good. Like I said, I didn't have any experience, but I dove right in—lips, teeth, tongue, and all. After a minute, the kiss started to feel awfully wet, but I was into it, so I kept going and going, not wanting to be the first one to pull away. Eventually, when we came up for air—literally since I'd almost sucked her face off—I realized why it had felt so wet. Reese had gotten a nosebleed in the middle of the kiss, and both of our faces were covered in smeared blood."

Martin and Bridget laughed, but I was too stunned to react.

Chase reached out and touched my arm. "Come on, Buttercup. Don't get embarrassed. Those were some good times we had. Remember?"

"How long were you two a couple?" Martin asked.

Just as Chase was about to respond, I reached over and touched his arm in the same patronizing way he'd touched mine. "Not too long. Right after *the other incident,* we broke up."

Bridget clapped her hands and bopped up and down in her seat like an excited child. "I wanna hear about the other incident!"

"I'm not sure I should actually share it, now that I think about it," I mused. "Is this your first date?"

Bridget nodded.

"Well, I don't want you to assume Chase has the same problem anymore. Since our *little incident* was so long ago." I leaned over to Bridget and whispered, "They gain better control as they grow older. *Usually.*"

Instead of being upset, Chase looked thoroughly pleased with my story. Proud, even. In fact, the rest of the evening went on pretty much the same way. Chase told elaborate stories about our fake childhood, unafraid to embarrass himself in the process, and kept us all amused. I sometimes added to his stories when my mouth wasn't hanging open at the crap he'd made up.

I hated to admit it, but the jerk had started to grow on me, even while telling stories about my bloody nose and the "unfortunate bra-stuffing incident." By the end of the evening, I was ordering coffee to stall the night's end—a far cry from our exchange in the bathroom hallway.

Outside of the restaurant, Martin, Chase, and I all handed the valet our tickets. I preferred to be in control of when a first date started and ended, so I'd met Martin at the restaurant. Of course Bridget had come in Chase's car like a normal date. She was also practically rubbing up against his side as she clung to his arm while we waited for our cars. When my shiny red Audi pulled up first, I wasn't sure how to say goodbye to...well...anyone. I took the keys and lingered with the door open.

"Nice car, Buttercup." Chase smiled. "Better than that hunk of junk you drove in high school, huh?"

I chuckled. "I suppose it is."

Martin stepped forward. "It was nice seeing you, Reese. I hope we can do this again sometime."

Rather than wait for him to attempt to kiss me, I went in for a hug. "Thank you for a nice dinner, Martin."

As I stepped back, Chase stepped forward and pulled me into a hug. Unlike the friendly back-pat I'd given Martin, Chase plastered me against his body. God, it felt good. Then he did the strangest thing... He wound my long hair around his hand a few times and closed it into a fist, using it to tug my head back. His eyes lingered on my lips as I looked up at him, and for a brief second, I thought he might kiss me.

Then he leaned down and kissed my forehead. "See you at the reunion next year?"

I nodded, feeling almost off-kilter. "Umm...sure thing." I glanced to Bridget after he released me. "Nice to meet you, Bridget."

Reluctantly, I folded into my car. Feeling eyes on me, I looked up while putting my seat belt on. Chase watched me intently. It looked like he wanted to say something, but after a few heartbeats, it felt strange to sit and wait any longer.

Taking a deep breath, I pulled away with one last wave, wondering why it felt like I was leaving something important behind.

CHAPTER
2

Reese – Four weeks later

One hundred and thirty-eight, one hundred and thirty-nine, one hundred and forty. The last ceiling tile—the one all the way in the corner of my bedroom closest to the window—had cracked. *That's new.* I needed to call the super and get that replaced before it screwed up my daily count and started to cause me stress instead of helping alleviate it.

I was still lying on my bedroom floor after hanging up with Bryant, a guy I'd met at the supermarket last week (instead of the usual bar pick-up, which never seemed to pan out that great). He'd called to tell me he was stuck at work and going to be an hour late for our second date, which was fine with me because I was tired and had no desire to get up anyway. Taking a deep, cleansing breath, I shut my eyes and focused on the sound of my own breathing. In and out, in and out. Eventually finding my calm, I hauled myself up off the carpet, freshened up my makeup, and poured a glass of wine before grabbing my laptop.

I browsed the New York marketing job posts on Monster. com for the sum total of five minutes before growing bored, and then I went on Facebook. As usual. *Because job hunting sucks.* Scrolling through my friends' posts, I saw the same old things—pictures of food, their kids, the lives they wanted us to believe they had. I sighed. A picture of a guy I went to middle school with cradling his newborn son popped up in my feed, and my mind immediately went to the man I *hadn't* gone to middle school with, *Chase Parker*.

I'd thought about my fake classmate more often than I cared to admit over the last month. Odd little things made him pop into my mind—Reese's Peanut Butter Cups on the impulse-buy shelf at the grocery store checkout (I bought them), a picture of Josh Duhamel as I thumbed through *People* magazine in the waiting room at my dentist (Chase could easily pass for his brother—I *might* have torn out the page), my vibrator in my nightstand drawer (I didn't, but I thought about it. I mean, I did have that page and all).

This time when the man leaped into my thoughts, before I knew it, I was typing *Chase Parker* into the Facebook search bar. My gasp was audible when his face popped up. The flutter I felt in my chest was pathetic. *God, he's even more gorgeous than I remembered.* I clicked to enlarge the photo. He was dressed casually, wearing a white T-shirt, jeans with a rip at the knee, and black Chucks. It was a good look for him. After spending a full minute appreciating his sexy face, I zoomed in and noticed the emblem on his T-shirt: *Iron Horse Gym*. There was one on the same block as the restaurant where we'd met. I wondered if he lived nearby.

Unfortunately, I wouldn't find out. None of his bio was set to public. In fact, the only picture I could see was that one profile picture. I'd need to send him a friend request and have him accept if I wanted to see more. Although tempted, I decided against it. He would probably think I was nuts sending a friend request to a guy who thought I was a bitch (and told me as much), who I'd met while we were both on dates with other people, and after a full month had passed.

But that didn't stop me from screenshotting his photo so I could look at it again later. After several more minutes of daydreaming about the man, I gave myself an adult pep talk. *You need to find a job. You need to find a job. You have only one week of work left after this one. Get your ass off of Facebook.*

It worked, and for the next fifty minutes I scoured the help wanted ads for something—anything—that sounded remotely cosmetics-marketing related, or even just remotely interesting. I knew I shouldn't bank on just the two interviews I had scheduled so far, but there wasn't much out there. By the time my doorbell buzzed, I felt deflated about ever finding a job to replace the one I'd held for the last seven years and, until recently, loved.

Bryant's kiss when I opened the door definitely went a long way toward changing my mood. It was only our second date, but he certainly had potential.

"Well, that was a nice hello," I breathed.

"I've been thinking about doing that all day."

I smiled up at him. "Come on in. I'm almost ready. I just need to grab my bag and get my phone from the charger."

He pointed to the front door after closing it behind him. "Did you have a break-in or something? What's with all the extra locks?"

My front door had a regular lock and three deadbolts. Normally, I would answer honestly and explain that I felt safer with an extra lock or two and leave it at that. But Bryant wasn't most dates. He was really trying to get to know me, and if he pried further—as I worried he might—I'd be forced to open up about some things I wasn't ready to yet.

So I lied. "The building manager is big on security."

He nodded. "Well, that's good."

As I was clasping on a necklace in my bedroom, I yelled out to Bryant, "There's wine in the fridge, if you want."

"I'm fine, thanks."

When I came out from the bedroom, he was sitting on the couch. My laptop was still open next to him from my job search.

I spoke as I fastened my earrings. "So what are we going to see?"

"I figured we could decide when we get there. There's a Vin Diesel flick I want to see. But since I'm an hour late, I won't argue if you aren't a fan."

I smiled. "Good, because I'm not. I was thinking more along the lines of that new Nicholas Sparks movie."

"Pretty steep punishment for being late. It was only an hour, not three days," he teased.

"That'll teach you."

Bryant stood as I walked over to shut my laptop. "By the way, who's the guy in your background?"

My brow furrowed. "What guy?"

He shrugged. "Tall. Messy hair that would like stupid on me. I'm hoping it isn't an ex-boyfriend you're secretly hung up on. Looks like he belongs on an Abercrombie bag."

Not having a clue what he was talking about, I opened my laptop back up to take a look. *Shit.* Chase Parker greeted me. When I'd saved his picture from Facebook, I must have inadvertently also set it as my screen background. Seeing that gorgeous face again, I grew flustered. Yet Bryant was waiting for an answer.

"Umm... That's my cousin."

It was the first thing that popped into my head. After I said it, I realized it was a little bizarre to have a picture of your male cousin set as your background. So I attempted to fix it with more lies—something out of character for me.

"He's a model. My aunt sent me some of his recent headshots and asked for an opinion on which I liked best, so I downloaded them to my laptop. My friend Jules was drooling over them and set one as my background. I'm so low-tech, I don't even know how to change it."

Bryant chuckled and seemed to accept what I'd said.

What is it with Chase Parker and made-up stories?

On Thursday, I had an interview in the morning and a second scheduled for the afternoon. The subway was jam-packed, and the air conditioning wasn't working. So, of course, that also meant the only train running was a local, not an express.

Beads of sweat trickled down my back as I stood sandwiched between other sweating commuters. The large guy to my right wore a T-shirt with cut-off sleeves and held on to the pole above him. My face was perfectly aligned with his hairy armpit, and his deodorant wasn't working. My left side wasn't exactly all sunshine and roses either. While I was pretty sure the woman didn't smell as bad, she was sneezing and coughing without covering her mouth. *I need to get off this train.*

Fortunately, I arrived at my interview a few minutes early and could make a quick stop in the ladies' room to fix myself up. The sweat and humidity had smeared my makeup, and my hair was a frizzy mess. *July in New York City*. It seemed like the heat got stuck between all the tall buildings.

Digging into my pocketbook, I fished out some hairpins and a brush and was able to pull my auburn locks back into a neat twist. The makeup would have to do with only a baby wipe as cleanup since I hadn't thought to bring any eyeliner.

I took off my suit jacket and realized I'd sweated through my silk shirt. *Shit*. I'd have to keep the hot jacket on for the entire interview.

A woman walked in while I was arm-deep inside my shirt with a damp paper towel, wiping sweat from my body. She caught what I was doing in the mirror.

"Sorry. It was so hot on the subway, and I have an interview," I offered as explanation. "I don't want to be a sweaty, smelly mess."

She smiled. "Been there. Gotta break down and take a cab in July when it's this humid and you have an interview for a job you really want."

"Yeah. I'm definitely going to do that for my afternoon interview. It's across town, and that's the job I really want, so I might go all out—even stop in at Duane Reade for some deodorant, too."

After I rushed to clean myself up, my morning appointment left me sitting in the lobby for over an hour before calling me in for the interview. It gave me some time to fully cool down and also check out their latest product catalogs. They were definitely in need of a new marketing campaign. I jotted down some notes on what I would change, in case the opportunity presented itself.

"Ms. Annesley?" a smiling woman called from the door leading to the inner office. I slipped on my suit jacket and followed her inside. "Sorry to keep you waiting. We had a small emergency this morning with one of our biggest vendors, and it had to be dealt with right away." She stepped aside as we arrived at a large corner office. "Have a seat. Ms. Donnelly will be right in."

"Oh. Okay. Thank you." I had thought she was my interviewer.

A few minutes later the vice president of Flora Cosmetics walked in. It was the woman from the hallway bathroom—the one who'd seen me washing my armpits. *Great.*

I was glad I'd at least done it without unbuttoning my shirt. I tried to recall what we'd spoken about, other than the weather. I didn't think there was much.

"I see you've cooled off." Her tone was very business-like, not at all friendly like it had been in the bathroom.

"Yes. Sorry about that. The heat really hit me hard today."

She shuffled some papers on her desk into a pile and fired off her first question without any further small talk. "So, Ms. Annesley, why are you in search of a new job? It says here you're currently employed."

"I am. I've been with Fresh Look Cosmetics for seven years. I started there right out of college, actually. I worked my way up from marketing intern to director of marketing during that time. I'll be honest, I've been happy there for my entire career. But I feel like I've hit a ceiling at Fresh Look, and it's time I started to look for other opportunities."

"A ceiling? How so?"

"Well, Fresh Look is still a family-owned company, and although I admire and respect Scott Eikman, the founder and president, most of the executive-level positions are taken by members of the Eikman family—one of whom, Derek Eikman, was just promoted over me to vice president." Saying it out loud still left a bitter taste in my mouth.

"So, people less deserving than you are promoted because of kinship? And that's why you're leaving?"

"I suppose that's a big part of it, yes. But it's also just time for me to move on."

"Isn't it possible that members of the Eikman family know the business better, having grown up in that world? Perhaps they are actually more qualified than other employees?"

What's the bug up this woman's ass? None of this nepotism is new. Hell, half of the Walmart execs are still blood-related to Sam Walton, and he's been gone for two decades.

It was definitely not the time to add that I'd had too much to drink at last year's company holiday party and slept with the then-director of sales, *Derek Eikman*. It was a one-time thing, a drunken mistake with a co-worker after a year-long dry spell. I'd known it was a mistake ten minutes after it was over. I just didn't how big of a mistake until two days later, when the asshole announced his engagement to his girlfriend of seven years. He'd told me he was single and unattached. When I'd marched into his office and told him off, he'd explained that we could still *fuck* even though he was engaged.

The man was a sleazebag, and there was no way I could work for him now that he'd been promoted to vice president. Aside from being a cheating pig, he also knew *nothing* about marketing.

"In my case, I'm relatively confident that I was the better candidate."

She gave me a completely fake smile and folded her hands on her desk. *Did I say something to upset her in the bathroom earlier?* I didn't think so... But her next question certainly jogged my memory.

"So tell me, what is it about your afternoon interview that makes the company seem superior? I mean, as a marketing expert, they must be doing something right to make you consider *paying for a cab*?"

Oh. *Shit.* I'd completely forgotten that I'd told her I was going to take a cab to my next interview—since that was the job I *really* wanted.

There was no digging myself out of the hole I was in after that. Even though, in spite of things, I thought I handled myself professionally, I could tell her mind was made up about me.

Just as the interview was coming to an end, an older gentleman popped his head into her office. "Sweetheart, are you coming for dinner tomorrow night? Your mother has been bugging me to get you to commit."

"Dad, umm...Daniel, I'm in the middle of an interview. Can we talk about it later?"

"Sure, sure. Sorry. Stop by my office later." He smiled politely at me and knocked on the door jamb as his goodbye before walking away.

My mouth hung open as I turned back to my interviewer. I already knew the answer, but asked anyway. "Daniel... Donnelly, the president of Flora Cosmetics, is your father?"

"Yes. And I'd like to think I *earned* the SVP of marketing job because of my qualifications, not because I'm his daughter."

Yeah, right. Since I'd inserted my foot into my mouth *twice* today, I saw no point in prolonging the pain.

I stood. "Thank you for your time, Ms. Donnelly."

My afternoon only got better after that. I'd just stepped out of my air-conditioned cab in front of the building where my two o'clock interview was scheduled when my phone started buzzing. The company I'd been excited about interviewing with—the company I'd essentially ruined my first interview over—was calling to cancel my interview and let me know the position had been filled already.

Great. Just great.

Shortly after that, I received a kiss-off email from Flora, thanking me for taking the time to interview but letting me know they were going a different direction in their hiring. *And it isn't even two o'clock yet.*

After a quick shower, my plan was to attempt to wait until closer to five o'clock and then get shitfaced. *Big plans.* I'd wasted a day off during my last weeks of work for this crap. Might as well enjoy myself.

I was lying on my bedroom floor in the middle of my counting routine when my cell rang. Reaching up to the bed, I patted the mattress until my hand landed on my phone. Seeing Bryant's name flash on the screen, I almost didn't answer because of my mood, but then decided to pick it up on the last ring.

"Hey. How did your interviews go?" he asked.

"I stopped on the way home and picked up two extra bottles of wine. Take a guess."

"Not good, huh?"

"You could say that."

"Well, you know what we should do about that?"

"Definitely. Get drunk."

He laughed as if I was joking. "I was thinking more along the lines of working out."

"Exercising?"

"Yeah. It helps to get stress out."

"So does wine."

"Yes, but with exercise, you feel great the day after."

"But with wine, I don't remember the day before."

He laughed. (Again, I wasn't joking.) "If you change your mind, I'm on my way to Iron Horse Gym."

"Iron Horse?"

"It's on 72nd. I'm a member there. I have guest passes you can use."

It had been more than a month since my bizarre encounter with Chase Parker, yet suddenly I found myself rethinking alcohol vs. exercise because the man wore an Iron Horse Gym T-shirt in his Facebook photo.

"You know what? You're right. I should exercise to help me relax. After all, I can get shitfaced later if it doesn't work."

"Now you're talking."

"I'll meet you there. How does an hour sound?"

"See you then."

I seriously should've had my head examined. I blowdried my hair and put on my sexiest exercise gear to go work out with a great guy I'd recently started dating, yet none of my efforts were really for him. Instead, I had far-fetched hopes of seeing a guy who owned a T-shirt with the gym name on it—a guy who thought I was a bitch and dated statuesque blondes with excessive cleavage, not five-foot-one, B-cup women with hips, even if I did have a tiny waist.

Forty minutes on the elliptical, and I was totally regretting my drinking-vs.-exercise choice. Bryant was lifting weights on the other side of the gym, and I should have been happy that a nice guy had invited me to come work out. Instead, I was out of breath, disappointed, and thirsty. *Glad I chilled two bottles of wine.*

When he was done, Bryant came over and asked if I wanted to go for a swim. I hadn't brought a suit, but I told him I'd keep him company in the pool area. While he went to change and rinse off, I walked on the treadmill to cool down. The slow speed allowed me to catch up on a backlog of emails on my phone. One of them was from a recruiting firm indicating that they'd found me the perfect job overseas—in the Middle East—and asking if I was interested in doing a video conference with the company. I thought the email was funny because there were so many misspelled words and grammar errors.

After Bryant changed, we walked to the pool area together. I read him the email as he opened the door. "It actually says in the qualification requirements, 'Must be sober, sane, and not overly dramatic'. Think they have a PMS problem in Yemen?" Looking down at my phone as I walked, I crashed straight into someone.

"Sorry, I wasn't looking where—"

I froze.

The sight of Chase standing there was almost enough to knock me over. I'd secretly hoped to see him, yet never thought I actually would. *What are the chances?* I did a double take, sure I was seeing things. But it was him all right, in the flesh. *And what flesh it is.* Standing there shirtless and wet—wearing nothing but a pair of low-slung swim trunks— he had me stuttering. *Literally.*

"Ch...Ch...Ch—" I couldn't get the word out.

Of course, Chase didn't miss a beat. He smirked and leaned in. "You do a cute train impression, Buttercup."

He remembers me.

I shook my head, attempting to snap myself out of it. But it was no use. He was so tall, and I was so short, I had no choice but to stare at his body. Water trickled down his abs. I was mesmerized watching it speed up and slow down as it crossed the rippled lines of his six-pack. *Damn.*

I cleared my throat and finally spoke. "Chase."

I was pretty freaking proud of myself for getting that much out. He had a towel slung around his neck and lifted it to dry off his dripping hair, revealing even more flesh. His pectoral muscles were carved and perfect. And—*oh, my God... is that... Holy shit. It is.* His nipples were cold and erect, and one of them was....was...pierced.

"Good to see you, Reese. We don't see each other for ten

years, and now we've run into each other twice in a month's time."

It took me a minute to realize he was referring to our fake middle school years. His wit snapped me out of my haze.

"Yes. Aren't I lucky?"

"I know you," Bryant said.

I'd completely forgotten he was standing next to me. Hell, I'd forgotten anyone else on Earth existed for a minute. I furrowed my brow. Did the two of them actually know each other?

"You're Reese's cousin. The model."

Shit! Shit! Shit! I wanted to crawl into a hole and die.

However, Chase (being Chase) went right along with it. He looked at me curiously as he spoke to Bryant. "That's right. I'm cousin Chase. Aunt Bea's youngest nephew. And you are?"

Bryant extended his hand, and Chase clasped it. "Bryant Chesney." Then he turned to me. "I thought your mom's name was Rosemarie? Same as my mom's."

Chase cut in smoothly. "It is. But some of us call her Bea. Nickname. She's allergic to bees. Got stung at a family barbecue once. Her face swelled up, and the kids all called her Bea after that."

Seriously, the man has to be a professional liar. He was so damn good at it, and he seemed to be turning me into one, too.

Bryant nodded like it all made sense. "Well, nice to meet you. I'll let you two catch up while I get in a few laps."

Just as Bryant began to walk away, Chase stopped him. "How did you know I was Chase? Aunt Bea showing off my pictures again?"

"Nah. Haven't met any of Reese's family yet. Saw your picture on her laptop."

"My picture?"

"It's Reese's background on her MacBook."

Forget the hole I wanted to crawl in to hide a minute ago. Now I closed my eyes and prayed for the Earth to swallow me up and never spit me back out. Or for the superpower of turning the Earth backward so time could rewind. I stood completely still and counted to thirty with my eyes tightly shut. When my time was up, I opened one eye, peeking to see if Chase had disappeared.

"Still here." He smirked.

I covered my face with my hands. "I'm so embarrassed."

"Don't be. We're not blood cousins, so it's not too weird for you to be dreaming about me at night."

"I was *not* dreaming about you at night!"

"So it's only during the day while you stare at my picture on your laptop, then?"

"It was an accident. I didn't mean to set it as my background."

He folded his arms over his chest. "Okay. I'll buy that."

"Good, because it's true."

"But how, exactly, *did* the picture get on your laptop in the first place? I don't remember you snapping a pic during our double date."

I snorted. "Double date?"

"Speaking of which, what happened to Oedipus? Kicked to the curb so soon? I gotta admit, even though you went about trying to get out of your date all wrong, you weren't wrong about that guy. Boring as shit."

"He was."

"So who's this new dope you're with?"

"Dope? You don't even know him."

"Left me standing here with his girl. Dope."

"He thinks we're cousins!"

"I told you, we're not blood-related."

"Yes, but—" I laughed. "You're bizarre, you know that?"

"Not any more bizarre than a woman who somehow took a photo of a perfect stranger and has it on her MacBook for her boyfriend to see."

"He's not my boyfriend." I had no idea why I said that. It was sort of true, but sort of not. "Well, we've gone out twice."

"Ah...so you haven't slept with him yet."

I hadn't, but how would he know that? "What makes you say that?"

"Because you're not the type of girl who sleeps with guys on the first or second date."

"How would you know?"

"I just do."

"What exactly *is* the type of girl who sleeps with a guy on a first date?"

"She sends signals—dresses a certain way, makes body contact. You know the type. I know you do."

"Like Bridget?" That woman had been pawing him by the end of the night.

He said nothing.

I thought it was oddly gentlemanly that he didn't agree about Bridget or confirm what I suspected happened after their date.

"So how *did* you get a picture of me anyway?" he asked instead.

I told the truth. Well, mostly. "I searched for you on Facebook after that night in the restaurant. I wanted to say thank you for saving me and making the evening fun."

"You sent me a message?"

"No. I never did. It sort of...felt creepy that I'd stalked you, so I changed my mind."

"And you liked my picture so much that you kept it?"

"I went to bookmark the page in case I changed my mind about sending you that note, and instead I saved the picture." I felt the blush creeping up my face. I'd always been a terrible liar. My mom used to say I was easier to read than a book.

Surprisingly, Chase nodded. I hadn't expected him to let me off the hook that easily. "Is this your regular gym? I haven't seen you here before."

"No. It's Bryant's gym. He invited me. I had a bad day and planned to wine away my stresses. But he suggested I come work them off at the gym instead."

"Told ya. Dope. Definitely not what I would have suggested to alleviate stress if I was Brandon."

"Bryant."

"Whatever."

"So what *would* you have suggested?"

"Nothing." He changed subjects. "So why was your day so bad, anyway?"

"Two job interviews. The first one I blew before I even walked into the office, and the second one blew me off just as I pulled up to their building."

"You're out of work?"

"Not yet. But I will be as of next Friday. Probably wasn't the smartest move to give notice in this economy before I found another job."

"What do you do?"

"Marketing. I was the director of marketing for Fresh Look Cosmetics."

"Small world. I'm friendly with Scott Eikman, the president of Fresh Look. We play golf together sometimes."

"Eight and a half million people in our little city, and my fake middle school boyfriend slash non-blood-related cousin golfs with the head of my company? That is bizarre."

Chase laughed. "Scott's retiring next year, right?"

"Yep. Moving to Florida and all. He has two sons who will probably take over." *Ugh. Derek.* I wished *he* was moving to Florida. Or Siberia.

Chase and I had been standing just in front of the pool door since we bumped into each other. A guy knocked on the glass and flashed a Dr. Pepper, dangling it in the air.

Chase held up two fingers in response, then explained. "We made a bet. I kicked his ass in lap times. That's my prize."

I arched a brow. "A Dr. Pepper?"

"It's good stuff. Don't knock it or I won't bring it to the next family barbecue."

After another minute, his friend banged again. This time, he waved his hand to Chase as if to say, *what the hell is taking you so long?*

Chase nodded. "I gotta run. We have a dinner meeting in a half hour, and I need to shower."

I tried to hide my disappointment. "Well, it was nice running into you, cuz."

Our eyes locked for a minute. Just like the end of the night at the restaurant, Chase looked like he wanted to say something. But instead, he glanced back over his shoulder to where Bryant was swimming, and then pulled me in for a hug, wrapping my ponytail around his fist and tugging my head back to look up at him.

His eyes lingered on my lips before he kissed my forehead. "Later, cuz."

He took a few steps toward the locker room door before stopping and turning back. "I have a friend who's a bulldog recruiter. Why don't I put you in touch with her? Maybe she can help find you something?"

"Sure, I'd love that. I'm not having much luck by myself. Thank you."

I handed him my cell, and he programmed in his number then sent a text to his own phone so we'd have each other's contact information. Then he was gone. Immediately, I felt longing. The odds of running into him a second time in this tremendous city were probably as long as being struck by lightning.

It would be less than a week before I found out sometimes lightning strikes twice.

CHAPTER
3

Chase – Seven years ago

I stared at Peyton's giant-sized face as I guzzled a bottle of water. The ad covered eight stories of brick on the corner building across from my new office.

"Stop slacking and get to work." The life-size Peyton let herself into my office, dropped her guitar case on the couch, and joined me at the window. "I cannot believe how big that thing is. You told me one billboard ad. That's a whole building. That tiny little chip in my front tooth is, like, three feet wide now."

"I love that chip."

"I hate it. The director at that callback I had yesterday told me I needed to get it fixed and lose ten pounds." She lifted her hand to her mouth. "I need to get a laminate or a veneer or something."

"You don't need to fix shit, and he's a moron with no taste."

She sighed. "I didn't get the part."

"See? Told you. No taste."

"You're biased because I have sex with you."

"No." I pulled her close. "I sat through a fucking opera last week because you have sex with me. I tell you you're a good musician because I've been to every show you've played since college, even when you're hidden in the orchestra pit. And since you started acting, I've seen every one of your off-Broadway shows."

"Off-off-Broadway shows."

"Wouldn't off-Broadway cover any show that isn't on Broadway?"

"No. Off-Broadway is a small show in Manhattan with less than five hundred people. Off-Off-Broadway is that show I did in the Village in the coffee house."

"You were really good in that."

Peyton gave me a skeptical face. "What part did I play?"

"The hot girl part."

"I played the mother who was dying of tuberculosis. You had your nose in a crossword puzzle the entire time."

Oh. That play. "I might have missed some of that one. In my defense, I had just found *crass*word puzzles. Come on... three-letter word for something that goes in dry and hard, but comes out wet and soft? I was busy counting the letters in *dick, cock, pecker,* and *prick* a dozen times each before figuring out the answer was *gum.*"

"You're such a perv."

I gave her a chaste kiss. "Where are we going for dinner, Chip?"

She covered her mouth but smiled. "Don't call me that. I could go for Thai. How about that little place in Chelsea we went to last month?"

"Sounds good." I took one last look at my new billboard as I flicked off the lights and closed my office door.

Outside, I turned left to head to the nearest subway station, but Peyton turned right.

"Could we catch the 3 train on Broadway instead of the usual one?" she asked. "I want to stop over at Little East."

"Sure." Peyton had started volunteering at food banks and shelters when we were in college. I loved that she was passionate about helping people. But this place had some rough, transient types. It wasn't unusual for a fight to break out a couple times a week. I'd tried to broach the subject of her safety. Unfortunately, her volunteering was one of the few areas where she wouldn't bend.

When she was five or six, her loser of a father walked out, leaving her mother with Peyton and two other kids. Her mom could barely make ends meet on two salaries, and with only one, she was forced to decide between food and rent. She chose rent, which meant they were regulars at the local food bank for a few years until things got better.

One of the more frequent visitors at this shelter was sitting out front when we arrived.

"Hey, Eddie," Peyton said.

I'd met the guy before. He was probably only in his forties, but the streets had aged him. His words were few and far between, but he seemed harmless enough. Peyton had a special bond with him—he'd say more to her than he did to most.

"What happened to your head?" I leaned down, careful to keep the distance I knew he needed. He had a wide gash near his temple.

"How'd that happen, Eddie?" Peyton asked.

He shrugged. "Kids."

Lately there'd been incidents of teenagers beating up on homeless people overnight out on the streets. Eddie wasn't big on sleeping in shelters. The places were almost always over capacity, and he had issues with people coming too close.

"New shelter on 41st opened," I said. "Just passed it the other day. Might not be too crowded since it's new, and the weather is warm."

"Yeah." Never more than a one-word answer for me.

"I think you should go to the police, Eddie," Peyton said.

With all the time she'd put in at these places, she still didn't get it. Homeless people didn't go to the police. They walked the other way when they saw them coming.

Eddie shook his head furiously and pulled his legs up to his chest.

"That looks serious. You probably should have had stitches. Do the kids who did that come to this shelter?" she asked.

Again, Eddie shook his head.

After a few minutes, I finally convinced her to leave the poor guy alone and go inside to do what she'd come to do. When we went in, the shelter manager, Nelson, was cleaning up dinner service.

Peyton immediately started to interrogate him. "Do you know what happened to Eddie's head?"

He stopped wiping down the table. "Nope. I asked. Got the usual response—nothing. You're the only one he says more than *please* and *thank you* to."

"Do you know where he sleeps at night?"

He shook his head. "Sorry. The city's got more than forty homeless communities, and that doesn't include setting up shop under a train trestle somewhere on your own. Could be anywhere."

Peyton frowned. "Okay."

"I know it's not easy. But we can't help the ones who won't take our help. He knows he's welcome to stay here anytime."

34

"I know." She pointed to the storage room in the back. "I forgot to take the inventory list. I have an audition tomorrow, so I'm going to do it online from home."

While Peyton was gone, I looked around the shelter. The place had recently been painted, and each volunteer had donated a framed poster with their favorite motivational quote. There were probably a dozen in matte black frames running down the long wall of the cafeteria. The first one read *Even at the end of the darkest night, the sun will rise again.*

"Is this one yours?" I asked when Peyton returned with a folder.

"Nope." She gave me a quick peck on the lips. "You can read them all another time, and I'll give you a reward if you find the one I brought. But I want to catch Eddie again before he's gone." She tugged my hand. "So let's go."

Eddie was no longer sitting outside, although he was easy enough to spot. Halfway up the block, he was ambling along. He had a limp on the right and a garbage bag slung over his left shoulder.

Peyton saw him just before he rounded the corner. "Let's follow him. See where he goes."

"Absolutely not."

"Why not?"

"Because it's dangerous—and an invasion of his privacy. We're not following a homeless person."

"But if we know where he sleeps at night, maybe the police would help."

"No."

"Please..."

"No."

"Fine."

I should have known she wasn't going to drop it so quick.

CHAPTER
4

Reese

My cell had rung bright and early this morning, and suddenly I had an unexpected lunch date I was rather looking forward to. Chase had mentioned he had a friend who was a recruiter, but he'd failed to include the part that the woman, Samantha, recruited for *Parker Industries—a company he owned*. I was instantly intrigued, and I'll admit I was a tad bit disappointed when she suggested we meet at a restaurant. Even though it was easy to get to—only a few stops on the subway from my soon-to-be-vacated office at Fresh Look—there wouldn't be any chance of running into Chase since we weren't meeting at his office.

But lunch had turned out to be pretty enlightening. We'd spent two hours at a restaurant, now followed by a long walk through the park. After we'd talked about my background and what I was looking for in an employer, the conversation turned to Parker Industries.

"So Chase actually invents the products himself?" I asked. Perhaps I should have spent time *Googling* the man instead of *ogling* him on Facebook.

"He used to, although these days he has an entire research and development team. But most of the ideas they work on are his. Believe it or not, that pretty boy is the smartest person I've ever met."

"What was the first product he ever invented?"

"The Pampered Pussy."

I stopped in place. "The what?"

Samantha laughed. "It's packaged as Divine Wax now that it's licensed in fifty countries. But back in college, it was The Pampered Pussy."

"He *invented* Divine Wax? I've heard that stuff is awesome."

"Sure did. During college, he lived in a frat with a bunch of muscleheads. Some of them were hardcore into working out. His sophomore year, a few had begun to compete in local bodybuilding contests. They had to wax their bodies, and these brawny tough guys used to bitch that the waxing hurt. Chase worked in the university's chem lab part-time and figured out how to incorporate a numbing agent into the wax. So after the hot wax was painted on the guys' chests and backs, they didn't feel anything as it was ripped off a few seconds later."

"And it turned into a household brand for women?"

"It took a while. Word spread at Brown that a hot guy could do waxing without the pain, and that evolved into The Pampered Pussy. He'd go to sororities and make a grand in an afternoon—*and* get laid by the prettiest girl in the house while he was there. It was unbelievable." Samantha laughed. "He was always easy on the eyes and a little arrogant because of his brains. Women love that combination."

We sure do. "That's pretty amazing. How did it get to the next level?"

"Junior year he was providing wax and doing whatever else to Dakota Canning, heir to Canning & Canning."

"The Fortune 100 pharmaceutical company?"

"That's the one. I guess Dakota told her father about the wax, and things just progressed from there. It was packaged and sold under a license agreement within six months. When Chase graduated Brown, he'd already made his first million."

"That's seriously unbelievable."

"Yep. He's like the Zuckerberg of vaginas now—has a dozen other products he's chemically improved. Most are in the health and beauty segment, but he also invented a burn cream that regenerates skin and decreases pain, and it only needs to be applied once a day. Most burn creams need multiple applications, and touching the skin after a severe burn is both excruciatingly painful and increases the chances of infection."

"Incredible."

"It is. Just don't tell him I said that." She smiled softly. "So how did you two meet again? He mentioned a double date but didn't get into details. Pulling anything personal from that man is like breaking into Fort Knox. And we've known each other since middle school."

"It's actually a bizarre story. I was on a bad date and hiding outside the restaurant bathroom leaving a message for my friend to call me back and pretend there was an emergency. Chase overheard me and basically called me out for being rude. After I went back to my date, he wound up coming over with his date and joining us."

"He knew your date?"

"Nope. He pretended we were old friends and joined us— told these elaborate stories about our fake childhood. Some of them were so detailed and real, I started to feel like they were actually true."

"The story part sounds like Chase. In high school, he wrote a creative writing paper for my friend Peyton once.

He handed it to her right before she had English class, so she didn't have time to read it beforehand. The guidance counselor called her down the next morning because her English teacher had become concerned about her well-being. He'd written some crazy story about being attacked by a wild boar during a camping trip with her parents, who were too drunk to help fight the thing off. The way he'd detailed the trip to the emergency room and all the stitches, it seemed too explicit not to be real."

"Yes! That's exactly what he did to me. He told some crazy story about our first kiss in eighth grade and how I'd gotten a bloody nose in the middle of it. It was so far-fetched that it was believable."

She shook her head and laughed. "There's a fine line between genius and unhinged."

When we arrived back at the street exit from the park, Samantha extended her hand. "It was really nice to get to meet you, Reese. I have to say, I was curious when Chase called me at home last night to ask me to look into helping you find something. He doesn't usually mix his personal life and business. But I get why he's so taken with you now. You're down-to-earth, smart, funny in a quick-witted type of way—a lot like Chase, actually."

"Oh...we're not...there isn't really a personal relationship to speak of. Just that one strange double date, and then we ran into each other again at the gym yesterday."

She looked at me skeptically. "Well, you must have made a good impression on him, then. He doesn't usually farm me out."

My brows drew together. "Farm you out?"

"I left industry recruiting three years ago. I usually just recruit for Parker Industries now."

"Oh! I just assumed...Chase said he knew a bulldog recruiter...I assumed you were also a corporate recruiter, not one exclusively for his corporation."

"That's what I used to do. But I'm glad he put us together. I have a lot of contacts in the women's product industry from Parker Industries. I'll put out some feelers to see who might be hiring. I actually know someone who might be in the market for a product brand manager. It's a lower-level position than what you're leaving, but it's soup-to-nuts advertising and marketing for a few products, so you'd get to do a full rebranding campaign. Although, they're looking for someone to start as soon as possible. Is that something you'd be interested in?"

"My last day at Fresh Look is next Friday, and I don't have anything lined up yet. I'm not the type of person who likes to sit around, so I'd definitely consider something like that."

"Great. Give me a day or two, and I'll see what I can do."

Tonight was my third date with Bryant—fourth if you counted the afternoon at the gym. He'd invited me over to his place for a home-cooked meal and a movie, and I knew that given the privacy, things were likely to progress physically between us. We'd shared some heated kisses, but that had pretty much been it so far.

In the shower, I thought about whether I was ready to have sex with him. By no means was I a prude, nor was there a certain number of hoops a guy had to jump through in order to get me into his bed. I'd had first dates that ended in sex, and I'd had four-month relationships that never progressed there. For me, it was what felt right. As I shaved my legs, I tried to wrap my arms around exactly how I felt about Bryant. He was a nice guy—thirty-one with no kids or ex baggage—handsome, held a solid job as a mutual fund manager, and wasn't afraid to show affection. Yet, as I ran the razor up my thigh, I found myself thinking of someone else entirely. *Chase Parker.*

I tried to tell myself it was because of the stories Samantha had shared today at lunch. His wax invention—I was shaving my legs. That's why I was thinking about him in the shower instead of my date. When I washed my torso, I thought of the small ring in his nipple. I might have let my hand linger a little too long as I sudsed up my breasts. *They need to be washed, after all.* And I was *only* thinking of Chase as I closed my eyes because I was curious about what his handsome face might look like if I took that ring between my teeth and tugged. I stopped my hand from lingering anywhere else, but it wasn't an easy feat. I had Chase on the brain when I should have had someone else.

On the way over to Bryant's, I stopped and picked up a bottle of wine I knew he liked. When he opened the door, he was sweet. "You look amazing," he said, then gave me a nice, welcome kiss.

A buzzer was going off in the kitchen, so he told me to follow him. I checked the apartment out as I walked through. It was clean and modern—even had some artwork on the walls. Most of my previous boyfriends thought decorating meant hanging a sixty-inch TV. *Progress.*

Bryant lifted the top off a pot and put it aside. Opening a box of rigatoni pasta, he smiled. "I make two dishes: rigatoni alla vodka and chicken parmigiana. You had pasta primavera the first time we went out, so I thought rigatoni was the safest bet."

It was thoughtful that he remembered what I ate. "Can I do anything to help?"

"You can grab two glasses from there." His chin pointed to a cabinet on his left as he poured the pasta into the boiling water. "There's a bottle of wine in the fridge I already opened. I'll get the pasta going. You can pour."

He watched me while I filled each glass. "What?"

"I want to say something, but it might come off as creepy."

"Well, now you have to say it." I sipped my wine and extended his glass.

"All right. I couldn't stop thinking about you when I was in the shower today—how gorgeous you are."

That should have made me feel good, but instead, it made me feel like complete shit. While the great guy I was dating had been thinking about me...I'd been feeling myself up to thoughts of another man.

I forced a weak smile. "That's sweet. Thank you."

He stepped closer and brushed a lock of hair behind my ear. "I mean it. I like you. You're smart, beautiful, and driven. I know it's early, but I feel like what's going on between us is a really good thing. It has legs."

I swallowed. I really did like him, too. But something was keeping me from jumping in with both feet. His words were what every single, twenty-eight-year-old woman wanted to hear from a great guy. Yet...I wasn't there yet.

He read it on my face.

Pulling back, he said, "I'm freaking you out, aren't I?"

I hated to make him feel bad, because I really did like him. "No...not at all. I like you, too. I just...I just think we should take it slow at the beginning. I haven't had much luck in the relationship department, and I tend to be gun-shy, I guess."

He nodded. And although he smiled, I could tell he was disappointed with my response. Hell, *I* was disappointed with my response. I'd been trying to talk myself into being crazy about him for a while now.

But that's what was missing—that crazy feeling I should have had. This early on, butterflies should have been flapping their colorful wings when he said those things or looked at me like he did when he opened the door. I was determined to keep trying. He seemed worth it.

Even though Bryant said he agreed we should take things slow, a damper was cast on the rest of the night. Still, I was relieved that I wouldn't have to make the choice about sleeping with him if things went in that direction. Because I'd realized I wasn't ready yet. As the night came to an early end, I wondered if I would ever be.

CHAPTER
5

Reese

"I really need to start taking taxis," I grumbled under my breath as I rushed up the subway stairs and headed down the block toward the building I would have already been at had my train not been stuck for twenty minutes. My interview was at eleven, and it was already eleven-oh-one. Perhaps changing my outfit *eight times* this morning hadn't helped my punctuality either.

The Maxim building was a modern, all-glass highrise with more than fifty floors. Inside the massive, sleek lobby, it took me a minute to even figure out where the company directory was—everything was silver and shiny. Finding it, I scanned for Parker Industries and ran my finger across the glass to locate the corresponding location. *Floor thirty-three.*

Running to the elevator bank, I saw that one car was just about to close, so I stuck my foot in to stop it. It worked but almost took off my toes in the process.

"Shit. Ouch." The doors bounced open, and I hobbled my way inside, unknowingly sticking my shoe's thin heel in the small gap of the door track. With my heel stuck, my body kept going, yet my foot didn't, and I wobbled, falling forward. An arm caught me and kept me from landing on my face.

"Goddamn it," I cursed under my breath, realizing my shoe was now completely off my foot and stuck in the elevator track.

"Nice to see you too, Reese."

My head whipped up as I realized for the first time exactly who was keeping me from falling. "You've got to be kidding me. How many bad impressions can one person possibly make on another?"

After steadying me, Chase kneeled and pried my wedged footwear loose from the elevator. He tapped my calf to signal me to lift my bare leg and then slipped the shoe back onto my foot.

"Definitely not a bad impression," he said, lingering on his knees longer than necessary. "You have great legs."

"Thank you—for unjamming my shoe, I mean."

He stood, and his eyebrows rose. "So you're not thanking me for complimenting your sexy legs, then?"

I felt a blush creeping up and was relieved when he turned his attention to the button panel. "What floor?"

"Umm…thirty-three?" *Is his company on more than one floor?*

"You're coming to Parker Industries? Are you here to meet Sam?"

"Yes. And Josh Lange."

"Josh?"

"Yes. He's who I'm interviewing with, right? The vice president of marketing?"

"Right. Yes. Josh is the VP of marketing," he agreed, but I had the distinct feeling Chase hadn't known I was coming to interview today.

We rode the elevator up in uncomfortable silence. When the doors slid open, he held out his arm for me to exit first, and we walked to the glass double doors of Parker Industries together.

The reception desk was empty.

"Why don't you have a seat, and I'll let them know you're here?" he said.

"Thank you."

A minute or two after he went inside, the receptionist returned to her desk. "Hi. Sorry, I had to make some copies. I hope you weren't waiting long."

"Not at all. Actually, I came in with Chase, and he was going to let Samantha Richmond and Josh Lange know I was here."

"You must be Reese Annesley. Sam asked me to bring you to the conference room when you got here." She waved me back. "Come on, I'll show you the way."

The conference room had a long mahogany table with a dozen chairs around it. The walls to the hallway were glass like a fishbowl, but the blinds on a track were partially closed. Once inside, I took out my Chapstick and lined my lips, adding some MAC Rebel lipstick on top. As I finished, I heard Chase's voice from the other side of the glass.

"I don't think it's a good idea to hire Reese."

My heart sank. Obviously, he didn't see me.

I recognized Samantha's voice when she responded. "Why? We have a position open that she would be perfect for."

"She wouldn't be a good fit."

"That's crap."

"Don't give me a hard time, Sam. Just don't hire her."

I couldn't see her, but I pictured her folding her arms across her chest. "Give me a reason."

"Because I said so."

"No."

"No?"

"That's right. No. You're punishing the woman because she's beautiful and you're attracted to her. That's just as wrong as punishing someone because they're old or have a certain color skin."

"You're totally off base."

"Okay. Then give me one good reason we shouldn't hire her. She's perfect for the job, and she's able to start right away. With Dimitria going out on maternity leave soon, the timing couldn't be better. Marketing is already understaffed, and Josh was planning on hiring someone for the branding team anyway. She can pick up some of Dimitria's projects and then start new ones after Dimitria is back from leave."

"Whatever. Do what you want, Sam."

Sam's voice became more distant. "I plan to." She must have begun to walk away.

I closed my eyes. I certainly didn't want to work somewhere I wasn't wanted. But I needed to thank Samantha for her consideration before I left. Deciding it would be a waste of everyone's time to even interview, I stood and began to walk back to the reception area. I would have the receptionist call Samantha for me. Of course Chase was coming down the hall as soon as I exited the conference room. I quickly turned and walked in the other direction, not even knowing where it would lead.

"Reese? Where are you going?"

"Why do you care?" I kept walking.

He caught up and fell in step with me. "What's the matter?"

It pissed me off that he was acting all innocent, so I stopped and faced him to continue. "I *overheard you* in the conference room. I'm leaving."

He closed his eyes. "*Shit.*"

"Yes. *Shit.* That's how you made me feel."

I began walking again, and Chase grabbed my elbow and steered me into an empty office, shutting the door behind him.

He raked his hand through his hair. *His stupid, sexy hair.* "I'm sorry. I was being an asshole."

"Yes. You were. A big one."

Chase dropped his head and chuckled. "You and Sam will get along great."

"I take it you didn't know Samantha had invited me here to interview today?"

He shook his head. "No, I didn't."

"Well, I don't want to be where I'm not wanted. Please thank Samantha for me."

"It's not what you think."

"I don't even know what I think. You have me so confused."

Chase stared at me for a moment, looking back and forth between my eyes. "Trust me, I'm trying to do the right thing."

"Trust you? Because you have such a great track record of *telling the truth* when you're around me?"

He glared at me.

I glared right back.

"Okay. Fine. You want the truth?"

I folded my arms over my chest. "That would be a refreshing change."

He took a step closer to me, inching into my personal space. "I'm attracted to you. *Really* attracted to you. Have been since the first time I saw you. Tried to be respectful, considering you were seeing someone. Done doing that. If you work here, I'm going to try to get you into my bed."

I opened my mouth to respond. Then closed it. Then opened it. "I can't believe you just said that to me."

He shrugged. "You wanted to know the truth. That's the truth."

"You do realize that I'd have to *agree* to sleep with you. Which wouldn't happen if you were my boss, so it wouldn't be a problem."

"Oh. Well, then... Sounds like we wouldn't have a problem after all. I was concerned for nothing. I'll hit on you, and you'll shut me down."

"And...I also have a boyfriend."

"Baron. We've met. The dope."

"Bryant. And he's not a dope."

"Then we're all set. Sam was right. You should work here if Josh wants to hire you. Won't be an issue."

He leaned in a little closer.

I stood my ground. *God, he smells amazing.*

"So we're good? I apologize, you accept? You're going to kick ass in the interview and get hired, then I'm going to try to get in your pants, and you're not going to let me."

I couldn't help but laugh. The man was truly absurd.

He extended his hand. "Deal?"

"I've probably lost my mind, but, hey, why not? I'm days from being unemployed." I put my hand in his, but instead of shaking it, he brought it to his mouth and kissed the top. I felt it all over. *God, I'm in trouble.*

He smiled wolfishly, revealing a dimple I hadn't noticed earlier. It was a good thing he hadn't taken that thing out before. *Dangerous.*

"All we have to do is get you hired now. You want some inside info?"

"Sure."

"Tell Josh he looks like Adrien Brody. He loves it."

I smiled warily. "Good to know."

"And for Sam…never say you're a Mets fan, even if you are. Yankees all the way."

I squinted suspiciously. "You think baseball will come up in my interview for a marketing position?"

"You never know."

"Why do I think you're screwing with me?"

"One other thing, Josh isn't hitting on you. That's a twitch he's got going on with his eye. Thought he was into me for the first week he worked here."

I laughed. "Okay."

Chase walked me back to the conference room, where Sam and a man I presumed to be Josh (since he looked exactly like Adrien Brody) were talking.

"Showed your interviewee the way to the ladies' room," Chase said and then introduced me to Josh. After we all shook hands and the three of us had taken seats in the conference room, Chase lingered in the doorway.

He held up a hand. "Nice to see you again, Reese. Good luck with your interview."

"Would you like to stay for the interview, Chase?" Sam asked.

"No. I'm good. I'm sure you two have it covered."

"Any questions or anything before you go?" she added.

"I don't think so." Chase pivoted to leave and then stopped. "Actually, I do have some quick questions. Do you mind, Reese?"

"Not at all." *What is he up to?*

"Great. Favorite baseball team?"

I squinted at him, debating whether I should trust him or not. He looked amused when my answer didn't come quickly.

I took a deep breath, followed by a leap of faith. "I'd have to say the Yankees."

"Good choice." Chase's eyes flashed to Samantha, whose face had brightened.

"One other question."

I knew exactly what it was before he asked, but played along anyway.

"Does Josh look like any particular celebrity to you?"

I turned to Josh and pretended to deliberate for a moment, then turned back to Chase. "Adrien Brody, except with glasses."

Sam looked at Chase like he'd lost his mind, and Josh sat a little taller.

"Good luck with the rest of the interview, Reese."

CHAPTER 6

Reese

It was still dark outside when I arrived at Parker Industries the following Monday morning. Considering the building lights were off, and the doors were locked, I realized I might have been a tad overeager for my first day. After loitering a few minutes in front of the building, waiting for someone to show up, I decided to head over to Starbucks for some coffee. It was next door to the restaurant where I'd first met Chase.

While it seemed no one was ready to go to work yet, there was a hell of a long line for coffee. I joined the brigade at the back of the line like a good little soldier and proceeded to catch up with reading emails on my phone. A hand at my back startled me, but it was the voice whispering over my shoulder that sent a shiver down my spine. "Am I the background on your iPhone, too?"

I jumped. "You scared the shit out of me."

"Sorry. I couldn't pass up the opportunity to sneak a peek. Figured since I'm your laptop background and all, the obsession might run pretty deep."

I turned and held out my phone. "I can see the similarities, but the photo is definitely not you."

Chase took the phone from my hand. "What the hell is that?"

"It's Tallulah."

"Is that thing real?"

"Of course it's real. *Really* ugly, isn't it?"

"Is it a cat?"

"Yep. It's a Sphynx. A hairless cat."

It was seriously the ugliest pet I'd ever seen. Her head was too small for her body, and her face looked like a devil's. Wrinkly, pale, fleshy-colored skin made her resemble a turkey before you stuck it in the oven.

"My stepfather bought it for my mother for her birthday because she has bad allergies, and she really wanted a pet. Turns out, it isn't the hair she's allergic to, it's the protein in animals' saliva and skin. So she dumped the thing on me this weekend while she tries to find it a new owner. He paid two thousand dollars for that ugly kitty."

"You do see the irony here, right?" Chase asked.

"Irony?"

"You have a hairless pussy, and today you're starting a job where the flagship product is—"

I covered my mouth. "Oh my God! You *would* find irony in that."

"What can I say? Bald is beautiful has made me a lot of money. That cat should be our company mascot."

I chuckled. "I'll keep that in mind for my first marketing project."

"What are you doing here so early, anyway?" He looked at his watch. It was then I realized he was dressed in running gear, not a shirt and tie like he had been at the office last week.

"I wanted to get an early start."

"Building doesn't open until six-thirty. I was just about to go for a run. But I'll show you how to get in when it's closed after we get our coffee."

"It's okay. I can wait until it opens. I don't want to interrupt your exercise."

"Fucking hate running. I'll take any excuse I can get to put it off. Showing a beautiful woman the way to my office is at the top of that list of excuses." He winked. "Especially one who's going to sleep with me eventually."

God, he is cocky. And apparently, cocky really works for me.

The line had moved up a few places, but I hadn't noticed since I was turned around talking to Chase. He lifted his chin to point to the gap between me and the person in front of me, and then put his hand on the small of my back to guide me forward. His touch felt so natural.

When it was our turn at the register, he told me to order first.

"I'll have a venti dark roast, black."

Chase smiled and added, "Make that two." Then he insisted on paying for both.

Caffeine in hand, we walked a block north and around to the back of the building, where he knocked on an unmarked set of steel doors. A guy opened one and greeted us as we entered.

"Mr. P., how's it going, man?"

"Not too shabby, Carlo. You?"

"Can't complain, can't complain. Wife's a bitch, but I can't blame her for that. She's married to a fat, lazy guy." The uniformed maintenance man patted his beer belly and smiled.

"Carlo, this is Reese Annesley. Today is her first day with Parker Industries."

"Nice to meet you, Ms. A." He wiped his hand off on his shirt and extended it to me while speaking to Chase. "You shooting a new catalog? You know those are my favorite times of the year."

"Not this week. Reese isn't a model, although she's pretty enough to be." Chase winked at me again, and I felt a flutter in my belly.

He's your boss, you pathetic thing. Maybe I *should* have sex with Bryant already, might help to take the edge off.

Chase punched a code into the keypad above the elevator call button, and the doors to the service elevator slid open. "The code is 6969."

"How will I ever remember that?" I teased.

As I went to step in, Chase wrapped his arm around my waist. "Wouldn't want you to trip again."

"Wiseass."

"I'm your boss now. You can't call me that."

I looked at my watch and smiled. "Not on the clock yet, *wiseass.*"

"Is that how this is going to be?"

"It is."

"Works both ways then. Before and after office hours, I can say whatever is on my mind as well. That's a game you might want to rethink playing with me." He pushed thirty-three and leaned closer. "Wanna know what's on my mind right now? I can shut my eyes and describe the visual in detail, if you'd like."

The elevator was suddenly very small. *And hot.* Very damn hot.

Just as the doors were about to close, a man in a suit stopped them and joined us. He grumbled something unintelligible and hit twenty-two.

Chase backed up a little and cleared his throat. "You'll need to use that service door before six-thirty and after eight."

"Okay."

In the tiny confines of the padded service elevator, Chase stood far enough away that it seemed normal, yet close enough that I could smell him. And he smelled incredible, woodsy and clean, which had me thinking... He probably doesn't get up and bathe just to go for a run. So that smell is how he wakes up in the morning? *Damn*. For some strange reason, I got a visual of Chase in the middle of the woods chopping down a tall oak. He was wearing jeans (with the top button left open, of course) and work boots, sans shirt.

Being this close to him had me losing my mind. I turned my head. "Do you have a cabin in the woods, by chance?"

He looked amused. "I don't. Do I need one?"

"Never mind."

Once we arrived on the floor, Chase gave me a quick tour. As we walked, I could feel the passion he had for his company while he gave me a brief overview of each department we passed. I'd lost flirty Chase and met CEO Chase Parker, and I liked him just as much.

He was so smart and fervent that I hadn't even noticed we'd spent more than an hour in the product development lab until people started coming in to start their workday. Chase showed me each product and gave me its history. When he came to the last product, Divine Wax, he left out some of the details Sam had filled me in about—namely, how The Pampered Pussy kept him busy getting laid through most of college.

"You should take home one of every product and try them out," he said.

"Already bought them all over the weekend and pampered myself a little. I want to use each one before attempting to do anything marketing-related with them."

"And?"

"I think it's interesting that such lovely products are developed by a man."

"What can I tell you? I'm in touch with my feminine side."

"Hmmm...I heard you utilized your products to *get* in touch with the feminine side in college."

Chase raised an eyebrow. "I see I have to keep you away from Sam."

"But she's such a wealth of knowledge."

His hand returned to the small of my back and guided me out of the product development lab. "That's the problem."

We walked to the marketing department side by side. "How long have you two known each other?"

"Middle school."

"Wow. As far back as we go, huh?"

"Yeah, but it wasn't her I was sucking face with in that hallway outside the gym."

A young guy walked out of the first office in the marketing department just as we passed. He was handsome, in an I-just-left-the-frat-house-and-scored-my-first-real-job type of adorable way.

Chase stopped and introduced me. "Reese, this is Travis. He's IT for marketing—does all of our SEO and web optimization."

He shook my hand with a goofy smile. "Please tell me she works here."

"She does."

"Damn, I love my job."

"You do, huh? Well, pop your eyes back in the sockets, and go read page fourteen of the employee handbook."

"Page fourteen?"

"The *no harassing fellow employees* policy."

Travis held up his hands and laughed. "All good. No harassment. Maybe just a few compliments on how beautiful she is."

This was definitely the type of office where everyone joked around, even with the boss.

Chase leaned over to me as we continued walking down the hall and whispered, "Stop worrying. Harassment policy only applies to employees, not to the owner. Checked this morning."

The big office at the far end of the hallway was Josh's. He was sitting with an obviously pregnant woman when we arrived. She slouched in her chair and rubbed her round stomach.

"I found your new employee trying to get in before the sun rose this morning," Chase announced. "Better put all that energy to good use." He looked at the woman I assumed was the one going out on maternity leave soon. "Looks like Dimitria is about to pop any second."

She looked seriously uncomfortable, gripping and ungripping one of those gel-filled stress balls as she spoke. "Why haven't you invented a product that stops pregnant women from peeing a little every time they sneeze or laugh? Or a product that makes the swelling go down in our ankles?" She pointed to her feet. "These are my *mother's* shoes. Nothing of mine fits me anymore. Not even my own damn shoes."

Chase shook his head. "Do you have any fears, Reese?"

"Fears? You mean like spiders and stuff?" *How much time you got?*

"Yeah. Something that makes you run out of the room irrationally when you come in contact with it because it scares the living shit out of you?"

"I'm not much of a pigeon person. I'll cross the street to avoid them."

Chase nodded. "My fear is pregnant women. So I'm gonna go hit the concrete for that run before it gets too hot outside."

Dimitria whipped the stress ball at Chase, hitting him in the shoulder. "Now I finally understand the use for those damn things."

Divine Wax. At the end of the day, I sat in my new office and spun the jar around on my desk a few times. Tomorrow I would sit in on the first official think tank strategy meeting as the marketing department kicked off a major rebranding project for Parker Industries' flagship product. I needed to get my brain into the mindset of a consumer doing home waxing. The only problem was, I didn't do my own waxing. So I'd made an appointment for eight tonight with my regular esthetician. She'd be doing my Brazilian using both her usual and Divine, so I could compare.

Most of the marketing department had gone, and I was nibbling on a protein bar and sipping a soda I'd gotten from the vending machine in the break room when Chase appeared in my doorway. Unlike this morning, he was dressed in business attire. He loosened his tie as he spoke. "Dr. Pepper, huh?"

I hadn't had one in years, but when I saw it in the machine today, it reminded me of when I'd run into Chase at the gym, and he'd told me how much he liked it. The memory had spurred me to push the button before I gave it any real thought.

"My cousin really likes them," I told him. "Thought I'd give it a try."

He smiled in that I'm-insanely-hot-and-I'm-not-even-trying-at-all kind of way he had. *God, stop doing that.*

"You like to work late?"

"I do my best work at night," I said.

Chase's eyebrows jumped. "It's after hours now, so I'm not the boss anymore. Isn't that how you told me it worked this morning?"

I leaned back in my chair. "It's after six. So say what's on your mind."

He moved to sit across from me and gave me his best dirty grin. "I was just going to say I do my best work at night, also."

"I'm sure you do. Although *I* was referring to brainstorming advertising ideas. I find I'm more creative in the evening. Sometimes after I've climbed into bed and shut off the lights, an idea will come to me for something I was trying all day to focus on."

"I'm very creative when I shut off the lights and slip into bed, too. Maybe we should try that together sometime? Probably produce some amazing results—twice as creative and all."

I shook my head but smiled, amused. "You're an HR nightmare, aren't you? I bet you make Samantha work hard for her salary."

"Actually, I'm usually not. You just keep hitting on me, and I can't help but react. It's kind of inappropriate, considering I'm your boss and all."

My eyes bulged. "I'm not hitting on you! You're the one—"

"Relax. I'm joking. I don't find it inappropriate at all. Keep doing it."

"Have you been sniffing wax chemicals all day?"

Chase's grin was contagious. "So how late you staying?" he asked.

"I have an appointment at eight. I figured I'd stick around until then since it's on my way home."

"Dinner with Braxton?"

"*Bryant.* And no. I have a wax appointment." I held up the small jar of Divine. "Figured I'd do a little product research."

"I should come."

"To get waxed?"

"To watch you get waxed." His eyes gleamed. "Research."

When Samantha suddenly appeared at my door, she gave us an odd smile. "I've been waiting in your office for ten minutes. Are we still grabbing a bite?"

Chase looked at me. "We're going over to Azuri's for falafel. Want to join us?"

"Thanks, I'd love to. But I have that appointment."

Later that night, after hanging up with Bryant, I was lying in the dark, replaying my day, when my phone buzzed. It wasn't a number I recognized, and the message seemed cryptic. It read, *Are you and Tallulah twins?*

It took me a minute to figure it out. For a moment I'd forgotten I gave Chase my number to pass to Samantha that day when we met at the gym. I closed my eyes and smiled to myself, suddenly not feeling sleepy at all.

CHAPTER
7

Reese

It was only day two, but I already loved my new job. It had rekindled something inside of me that I hadn't felt in a long time. I hadn't even realized it was missing until now. *Passion.* I couldn't wait to go to work when I woke up this morning. I'd been there at one point with my previous job, but where had that feeling gone? Parker Industries made me feel alive again.

I'd spent all morning in a marketing think tank session listening to the group come up with ideas. These people fed off of each other—building off each other's thoughts to come up with the best single idea, rather than competing with one another. Since I was new, I listened more than I spoke.

We'd returned from lunch, and Josh was standing at the whiteboard, scribbling random words that people called out, when Chase slipped into the back of the room. He stood quietly, observing. Feeling his eyes on me, I glanced back a few times, and his gaze was always waiting for mine.

There were two empty seats in the room. One was next to me. After a few minutes, Chase silently walked up the side of the room and slipped into the seat to my right. We exchanged a sidelong glance, and then Josh stepped away from what he'd been writing and cleared his throat.

What do women want? he'd written on the whiteboard in big, black letters.

"Before we get started again this afternoon, let's talk about the things we know." He counted off facts with his fingers, beginning with his pointer: "One, our customers are ninety-six percent women. Two, women's buying habits are different than men's. Three, ninety-one percent of women in the survey we did last year said advertisers don't understand them." He ticked up his pinky as he started his fourth point. "Four, men shop for their needs. Women shop for their wants." Then he tapped on the board. "*What do women want?* If we're going to sell them a product, let's start at the very beginning."

He pointed to easels set up on both sides of the room. "We're going to split up into two teams. There are two whiteboards. Let's make this interesting, shall we? All the women work together on the right side of the room, and all the men work together on the left. I want a minimum of five wants on each of your lists. More is fine. I'll be the scrivener for the men." He looked to Chase, who offered a single nod. "Chase will be the scrivener for the women."

Chase leaned over to me and whispered, "You smell incredible—like the beach in the summer." He breathed in deep through his nose. "Coconut, maybe some honeysuckle, mixed with a little citrus."

I shook my head, but whispered back, "Thank you." Then I pointed to my watch. "Inappropriate during the work day."

"Oh yeah? Adrien Brody needs a raise. I'm about to get a roadmap into what makes you tick, and I get to call it actual work. Love this job sometimes."

After the room had been rearranged and everyone was comfortable in their new seats, Chase suggested each woman take five minutes to make her own list, and then we could see what the group collectively came up with. He tried to peek at mine a few times, but I covered my notepad and grinned. After everyone's pens had slowed, Chase stood, swiped the marker from the tray, opened it, and scribbled *What women want* with a thick slash underlining it.

"Of course, I already know the answer to this one, but since I'm the facilitator, I'll let you ladies take your best shot." He smiled playfully, and there was that damn dimple again.

Go away! You're like kryptonite to my brain.

At first, the wants being tossed around were typical—money, love, security, adventure, health, beauty, fun, simplicity. The ladies in the group argued over a few, but most of their note pages were full of crossouts that we'd listed on the whiteboard or disregarded. I was mostly quiet, and my list still had a few items not already mentioned. Chase looked over and tried to read my list upside down.

"What do you want, Reese? Anything left on your list?"

I nibbled on my bottom lip as I looked down at my notepad. "Recognition, safety, power, family." Checking off as I went, I found one left. I hesitated, but then looked up and said, "Orgasms."

Pointing to love on the whiteboard, Chase asked, "Are orgasms not covered here?"

I tilted my head. "The two aren't mutually inclusive to most women, believe it or not."

"Fair enough." Chase added orgasms to our list. Of course, he made it twice the size of the other wants. He also added family, safety, and recognition to the list. "Power? What does that mean? As in strength?"

64

"No, meaning the ability to influence the behavior of others."

"In order for you to have power, you need to strip it from the others you're going to influence? So you want to be a dictator? *Women* want to be dictators?"

"No. You're taking the concept of power to an extreme. A dictator rules by force and oppression. Women want to rule by influence. We like a softer touch."

"I don't think women want the power in *everything*."

Abbey, one of the brand managers, cackled at Chase's statement. "That's because you're a man."

"Our goal is to get to the root of what women want so we can connect our product to that want. So let's be honest with ourselves. There are times when a woman wants to cede control to a man." Chase pointed to the big O in orgasm. "In the bedroom. A lot of women like a dominant lover."

The women mumbled and shook their heads, but I spoke up. "That's true, but we still want to hold the power there. It's the woman who decides when it's time to have sex in a relationship. It's our influence that controls whether the act happens or not. Even in a true dominant-submissive relationship, when a woman is submissive to her male partner, she still holds the power even as she's being paddled. She has a safe word, and that gives her all the control. She has the *power* and *influence* even from the physically submissive position."

I was mindlessly twisting one of my bracelets, a nervous habit I had, and when I looked up, I found Chase staring at my wrists. He cleared his throat and capped the marker abruptly.

"Good work, everyone. I think our list is complete. Gotta run to an afternoon appointment. I'm looking forward to seeing which want will be the center of our rebranding campaign."

It was after eight, and the night cleaning crew was vacuuming, so I didn't hear Chase coming down the hall until he was in my doorway.

"Fourteen hours a day. You're even making me look bad."

He had changed out of his suit and into running shorts and a T-shirt.

God, his thighs are thick and muscular.

I had my hair piled up on top of my head, a bunch of pencils sticking out of it. I caught the quizzical look on Chase's face as he examined it. "I forgot a hair tie. By the end of the day, I need my hair off my neck."

Chase's eyes traced my neckline. I felt a flutter in my belly at the way he seemed to be unable to stop staring.

"So what was the consensus today?" he asked. "The strategy for the rebranding campaign? What *does* a woman want?"

"We're not there yet. We've narrowed it down to three, and we're going to map out ideas for them and see which takes us in the right direction."

"Which three?"

"Power, adventure, and orgasms."

"Well, we know those three combined did well for those *Fifty Shades* books."

"This is true."

He tilted his head. "You read those?"

"I did."

"And?"

"Loved them. Women love a fantasy."

His eyes never left mine. "It's after business hours, right?"

I looked down at my watch. "I'd say so."

"You into that sort of thing?"

The color on my face answered the question. I avoided meeting his gaze as I stared down, twisting my bracelet. "I don't think so. But I've never actually tried it."

Forcing my eyes up to his, I asked, "How about you?"

"Not something I ever gave any thought to myself. But I could see the appeal of tying a woman up, having her vulnerable before me—a certain element of power for both people, in a way."

His eyes fell to my throat when I swallowed.

"Maybe seeing my pink hand mark on her pale skin...on her ass, the inside of her thighs..." He paused, staring at my wrists. "Bound, a blindfold, maybe a toy or two."

"Thought you said you never gave any thought to it?"

"I didn't." He waited until our eyes locked. "Until today. Didn't get shit done thinking about your tiny little wrists and how much I look forward to seeing them tied to my headboard someday."

Just then, my cell started to buzz. I looked down, seeing the name, and my eyes flicked back and forth between Chase and my iPhone. He wasn't going to give me any privacy.

"Excuse me one second." I swiped and answered. "Hello?...Yes, I'm almost done. Why don't I meet you there?... Okay. See you in a half hour."

"Date?"

"I'm meeting Bryant for drinks."

Chase's jaw tightened. He nodded. "Have a good night, Buttercup."

CHAPTER
8

Reese

I had sex on the brain.

It just wasn't Bryant I wanted to have it with.

We'd had two drinks. I told him all about my new job, and he *actually listened*. Now we were sitting at the bar, and he put his hand on my knee.

"I was thinking...how about we go down to the Jersey Shore this weekend? A weekend on the beach, dinner at a shack that sells cold beer and clams by the bucket? My friend has a place down in Long Beach Island, and he isn't using it this weekend."

I loved the beach, and a clam bar and beer was totally my thing. Yet...I was hesitant to commit on the spot for some reason. I needed time to think about it a little more. "Can I get back to you in a day or two? We just started this big project I'm working on, and they may expect me to come in over the weekend. I'm not really sure yet."

As usual, Bryant was a good sport. "Sure. Of course."

We called it an early night after that since both of us were early risers. Back at my apartment, Tallulah, that damn ugly cat, scared the crap out of me when I walked in. The sound of my collection of deadbolts unlocking had become her personal Pavlovian call to action. The living room was dark except for two bright green globes staring directly at me. She was perched on the top of the back of the couch waiting for me when I flicked on the lights.

"God, you really are ugly as sin."

"Meow."

"I know, I know, you can't help it." I scratched my fingernails on her back. It felt so odd without any fur. "How about if I get you one of those little cat sweaters? Maybe something sleek-looking and black? Or maybe something with faux fur on it, huh? Would you like that, ugly girl? You need some fur for this Butterball-looking body."

"Meow."

I carried her with me as I did my daily entry ritual—opening all the closets and doors, checking behind the curtains and under the bed. Finding all clear, I took a quick shower, moisturized my body, and climbed into bed. Tallulah hopped up and planted herself on the pillow next to me.

After a fourteen-hour day at a new job, followed by two martinis, I should have been tired. But I wasn't. I was... *horny*. My problem could have been easily remedied. I was certain all I had to do was invite Bryant back to my place, and he would have gladly taken care of my needs. Yet I chose to be alone.

Tallulah purred next to me, then hit me in the face with her paw. When I ignored her, she did it again. The second time, I took a paw to the nose. Giving in, I reached over and scratched her fleshy pink belly again. She rolled on her back to give me full access. With her paws drawn and bent at her sides, her arms and legs looked like wings. She really did look like an uncooked turkey. Reaching over to my nightstand, I grabbed my phone and snapped a couple of pictures I intended to email to my mother in the morning, but then I remembered the message Chase had sent me the other night about Tallulah.

I typed out a text, attaching the photo of Tallulah on her back.

Reese: *Pretty sure her twin is a Butterball in a grocery freezer somewhere.*

It had been less than a minute when my phone buzzed with an incoming text.

Chase: *I flipped my phone around a few times before I realized what I was looking at. That is seriously one ugly pussy.*

Reese: *LOL. Who has taken over half my bed. She's also very demanding and keeps pawing me in the face if I stop scratching her.*

Chase: *Just you two sharing that big bed tonight?*

He knew I'd been meeting Bryant after I left the office.

Reese: *Yup. Just me and my ugly kitty.*

Chase: *Good to know.*

Reese: *Well, sweet dreams.*

Chase: *You can count on it now. Night, Buttercup.*

My best friend Jules and I met for coffee the next morning before work. It had been the longest I'd gone without seeing her since we both started at Fresh Look on the same day seven years ago.

"The place sucks without you," she pouted as we sat near the window with our coffees.

"Of course it does. You have no one to gossip with."

"I had lunch with Ena from media relations the other day and told her about a new vibrator I bought. I'm pretty sure I scared her away for life."

"Some people are uptight about sharing that type of information."

She shrugged.

Jules was the most open and non-uptight person I'd ever met. Her parents were actual hippies, and she grew up with the *share the love* vibe in her house. Once she told me her parents had separate bedrooms for when the other had company. Sharing highlights about your new vibrator purchase seems tame when you grew up with your parents sharing partners.

"Well...not that you need it since you have Bryant now, but Lovehoney just came out with a new triple-whammy Jessica Rabbit, and it's seriously better than my last two partners. It actually finds your clit."

"I'll have to check it out."

"Don't tell me Bryant's a dud?"

I sipped my coffee. "Wouldn't know. Haven't slept with him yet. But he's pretty attentive in general. So that's a good sign, I suppose."

"Just not feeling it with him, or is something else going on?"

The fact that my mind immediately went to Chase made it clear it was more about *something else* than it was about Bryant. *Someone* else, actually. "He's great. He really is."

"But..."

"I don't know. Something has been holding me back from taking our relationship to the next level."

"Something or someone?"

Jules knew me too well.

"Remember that guy I told you about who I met at the restaurant on my date with Martin?"

"The hot one who made up all the stories?"

"That's the one."

"I sort of ran into him again."

"Sort of?"

"Well...I've run into him a few times."

"Where?"

I hesitated and then responded with a question, as if I were trying out the response. "In the office?"

Jules put her coffee down on the table between us. "He works at the new office? You've got to be kidding me. You know what happened last time you had sex with a co-worker."

"Chase isn't exactly a co-worker." Just as I said the words, my boss walked into the coffee shop. Well, technically he wasn't my boss. He was my boss's boss. I wasn't sure if that made it better or worse. *Worse, I'm sure.*

Jules and I were in the corner, so I hoped maybe Chase wouldn't see us. Not that I didn't enjoy looking at the man every time an opportunity came my way, but I knew Jules wouldn't be discreet. He walked in, stood in line, and within seconds turned and scanned the room. I briefly wondered if he was looking for me, although I didn't have time to deliberate long because suddenly he was heading right toward us.

Unlike my first day when I'd run into him here, this morning he was already dressed in a suit. And, *shit*—he looked even hotter than usual. His hair was still wet and mussed in that way that said he didn't give a shit, and it worked for him by setting him apart from the other suit-wearing, slicked-back-haired men. He had on a French blue dress shirt and a tie of the same color, only darker. It hung untied around his neck like he'd thrown it on and run out the door in a rush.

There was zero doubt in my mind that his shirt was custom made, the way it stretched across his wide chest—fitted, yet not too tight. It hinted at the carved lines I knew were below, but didn't flaunt them on full display.

While *I* was discreet in checking him out as he walked over, Jules' eyes lit up, and she openly ogled.

"Morning." He smiled at me and nodded to Jules. "How'd you and Ugly Kitty make out last night? She let you get some sleep?"

"She did. Might have to keep her as a bedmate."

"Shame."

Jules quirked an eyebrow. "Ugly Kitty? And who is this handsome man speaking to us?" Like I said, Jules came from a *very* open house. She had no filter. If she thought it, it slid right down a steep slide from her brain and popped out her pink-painted lips.

Chase blessed us with his full, mega-watt dimpled smile and extended his hand down to Jules. "Chase Parker. Reese and I work together."

Jules turned to me, bug-eyed. "Chase as in *Chase*, who we were just talking about?"

Chase raised an eyebrow. "All good, I hope?"

"Look at you! What could possibly be bad?" she said.

Chase chuckled and shook his head. "You ladies want a refill? I have an early meeting I need to run to after I get my caffeine fix."

"I think we're good. But thanks."

"See you in the office later, then."

"Highlight of my day," I teased.

Chase was barely out of earshot when Jules started in.

She held up her hand, showing me her palm. "No need to explain why you've lost interest in Bryant. That man is delicious. You know my theory that handsome men aren't as good in bed as the non-handsome crowd because they've never had to work for it hard enough?"

"Yes. What about it?"

"One look at that man and I can tell you, *he's* the exception."

"You know he's good in bed just by looking at him and that short conversation?"

She put on a serious face. "Without a shadow of a doubt, I do."

Jules was nutty, but I tended to agree with her. I knew from Chase's personality that he would perfect anything he focused on. He was also naturally aggressive, which I was certain would translate into dominant in bed.

I sighed. "He's really smart, too."

"Poor guy. Gorgeous, smart, and good in bed. What does he do at the new job? Let me guess—sales. Whatever he's selling, I'm buying."

"I guess you could say he does a little of everything."

Jules thought she understood. She shook her head. "Admin assistant? That's okay. You have a good job. You can be his sugar momma."

"He's actually the CEO. Chase Parker *owns* Parker Industries. And not in the same way that sleazy Derek Eikman will someday own Fresh Look. Chase is self-made. He invented most of the products the company sells, and he runs the company himself."

"Oh, Jesus. All right, all right. Let me think." She tapped her pointer finger to her chin a few times. "So you obviously shouldn't sleep with him, because we know how that can turn out from your little moment of temporary insanity with Derek. But there is absolutely no reason whatsoever that

I shouldn't hop in the sack with that pimped ride." Jules wiggled her eyebrows.

"Pimped ride?"

"I'm trying a new phrase on for size. How's it working?"

"It's not."

"Well, this could work out for both of us. Actually, it works for *four* of us. Think about it. If I sleep with him, you'll think it's too weird to sleep with him, too. You're not the kind of person who can explore where your friends have already planted their flags. So he'll mentally become off limits to you. Eventually you'll look at him like art you admire instead of a steak you want to eat, and that will free up your appetite for other food—like Bryant. That will make both you and Bryant happy. And, of course, Chase and I are going to be extremely happy...because we will both have had the best sex of our lives." She shrugged. "Problem solved. You're welcome."

I laughed. "I really do miss having you around all the time."

"Me too. It really sucks without you. Someday we need to start our own advertising firm. We'll hire only powerful women as management and hot men as assistants."

"Sounds like a plan to me."

"So what are you going to do with Bryant and Bossman?"

"I need to give things a real try with Bryant. My dating life hasn't exactly been full of eligible bachelors. I've had one relationship that lasted more than two months in the last five years. And you know how that ended. Alec was a nice guy, but he was still so hung up on his ex that he called me Allison every time we were in bed—usually during his grand finale."

I sighed. "Bryant really seems to be a great guy without baggage. I should just sleep with him and get it over with."

"Now that sounds like how I'd want the person I was

dating to think of having sex with me for the first time. *Get it over with*."

CHAPTER
9

Chase – Seven years ago

Eddie had been missing from his usual spot for three days. After lunch, Peyton made me walk around the neighborhood with her to see if he'd turned up yet. I had a bad feeling after seeing that gash on his head last week. Peyton must have, too. As we rounded the corner, a sense of relief came over me when I saw him. Only he wasn't alone. He was being hassled by two cops. The taller one—Officer Canatalli, according to the badge on his puffed-out chest—had just kicked Eddie's feet.

"Afternoon, officers," I called. "New beat?"

The cop, who wasn't much older than me, gave Peyton a leering once-over, then squared his shoulders and widened his stance. "You got a problem?"

"No problem. Just usually see Officer Connolly around this block. I work around the corner." I tilted my head to Eddie. "This is Eddie."

Peyton added. "Eddie is a friend of mine. I volunteer over at Little East Open Kitchen. It's a local food bank on—"

"I know where it is. Little thing like yourself shouldn't be around these type of people. They're dangerous. You could get hurt."

I closed my eyes, knowing how Peyton was about respond.

"*They're* dangerous? Don't you think that's kind of a generalized statement? It's no different than talking about Italians and saying *they're* all a bunch of mobsters, Officer *Canatalli*."

I tried to temper where the conversation was heading. "Eddie here has been getting hassled by some teenagers lately. That's how he got that gash there on his head. Peyton went down to the precinct to report it, but nothing was done about it."

"Yet another reason why he shouldn't be hanging out here on the street. We were just telling him it was time to move on for today. Sergeant wants the street cleaned up." The cop kicked Eddie's foot again, and Eddie's leg recoiled as he balled himself into a position to protect his head.

"Eddie doesn't like to be touched. He prefers people to keep a few feet away."

"So do I. That's why I don't sit on the sidewalk where someone will physically remove me if I don't get up."

Rookie asshole.

"Come on, Eddie. Come with me." Peyton extended her hand.

Eddie looked at me, then the officers, then back to me before taking her hand to get up. He lifted his black garbage bag over his shoulder. The bag was bulging, and after two steps, a small hole in the bottom spread wide, and everything he owned began to spill onto the sidewalk. The impatient policemen started to complain. They had no compassion.

Peyton had her guitar case slung over her shoulder, and she kneeled down, setting it on the sidewalk, and removed the instrument.

"Here, Eddie. Use this. The case just made it heavy anyway." She slipped the guitar's strap over her shoulder, and Eddie eventually bent and stuffed everything into her case.

As we walked back toward my office, I whispered to Peyton, "What are we going to do with him?"

She shrugged and gave me that sweet smile I could never resist. "I don't know, but there's plenty of room in that big, new office of yours."

CHAPTER
10

Reese

I was busy with work the entire day, although that didn't keep me from thinking about the boss at random times. It sort of helped to break my day into segments. Work on a tagline for Divine. *Daydream about the boss.* Research SEO keywords. *Daydream about the boss.* Lunch. *Daydream about the boss.* No wonder I was still at work at eight o'clock with all the time I'd slacked off.

When footsteps approached my door, my pulse quickened, anticipating it might be Chase. I hid my disappointment by being extra bubbly.

"Hi, Josh!"

"Burning the midnight oil again, huh?"

"I'm playing catch-up with so many things, and I want to be able to participate. Your team is incredible. They know these products inside out."

"They are pretty great. But sometimes a fresh look at things wins out over experience. Chase told me two out of the three concepts we're working with originated from you."

"It was a team effort."

He smiled warmly. "Gonna head out. Don't stay too late."

"I won't."

Just as he turned away, I thought of something I kept forgetting to ask. "Hey, Josh. Do you think we'll work this weekend? A...friend asked me to go away for the weekend, but I wasn't sure if you planned to come in or not. Lindsey mentioned that sometimes the team works weekends when they have a big project going on."

"I don't think so. But I'll check with Chase tomorrow, see if he has any plans. He likes to get us out of the office when we do weekend brainstorming sessions."

"Okay. Thanks. Have a good night."

A few minutes later, I was shutting down my laptop and packing up my desk when Chase walked in. He was in gym clothes—loose shorts and a faded Mets T-shirt. *God, he looks sexy.* I was beginning to realize I thought the man looked good in anything.

"You wear that T-shirt around Samantha?"

"I wear this T-shirt *because* of Sam. Drives her nuts."

"You two have an interesting dynamic, that's for sure."

"How was the rest of your coffee with your friend? You two talk about me some more after I left?"

"I was just telling her the story of how we met, that was all. Don't let it go to your head." Of course, what we were discussing *would* have inflated his ego, but he really didn't need to know that.

"That's disappointing. Was hoping maybe you were telling her how *hot* you thought your boss was."

"Josh is handsome, although I'm not really the Adrien Brody type myself."

"Smartass."

"You heading to the gym?"

"Yeah. Didn't get a chance to run this morning because of that early meeting I had. You heading out?"

"Yep. Home to Ugly Kitty. I think she gets pissed when I leave her alone for too many hours. She waits for me near the door and scares the shit out of me with her glowing green eyes."

Chase tapped his finger against the door jamb like he was considering something. "No Brian tonight?"

"*Bryant*. And no, not tonight. Just me and Ugly Kitty." The mention of Bryant reminded me of this weekend again. "By the way, do you know yet if you're planning on working this weekend?"

"Working this weekend?"

"The marketing department, I mean. Lindsey said sometimes during a big project everyone will go offsite for brainstorming."

"Haven't talked about it yet."

"Okay."

"You have plans this weekend or something?"

"Not really. Well...sort of. A...friend asked me if I was free."

He stared at me for a few seconds then squinted. "Anything good?"

"Long Beach Island."

I was pretty sure he really wanted to know whether my plans were with Bryant, but I intentionally kept being vague. And he intentionally kept prodding. It was almost like a game.

"Got a house there?"

"No. Friend-of-a-friend sort of thing."

He squinted again, staring at me, but I still didn't give in. "Girls' weekend?"

I shook my head.

He nodded. "See you in the morning. Don't stay too late."

"Okay. Goodnight."

Chase turned like he was going to leave, then turned back. "On second thought, you know what? I think we do need to work this weekend."

I smiled brightly—although I wasn't sure why the hell I was smiling when he'd just put the kibosh on my weekend at the beach.

Maybe because I didn't really want to go with Bryant. Or maybe because the thought of working with Chase all weekend was more exciting than a romantic beach weekend with the guy I was dating. Either way, I was looking forward to working *a little too much.*

After I left the office that night, I stopped at the restaurant a few doors down and picked up a meatball parm hero, knowing I'd be too lazy to cook when I got home. Between the long hours at the office, late-night meals, and skipping the gym, I was definitely going to gain weight if I didn't do something about it.

Maybe I should join a new gym? Iron Horse was nice. And Bryant would probably like it if I joined. But who would I be kidding? Myself. I already spent half the day glancing up to spot a certain someone around the office. I sure as hell didn't need any more distractions from that man.

My phone buzzed as I crossed the street on the way to my subway station. Bryant's name flashed on the screen. Knowing I only had a minute before I lost service, I hit ignore, figuring I would call him back when I got home.

Outside of my train station, a man with longish gray hair sat on the concrete. He had a long beard to match. His skin was dark and leathery, likely from long hours baking in the sun. But it was the light blue of his eyes that caught my attention when he looked up. I have no idea why, even though I knew he was obviously homeless, he didn't look like someone who was *supposed* to be homeless. He seemed soft and sad, rather than drunk or scary like a lot of the people I'd learned to speed past growing up in New York City. He had a guitar case sitting next to him with the lid open, but it was filled with piles of neatly organized clothing. I offered a smile and kept going. He returned the smile, but quickly looked away—like he wasn't supposed to be looking at me.

Halfway down the subway stairs, I remembered my giant meatball hero. Walking back up, I split it in two and gave half to the man with the sad blue eyes. He smiled gratefully and nodded.

It felt good, and my ass certainly didn't need an entire hero.

CHAPTER
11

Reese

I'd forgotten how much I loved happy hour. Jules and I used to do it every Thursday night when we first started at Fresh Look, but as time went by, one of us was always working late. We'd apologize and promise to do it the following week, but then the other person would be on deadline and not be able to go. Eventually, we just stopped even trying to make plans.

But the employees at Parker Industries made time for happy hour, and I'd managed to leave the office at a reasonable hour, too. Lindsey was another brand manager in the marketing department, and we'd hit it off on my first day. We were sitting at a bar, drinking Godiva chocolate martinis and enjoying the free appetizers as she filled me in on all the office gossip.

"And Karen in payroll is engaged to a guy who used to be in porn."

"Porn?"

"It was soft stuff. But if you want to see his dick, just Google John Summers."

"It would be really weird to Google someone in the office's fiancé to look at him naked."

Lindsey crinkled up her nose. "It's not circumcised. It's really ugly. But it's huge." She held out her hands nearly twelve inches apart. "Like a baseball bat. Now every time I look at her, I can't stop wondering how that thing fits. I mean, she's so tiny."

"You need to meet my friend Jules. It's uncanny how much you remind me of her."

Lindsey tossed back the rest of her martini and held the empty glass up for the bartender. "So tell me about you. Boyfriend, husband, sister-wife? What's going on in your life?"

Answering should have been easier. "I've been on four dates with a guy who's really sweet. We talk almost every day."

"Really sweet, huh? Are you exclusive?"

Huh? Are we? "We haven't really talked about it. But I haven't been dating anyone else."

The bartender came by with a shaker and refilled both our glasses. Lindsey eyed me over the top of hers as she sipped. "You're not that into him."

"What makes you say that?"

"You didn't perk up when you talked about him, you described him as 'sweet', you aren't sure if you're exclusive, and it seems like thirty seconds ago was the first time you'd even considered the question. That means you don't care if he isn't." She shrugged and said pointedly, "You're not that into him."

I exhaled a deep breath. "I think you're right. He's great—he really is. But there's just something missing."

"Can't force it."

She was right. Although the thought of breaking things off with a guy like Bryant—one who didn't come along that often in New York City—was pretty depressing. I needed to think about something else.

"Tell me more gossip? What about Samantha?"

"She's pretty much what you see. Been with the company about four years now, I think. Married, no kids that I'm aware of. She and Chase go way back. I heard a rumor that she was best friends with his girlfriend who died."

"His girlfriend *died*?"

"Yep. Years ago. I think she was only twenty-one at the time." Lindsey shook hear head. "Tragic."

"How did she die? Was she sick or something?"

"Some sort of an accident, I think. It was before I started. But I heard Chase was screwed up for a long time. It's why he licensed all his products originally instead of distributing them himself. A lot of those licenses are expiring, and that's why we're marketing some of the products for the first time."

"Wow."

"Yeah. He seems really good now, though. He's usually in a good mood, anyway." Lindsey grinned. "But I would be too if I got up every morning and looked at that face. The man is obscenely hot—if you're into that sort of thing, that is."

I laughed. "Not your type?"

"Apparently I like my men balding with a beer belly and propensity to be unemployed. I've been with Al since I was sixteen."

"He's gained some weight, huh?"

She snorted. "Actually, no. He's pretty much always looked the same way. But the man thinks I walk on water for reasons I'll never understand. Treats me like a princess."

"Good for you."

A couple of people from sales came into the bar and joined us, effectively ending my gossip session with Lindsey.

After that, we mingled, and I got to meet a few new people. But I couldn't stop thinking about what I'd learned about Chase. He'd lost someone. Something like that had to have a big impact on your life, no matter how smart and well-adjusted you were.

Even if it didn't break you, it left cracks and tiny fissures that could never be repaired.

Although the bar had grown busier by nine, the office crowd had begun to thin out. Lindsey went home, and there was only one other person from marketing left. It was time to call it a night. I attempted to get the bartender's attention, but she was swamped down at the other end of the bar.

A man who'd clearly been overserved squeezed in next to me and tried to strike up a conversation while standing too close.

"Is that your real hair color?" he asked.

"Don't you know you're never supposed to ask a woman her age, weight, or if she dyes her hair?"

"Didn't know that." He swayed back and forth. "So asking for a phone number is okay?"

I attempted to be polite. "I suppose, if she isn't married and seems interested."

Feeling the need to escape, I tried again to get the bartender's attention so I could close my tab. She held up her hand to let me know she'd seen me, but she was still busy making drinks at the other end of the bar. They really needed another bartender with this crowd.

Since I was stuck standing there, drunk guy assumed that meant I was interested. "What's your name, red?" He reached out and touched my hair.

"Please don't touch me."

He raised his hands in mock surrender. "You like women or something?"

This guy was amusing. For the first time since he'd walked over, I finally gave him my full attention, turning my body to face him before answering. "You assume I like women, just because I don't want you to touch me?"

He ignored me. "Let me buy you a drink, pretty girl."

"No, thanks."

He leaned in closer, wobbling as he spoke. "You're feisty. I like that. The red hair must be real."

A voice from behind me caught me by surprise.

"Go stand somewhere else." Chase's voice was low but stern. He took a step and partially inserted himself between us, facing the drunk.

"I saw her first," the man whined.

"I don't think so, buddy. I sucked her face in middle school. Take a hike."

The drunk grumbled something, but staggered away. Chase turned to face me, standing in his place. *Wow. Much better view.*

"Thank you. Polite wasn't working."

Of course, as soon as the drunk was no longer a problem, the bartender came to settle my tab. "What can I get you, Chase?" *Or maybe not.*

"I'll take a Sam Adams."

She turned to me. "You want me to close out your tab, right?"

"You're leaving? I just got here. You have to have one drink with me."

I wanted to. I *really* wanted to. But I knew I should probably go. Chase read the hesitation on my face.

"Close her tab. Bring another of whatever she's drinking, and put it on my tab. We're going to move to a table where it's quieter."

The bartender took his direction, and I shook my head, even though I was smiling.

"No one ever says no to you, do they?" I asked.

"Not if I have anything to say about it."

A minute later, Chase had both of our drinks in one hand and used the other to guide me toward a quiet table in the back. Once settled, he sipped his beer, watching me over the bottle. "Thanks for the invite tonight, by the way."

I stopped with my drink mid-way to my lips. "I didn't even know everyone went out on Thursday nights. I'm the new girl. You could have told me about it."

"Tried to. Came by your office, but you were already gone."

I'd actually sat at my desk and thought about stopping by Chase's office to mention everyone was going for drinks. But in my head, it had felt like I would be asking him for more than just joining a group for happy hour.

"Well...we're both here now," I said. "You worked pretty late tonight."

"I had dinner plans, actually."

His answer made me feel anxious...and maybe a *teeny bit* jealous. "Oh."

I felt him staring at me, yet avoided his eyes as I stirred my drink. When I finally looked up, his eyes searched for something in mine.

"With my sister, not a date. It's a regular weekly thing."

"I wasn't asking."

"No. You didn't ask. But you were disappointed when I said I had dinner plans."

"I was not."

"Looked that way to me."

"I think your conceitedness clouds your judgment of what you see sometimes."

"Is that so?"

"It is."

"So it wouldn't stir any feelings inside of you if I told you I was late because I was busy fucking someone?"

My jaw clenched, but I forced a mask onto my face and shrugged. "Not at all. Why would it bother me? You're my boss, not my boyfriend."

Surprising me, Chase dropped it and changed the subject. "So how do you like it so far at Parker Industries?"

"I love it, actually. It reminds me a lot of when I first started at Fresh Look. Everyone is so open-minded and in touch with the people who actually use the products. Even though Fresh Look is a smaller company than Parker, it took on investors over the years, and they began to control more and more of how Fresh Look marketed. Eventually, management started to lose sight of who we were marketing to—the board of directors or the women who used the cosmetics."

Chase nodded like he understood. "There's definitely a trade-off when you go outside for money. Control isn't something I ever want to give up again. It would drive me crazy to have to answer to a bunch of suits who didn't have a clue about what's important to the women who buy my products. Is that why you left? Because you lost your ability to market the way you believed it needed to be done?"

"I wish I could say it was. But I honestly didn't realize how restrained I'd felt until this week with Josh and his team."

Chase stared at me for several seconds. "Sometimes you don't know what you're missing until you find it."

I knew, by the way my body reacted to watching his Adam's apple bob up and down, that I was in trouble if I didn't redirect our conversation. I cleared my throat and blinked to disconnect my eyes from his neck.

"So...how was dinner with your sister?"

"She's very pregnant. All she talked about was hemorrhoids and leaking breasts. I lost my appetite."

I laughed. "Is this her first?"

"Pretty sure she thinks it's the *world's first* baby being born. I could see the pain in her husband's eyes as she talked tonight."

"I'm sure she isn't *that bad*."

"Over dinner, she yelled at him for *breathing* too loud. *Breathing*. He also wasn't allowed to order sushi at the Japanese restaurant we went to because she can't have it."

"I can't tell if you're making that up or not, considering your propensity for telling random stories."

"Sadly enough for my brother-in-law, I'm telling the truth."

"Does your sister live here in the city?"

"Upper East Side. Moved from downtown near her husband's job last year to be closer to her job at the Guggenheim. Now she can walk to the museum in three minutes, and her husband's commute is three times as long as it was. So of course, she quit her job as soon as she found out she was pregnant."

"You're being hard on her."

"She sure as shit makes it easy." He finished the rest of his beer. "I'm going to grab another one. You ready for a refill?"

"I probably shouldn't."

He grinned. "One refill coming right up."

While he was off getting our drinks, I sat pondering who, exactly, Chase Parker was. I'd never met a man quite like him before. He was someone I couldn't put my finger on... he didn't seem to fit into any one box. A businessman who ran a massively successful company—yet he looked more like a rock star with his shaggy hair and frequent five o'clock shadow. Custom-tailored, conservative suits covered a carved body and pierced nipple. He dated buxom blondes and joined strangers for dinner, yet had a standing weekly date with his sister. Even without factoring in what I'd learned tonight from Lindsey, the man was a complex package.

He returned a few minutes later with drinks in hand. "Miss me?"

Yes. "Were you gone?"

"So where is Becker tonight?"

"*Bryant.* And I'm not sure. We didn't have plans. I suppose he's home."

"Tell me about him?"

"Why?"

"I don't know. I'm curious, I guess. I'm wondering what kind of a man you're interested in."

You. "What do you want to know?"

"What does he do for a living?"

"He's in financial services. Manages mutual funds and stuff."

"What's his favorite movie?"

"I have no idea. We haven't been seeing each other that long."

"Does he snore?" He tried to hide his sneaky grin.

"Does Bridget?" I countered.

"I wouldn't know. She hasn't been in my bed. Then again, I'm sure I wouldn't know if you snored even if you were in my bed."

"Why is that? You're a sound sleeper or something?"

"You wouldn't be sleeping."

I laughed. "I walked right into that, didn't I?"

"You should get rid of Baxter and walk right into my bedroom."

Why was I laughing when he'd just told me to dump the guy I was dating and hop in his bed? This man made me lose all sense of judgment.

"So...any other siblings, besides your pregnant one?" I asked.

"If you're trying to cool me off, that's one way to do it. Mention Anna."

I sipped my drink. "Good to know."

"It's just me and preggo. How about you? Any brothers or sisters?"

"Just one. Owen. He's a year older. Lives in Connecticut, not too far from my parents."

"You two close?"

"We don't get to have dinner once a week, but yes, I like to think we're close. Owen's deaf, so it's not as easy as picking up the phone to actually talk, but we text all the time. And we do FaceConnect where we can type and see each other. When we were younger, we were inseparable."

"Wow. Do you know sign language or anything?"

"Not really. Owen lost his hearing at ten from...an injury. He took to reading lips faster than signing. I'm pretty good at reading lips. I used to put in earplugs and pretend to be deaf like him."

"Really? What I am saying?"

Chase mouthed something. I caught it on the first try, but screwed with him a bit. "Hmmm...not sure. Do it again."

Again his lips moved. This time, he'd over-accentuated each word, but he'd mouthed *You should come home with me* clear as day.

"Sorry. Guess I'm rusty." I smirked.

Chase bent his head back in laughter, and his throat vibrated.

God, that Adam's apple really works for me. The damn thing was taunting me, jumping around, showing off. I needed to get the hell out of the bar before I did something I'd regret for a multitude of reasons.

Finishing my drink, I stood. "I should get going. It's late. And I like to get to the office early to make a good impression with the boss."

"Pretty sure you've already done that."

"Goodnight, Chase."

"'Night, Buttercup."

CHAPTER
12

Reese

Saturday morning, I woke up feeling anxious. Not anxious in a nervous sort of way, it was more like the type of anxious I'd get for a date I was looking forward to. Only it wasn't a date, I was working. *On a Saturday.*

After going for a run to try to shake off my anticipation, I took a cool shower to clear my head. I let the water sluice over my shoulders and closed my eyes as I hummed. While humming had always been something I did to soothe myself, to soothe Owen, when I realized I was humming Kylie Minogue's *Can't Get You Out of My Head*, my eyes sprang open.

Of course they landed on one of the half-dozen Parker products that now filled my shower and bathroom. I truly could not get the man out of my mind, as he was all around me—in my thoughts, at work, *in my shower*. The small purple canister of Divine Scrub peeked out from behind my shampoo, catching my eye. I thought it was possible there was some deeper meaning—Divine Scrub, scrub away dead skin, scrub away thoughts of the man.

I scrubbed my body for nearly fifteen minutes, trying to rid my mind of Chase. The new body scrub supposedly not only scraped away dead skin but also included some chemical compound that regenerated new skin. When I was done and drying off, I was pissed that my skin felt incredibly soft instead of raw and cleansed of what I was trying to get rid of.

I threw a short, silky robe over my naked body, left it untied, and went to my bedroom for some lotion to rub into my new baby-soft skin. My vibrator was tucked away in the back of my nightstand where I also kept my favorite skin oil. Putting my hand on it, I considered getting myself off. Could I do that? Would it work to get Chase out of my system? Maybe that was exactly what I needed. It *had* been a long time since I'd been with a man. Probably close to eight months now.

I was getting myself all worked up over a good-looking man because of my pent-up sexual frustrations. Yeah, that was probably it.

But why wasn't I desperate to chase my orgasm with thoughts of Bryant in my head? Bryant was good looking. And sweet. And nice. And wanted me. *And isn't my damn boss.* Letting my robe fall open, I slipped my battery-operated man from my drawer and laid back on my bed, shutting my eyes.

Bryant. Bryant. Think of Bryant.

A vision of Chase the day I ran into him at the gym popped into my head. *God, he is gorgeous.*

No. What are you doing? Bryant. Think of Bryant. Bryant. Bryant. Bryant. Bryant, who bought me flowers last week for no reason other than to make me smile. Bryant, who texts me sweet little messages. **Thinking of you. Hope to see you soon. How is your pussy doing?** Wait. No. That last one was Chase. Who texts that sentence to a woman, even if he was talking about a cat? *And why the hell do I like it when he does?*

Bryant.

Chase.

Bryant.

Chase.

The soft hum of my vibrator relaxed me as I closed my eyes.

Bryant.

Bryant. Think of Bryant.

Water dripping from Chase's hard pec.

That V. That deep, carved V.

Pierced nipple.

Stop it. Bryant.

Chase.

Bryant.

Chase.

Chase.

Chase.

Argh. I groaned, frustrated with my mind, as I lowered my hand down my body.

I needed to stop thinking about the man, rid my system of dirty thoughts of my boss. I'd tried everything else—why not try to *coax* him from my system? After all, at least this method was more fun.

Chase's building was a three-story brownstone. I had assumed he'd live in a sleek highrise with a doorman, maybe even a penthouse. But when I walked down his beautiful tree-lined street, the neighborhood somehow fit him better. Nothing with that man was what I'd expect.

Steep stairs climbed from the street level up to an almost second-story entry. The front door was massive. It had to be at least fifteen feet high with thick, leaded glass and dark mahogany wood. Three buzzers lined up next to each other inside the archway of the door, but only one was labeled— *Parker*. I took a deep breath, buzzed, and waited.

After a few minutes, I buzzed a second time. When no one came to the door, I looked at my watch. Three minutes to eleven. I was early, but only by a hair. More time went by, and it became clear no one was home. Retreating a few steps down the stairs, I checked the house number, which was set into the back of the third-from-the-top stair. Three twenty-nine—I was definitely at the right house.

Maybe I'm hitting the wrong buzzer. I pressed the one to the right of the one marked Parker and waited some more. Still nothing. Pulling my phone from my purse, I scrolled through my emails to find the one Josh's secretary had sent so I could double-check the address, even though I was positive it was right. I remember thinking it was a pretty big coincidence that Chase's house number was the same as my apartment number—three twenty-nine.

Opening the email, I verified I was definitely at the right address...but then I saw the problem. The email read, *Dress comfortably, come hungry, and bring only your creativity. See you at 1!* Shit. I had looked at it too fast the first time and mistakenly read the one with an exclamation point as an eleven. I was two hours early. No wonder no one was here yet.

I'd made it halfway back down the stairs when I heard the clank of a lock behind me. Glancing back as the door opened, I froze mid-step at the sight of Chase wearing only a towel wrapped around his waist.

"No, really, I can go. I have errands I've been avoiding forever, and it was my screw up. I'm two hours early, and I'm sure you have things to do."

Chase had insisted I come inside.

He put his hands on my shoulders. "You're staying. I'm going to go upstairs and get dressed, and then I'll make us something to eat." He motioned to a huge living room off to the left. "Make yourself comfortable. I'll be down in a few."

I nodded and did my best *not* to check him out. But he was only in a towel, for God's sake, and a girl only has so much discipline. Against my better judgment, I did a quick scan of his chest. When I caught sight of a noticeable bulge in *that area* of his towel, my eyes lingered, and Chase noticed.

He arched an eyebrow. "Unless you'd like me to stay this way."

Embarrassed, I shook my head and walked into the living room to hide my blush. I thought I heard him chuckle as he went up the stairs.

While he was gone, I took the opportunity to check out the living room. There was a huge fireplace with a mantel above it. A few framed pictures were displayed, and I lifted each one to take a closer look. Chase and what must have been his parents at his college graduation—they beamed proudly, and he wore his signature messy hair and a crooked grin. There were a few other family photos and a photo of him with the mayor. But the picture on the end of the shelf stole my heart. It was a sonogram dated two weeks earlier, bearing the patient's name *Anna Parker-Flynn*. He'd complained about his sister to me at happy hour, yet framed her baby-to-be photo.

Behind the couch was an alcove with the tallest windows I'd ever seen—at least nine feet in height, and they started two or three feet off the ground. The glass had colorful leaded panels, and light streamed in, beaming a kaleidoscope prism of colors across the room. Beneath the windows were built-in bookshelves. I checked out the titles—you can tell a lot about a person by what they read. *Steve Jobs: American Genius,* Stephen King, David Baldacci, a few classics, and... *Our Endangered Values: America's Moral Crisis* by Jimmy Carter.

Huh?

Now dressed, Chase came into the room and groaned when his cell phone immediately rang. He apologized, saying he needed to take an overseas call. I really didn't mind. I'd intruded two hours early, and snooping at glimpses of his private life was fascinating to me. He was barking at someone on the phone from the other room when I picked up an old, beat-up Gibson acoustic guitar that was leaning against the corner of the alcove.

I strummed lightly, and the sound brought back old memories. Owen and I used to have the same guitar when we were kids. Instinctively, my fingers began to press down on the chords to "Blackbird" as I strummed. It had been years since I played, yet it still flowed from my memory with ease.

When I was done, I found Chase standing in the archway, watching me. His face, which was usually easy to read, was impassive, stern almost. He just stood there, staring at me. Maybe I'd overstepped my bounds by picking it up.

"I'm sorry. I shouldn't have touched it." I gently placed the guitar back where I'd found it, leaning in the corner.

"It's fine." He turned abruptly and walked out of the room.

I opened my mouth to call after him, but could find nothing to say.

When he came back a few minutes later, he smiled, but still wasn't his usual flirty self. "Come on. I'll make us a bite to eat."

I followed him into the kitchen. The historic architecture of the brownstone had been carefully maintained, yet the entire kitchen was stocked with high-end, modern appliances and granite. Somehow the old and new blended together beautifully.

"Wow. This is amazing." I looked up at the soaring ceilings and all the tile-work on the walls. There was an island with copper pots and pans hanging from a rack above it. Chase grabbed a pan and started taking things out of the refrigerator.

Without looking at me, he spoke. "Paul McCartney or Dave Grohl?"

He wanted to know what version I'd had in my head as I played "Blackbird."

"Paul McCartney. Always."

"Big Beatles fan?"

"No, actually. But my brother is. He knows every word to every song."

Chase finally turned around. His face had softened. "Your brother who's deaf."

"Only one I have."

"Do you play often?"

"It's been years since I played. I'm kind of shocked I remembered the chords. My fingers just started playing it— probably because I played it about ten thousand times when we were kids. I only know four songs. 'Blackbird' was Owen's favorite before he lost his hearing. I learned to play it for him after he'd completely lost all audio reception. He would hold the guitar and feel the vibrations and sing along."

"That's cool."

"Yeah. Oddly enough, music was a big bond between us growing up. We used to play this game where I would hum songs, and he would touch my face and try to guess the song from the vibration. He was really good at it. I mean *really* good at it. I only had to hum a few bars, and he would know the song. Over the years, it became our secret little language—a way of communicating what I was thinking to him without anyone knowing. Like, sometimes we would go to our Aunt Sophie's house, and she would sneak and pour gin into a coffee mug. She thought none of us knew. But after her third cup of 'caffeine', she would start to slur a bit. So when she called our house, I'd answer, give our mom the phone, and then hum Pink Floyd's 'Comfortably Numb'. Owen would hold my face for two seconds and then guess who was on the phone."

Chase laughed. "That's great."

"Except I often still do it, and I don't even realize. I'll be in the middle of something and notice I'm humming a song that expresses my thoughts."

"Well, hopefully you won't be humming Johnny Paycheck anytime soon."

"Johnny Paycheck?"

"Sings 'Take this Job and Shove It'. I'd rather hear some Marvin Gaye flowing from those lips."

"Let me guess, 'Let's Get it On'?"

"You know you'll be humming it, too, huh?"

"You have a one-track mind."

He looked at me funny, seeming almost perplexed at his own answer. "Lately, I think you're right. Got this spitfire on my mind all the time. Her attitude is as fiery as her hair."

I laughed it off like it was a joke, but something told me he was being honest, that he really *was* thinking about me all the time. Or maybe it was just wishful thinking from my own one-track mind.

"So how did your brother lose his hearing anyway? You mentioned it was an accident. Was it a sports injury or something?"

While I never liked telling the story, I figured Chase of all people would understand, considering what I'd learned about his girlfriend. I'd pretty much obsessed over what Lindsey had told me the other day. It made me wonder if the past experiences Chase and I shared were some sort of unspoken connection between us.

"When I was nine, and Owen was ten, there was a string of home break-ins in our neighborhood—mostly just burglaries while the homeowners were out. Owen and I were latchkey kids. Our parents went to work before we left for school and came home after us. They also didn't get along, and my dad would frequently take off for a few days at a time, so the house was pretty much empty most days. One Tuesday, we had a half-day of school because the teachers were having some sort of a development conference. When we came home early, we walked into our house being robbed by two men."

"Shit. I had no idea, Reese. I'm sorry. I shouldn't have assumed."

"It's okay. I don't talk about it much. But it's part of who I am, part of who Owen is, for better or worse. Even though Owen was only ten, he pushed me back out the door and started screaming for help. One of the guys was holding our Xbox and used it like a bat to Owen's head—fractured the temporal bone and severed a nerve that sent Owen to the hospital with a concussion for a few days and left permanent sensorineural hearing loss."

"Jesus Christ. You were just kids."

"It could have been worse—at least that's what Owen's always said. He was still a pretty happy kid even after he lost his hearing."

"And you? Were you hurt at all?"

"I fell waiting for the ambulance while I was trying to take care of Owen, cut my hand on a piece of jagged metal on the broken Xbox." I held up my right hand and showed him the faint star-shaped scar between my thumb and pointer. "Didn't even need a stitch, healed itself." I laughed. "It's funny. Owen bore all the physical injuries, and he walks around pretty much carefree. I, on the other hand, walked away unscathed, yet I'm the one with a half dozen locks on her door and a compulsion for checking the backseat of my car and behind the shower curtain multiple times a day. I'm sort of afraid of my own shadow."

"But you look in the backseat instead of not driving?"

I wasn't sure what he was getting at. "I guess so. Yes."

"That's not being afraid. Being afraid is when you let fear control your life, let it stop you from doing what you want. When you're afraid, but you look your fear in the eye and live, that's courageous."

And there it was again. That invisible connection I'd felt to him since the first night we met. I didn't understand it, couldn't explain it or see it, yet I was certain it was there. I just *knew* he understood me, and it made me want to understand him, too. He couldn't have chosen anything more perfect to say.

"Thank you for saying that. I don't know why, but it always feels like you know what I need to hear." I scoffed.

"Even when you told me I was being a bitch in that restaurant hallway, I suppose."

Chase stared at me. "Did they catch the guys who did it?"

"Took a few months, but eventually they did. I think I slept for twenty-four hours the day after they were arrested. I had taken to sleeping on the floor in Owen's room, and any little sound would wake me."

"I'm sorry that happened to you."

"Thank you." Talking about that day always made me feel sad, but somehow, today, it felt oddly cathartic, and I was ready to move on to lighter topics. "So, you cook, huh?"

"I have a few tricks up my sleeve."

"Let's see what you can do, Bossman."

Chase turned on the griddle of his big stove and tossed a few slices of whole wheat bread on to grill. He then took out the strangest combination of things...including pineapple, cream cheese, and a bag of nuts.

As he began slicing the pineapple, he smiled and extended a piece to me across the island. "Are you a picky eater?"

"Not usually. I like to experiment."

"So you'll let me feed you whatever I want?"

My eyebrows jumped.

"I was talking about pineapple-cream cheese-cashew surprise. But I like the way you're thinking better."

The flirty banter was back, and the awkwardness from the living room seemed to be behind us, though I still felt the need to address it.

I looked up at him and spoke softly. "I'm sorry about before—for picking up the guitar and helping myself to it. I shouldn't have done that. It looked like it upset you."

He looked away briefly. "It's fine. Don't worry about it. It's been collecting dust for years anyway. Someone should play it."

"You don't play?"

"No, I don't."

He offered nothing else, so I left it be.

The bizarre sandwiches he made us turned out to be delicious, and we sat in the kitchen, talking as we ate.

"This house is beautiful," I told him. "I'll admit, I would have guessed you more of a penthouse/highrise type than a brownstone guy before today. But seeing this, it fits you."

"Oh yeah? I'm not really sure what that means. Is it good?"

I smiled. "It is."

"Tell me, does Brice live in a penthouse or a brownstone?"

"*Bryant.* And he lives in a regular apartment building, I guess. Like me."

"And is that the type of guy you normally go for?"

"My type seems to be more the liars, losers, and leeches. I haven't had the best luck in my love life the last...I don't know...dozen or so years."

"Is that all, just a dozen years? It's a dry spell. I'm sure it will clear up any day."

I chuckled. "Yeah, I'm sure."

"Tell me about Barclay. Which one is he? Liar, loser, or leech?"

I shook my head. "*Bryant* isn't any of them." Popping the last piece of the snack Chase had made into my mouth, I figured it was his turn to talk. But he didn't. Instead he watched me chew and waited for me to continue. "I'm pretty sure he's a genuinely nice guy."

"So why haven't you slept with him yet?"

"I think you have an unhealthy obsession with my sex life. This is, like, the third time you've asked me about my relationship with Bryant."

Chase shrugged. "I'm curious."

"About my sex life?"

"Or lack thereof. Yes."

"Why?"

"I honestly have no fucking clue."

"Well...when was the last time *you* had sex?"

Chase sat back in his seat and folded his arms over his chest. "Before I met you."

I had no idea where the conversation was going or what it meant, but every nerve in my body was excited we were having it.

"Dry spell?" I asked.

"You could say that," he responded.

"I could say that? What kind of an answer is that? Is there anything else I could say?"

Chase leaned in. "You could say I'm waiting for the woman I really want to sleep with to become available so I can make my move."

I swallowed. We sat in silence for a few minutes, just looking at each other. A part of me wanted to pick up the phone and break things off with Bryant, right then and there. But the other, more sane, part of me remembered that the beautiful creature sitting across the table was my boss.

"Have you ever had an office fling?" I asked, tilting my head.

I could see a million questions run through Chase's mind. He wasn't sure how to answer. Smartly, he settled on the truth. "I have."

"So have I. It didn't work out too well."

He held my eyes, not backing down. "Shame. You know the old saying, if at first you don't succeed, try, try, again."

When his eyes moved from mine down to my mouth, and he

licked his lips before they finally returned, I knew it was time to change the subject.

Abruptly, I stood. "How about a tour of the house?"

"Absolutely. There's one room in particular I'd like to show you."

CHAPTER
13

Reese

I was exhilarated after spending the day working, almost high. It was only me and Josh left sitting on Chase's rooftop deck—and Chase, of course. The other four, including Lindsey, were gone. Josh and I had stayed to have a beer now that work was done.

I was sporting a ridiculously large smile. "At the risk of sounding like a complete goofball, I need to tell you, today was amazing. I can't remember when I've enjoyed working on anything this much. I'm not sure I ever have."

Josh tipped his beer in my direction. "It did feel good. Damn good. But I think you have a lot to do with that, Reese. You being new to the group seemed to bring out something in all of us—Chase especially." He shifted his eyes to Chase. "I haven't seen you this fired up in years. Today felt more like a new product launch than a rebranding campaign. Everything seemed new again."

Chase was sitting back in a lounge chair. He wore dark sunglasses, but I could feel his eyes on me nonetheless.

Nodding, he said, "It felt right. Been a long time since anything felt so right."

After a few more minutes, Josh guzzled back the rest of his beer. "Gotta head out. Elizabeth is making me go to a cake-tasting party tonight. Since when did everything about weddings turn into a damn event? I've had to go to a food tasting, a band showcase, and a floral-presentation party. Vegas is sounding better and better."

"Just wait." Chase stood. "Anna had a bridal shower, a pregnancy-announcement party, and a gender-reveal party. You're just getting started, buddy."

"What the hell is a gender-reveal party?"

"The parents-to-be give a sealed envelope that contains the sex of the baby to a bakery, and the baker puts pink frosting inside the cupcakes if it's a girl and blue if it's a boy. Then they have a party, and everyone finds out at the same time, including the parents-to-be. Pure. Fucking. Torture. Whatever happened to the kid popping out and the doctor giving it a smack and yelling *it's a boy* over the thing crying?"

"Thanks. More to look forward to."

Chase slapped Josh on the back as we walked to the stairs. "You're welcome."

Arriving on the first floor, I eyed the mess we'd left in the living room and dining room. Chase had dinner brought in, and there were dishes and balled-up papers from our work session all over the place.

"Where you heading, Reese?" Josh asked. "I'm going to grab a cab downtown if you want to split one."

"I'm cross town. But I'm going to stay for another minute and help Chase pick up a bit."

Josh looked over my shoulder, seeing the mess for the first time. "Crap. Thanks. I owe you one, Reese. See you Monday."

Before Chase even returned from walking Josh out, I had the place halfway cleaned. I picked up the garbage, and I was rinsing dishes and loading them into the dishwasher when I felt Chase come up behind me. He gently placed a hand on my face, and I stopped what I was doing.

"Keep going."

At first, I thought he meant to continue loading the dishwasher. Then I realized I'd been humming. Smiling, I continued with my tune. Luckily, he was no Owen. I would have been mortified had he guessed the song I was humming.

"'Thinking Out Loud', Ed Sheeran."

"Not even close." I laughed.

"'I Don't Mind', Usher."

I shook my head. "You do realize those two songs sound nothing alike?"

I finished loading the dishwasher while Chase moved the furniture we'd rearranged back. We glanced up at each other as we worked.

"Plans for tonight?" he asked.

"No. I wasn't sure what time we'd be done. You?"

"Nope. Wanna share another beer with me?"

"Sure. Why not?"

He grabbed two Sam Adams bottles from the fridge, and we sat down on the living room couch. Opening one, he took a sip and handed me the bottle, setting the other unopened one on the end table next to him.

I took the bottle. "I didn't realize you meant *literally* share a beer." I sipped and then offered it back to him. Raising my fingers to my wet lips, my instinct was to wipe away the beer remnants. But then I realized it wasn't just beer on my lips—it was *Chase* on my lips. His eyes followed the path of my tongue as I instead licked the wet spot off. The way he looked at me sent tingles of arousal through my body, hitting *certain places* more than others.

Desire built as we quietly finished one beer, and then he cracked open the other. I never knew something so innocent could seem so much like foreplay. *There goes my theory of getting him out of my system this morning.*

"We're off the clock now, aren't we?" He passed me the bottle.

"Hmmm...not sure how weekends work. It's technically not a workday, yet we did work today. Still, I'd have to say even if Saturday counts as part of the workweek, we're off the clock by now."

"So I'm not your boss right now, then?"

"Suppose not." I grinned and took a long sip from our beer.

"Well, then...it wouldn't be inappropriate to tell you that while I was in the shower this morning, I closed my eyes and thought of you as I took care of myself."

I was mid-swallow when what he'd said registered.

I choked, sputtering and spraying beer all over the place. Coughing, my voice was hoarse. "You what?"

"From your reaction, I'd say you heard me correctly." He took the beer from my hand.

"Why would you tell me that?"

"Because it's true. And I figured I'd lay all my cards on the table. You're not having sex. I'm not having sex. Thought maybe we could work through our problem together."

"I don't have a problem."

"So why aren't you having sex, then?"

"Why aren't you?"

"Because I'd like to have it with you, and you haven't given in to me. *Yet.*" He brought the beer to his lips and watched me as he drank.

"I can't believe we're having this conversation. You know I'm seeing someone."

"I do. That's why we're having this conversation. If you weren't seeing someone, I'd have you up on that kitchen island *showing you* what I want to do to you, rather than telling you."

"Is that so?"

He moved closer. "It is."

"What if I'm not into you in that way?"

Chase looked down, his eyes lingering on my nipples. *My very erect nipples.* "Your body says otherwise."

"Maybe I'm just cold."

He inched closer. "Is that it? Are you cold, Reese? Because you actually look a little warm. Flushed, even."

"You're my boss."

"Not now. You just said so yourself."

"But...even if I wasn't dating Brice—"

"Bryant," Chase corrected me with a smirk.

Oh my God. "Bryant. Even if I wasn't dating *Bryant*. And even if I was attracted to you—"

"You are."

"Quit interrupting. You're trying to confuse me. Like I was saying, even without Bryant in the picture and me being *slightly* attracted to you, it still can't happen. I really like this job, and I don't want to screw things up."

"What if I fired you?"

"That probably wouldn't be the best way to get into my pants."

"Tell me what is."

I chuckled. "You sound pretty desperate."

Although we'd been teasing, his response was serious. "I feel pretty damn desperate right about now."

So did I, but I wanted him to truly understand where my head was. "Can I be honest with you?"

"I'd be upset if you weren't."

"I sort of...had an office relationship...Well...it wasn't really a relationship. It was more like a momentary lapse in judgment caused by excessive imbibing in holiday cheer. Anyway, you get the picture."

"Yes. Unfortunately, I do. You slept with someone from work. Hang on. I should get another beer. I'm taking it this story isn't going to bode well for me."

Chase got up and grabbed two more beers. This time, he opened both and handed me one.

"I get my own?"

"Story sounds like you might need it."

I smiled gratefully. "Thank you. You're right. I do." Taking a deep breath, I continued. "Anyway, I loved my old job. It was pretty much my life for the last seven years. I worked my way up from intern to director. I dated, but hadn't had a serious relationship for the last five years. Make a long story short, I accidentally slept with a co-worker."

"Accidentally?"

"Peppermint Schnapps martinis at the office Christmas party. Don't judge."

Chase looked entertained, his eyes sparkling. He held up his hands. "No judgment here. Tough night and you let loose. Been there."

"The guy turned out to be a total dirtbag. Two days later he announced he'd gotten engaged over Christmas to his long-time girlfriend. He'd told me he was single."

"Sounds like an asshole."

"He was. And that's not the worst part. I told him what I thought of him and went out of my way to be an asshole to the jerk. A few months later, he was promoted to being my boss."

"Shit."

"Yeah. And to make it even worse, he knows nothing about marketing."

"How did he get the job?"

"He's the owner's son."

Chase's face was glum, but he nodded. "I get it. I'm not gonna lie and say I'm not disappointed, but I get it."

"You do?"

"Of course. You don't want to screw up your career for a night of physical gratification."

"Exactly."

"Even though that physical gratification would begin with me starting at your toes and working my way up. Slowly. Over hours."

"Hours?" My low voice came out with a high pitch.

Chase nodded with a sexy grin. "I'm up for the challenge."

"What challenge?"

"Waiting it out. Or breaking you down. One or the other."

"You're going to wait until I don't work here any more? What if I stay for years?"

"It won't be years."

I furrowed my brow.

"You'll break before then."

Bryant: *How was work today?*

I'd just gotten off the train at my stop when the text came in. I took a deep breath, dreading what I was about to do, but knowing in my heart it was right.

Reese: *It was good. Very productive, actually. I'm almost home, but could go for a drink. You up to join me for one? Maybe at The Pony Pub?*

The small bar was quiet and halfway between our apartments. We'd met there for our first date.

Bryant: *Absolutely. Meet you there in a half hour?*

Reese: *Perfect. See you soon.*

CHAPTER
14

Chase – Seven years ago

"Another Jack and Coke." I held my hand up to the bartender. I was usually halfway through my first drink by the time Peyton showed up, but starting on my second one was late even for her. Picking up my phone, I thumbed off a text.

Chase: *You're later than your usual late.*

Peyton: *I'll be there in ten minutes. If I'm not, read this text again.*

I chuckled.

She showed halfway through my second. Her arms wrapped around me from behind. "Can I buy you a drink?"

"Sure. My girlfriend is on her way, but she's late, so I could use some company."

She smacked my abs. "Some company, huh?"

I reached around, hooked my hand on her waist and pulled her from behind me to my lap in one fell swoop. She giggled, and any annoyance about her being forty-five minutes late was instantly gone. Again.

"What's your excuse this time?"

"I had some stuff I needed to take care of." She looked away when she said it, which told me I needed to pry more.

"What stuff?"

She shrugged. "Just some stuff. For the shelter."

I squinted. "Like...unpacking boxes of donated food? Or cleaning up the dishes after dinner service?"

"Yep. Just some errands. Stuff like that." She quickly tried to change the subject. "What are you drinking? Is that a Jack and Coke?"

Now I knew she was up to something. And I was pretty sure I knew what it was. "Yep. Jack and Coke. You want your usual?"

She hopped down off my lap and pulled up the stool next to me. "Yes, please. How was your day?"

After I called the bartender over and ordered her Merlot, I swiveled her chair in my direction. "You followed him again tonight, didn't you?"

Her shoulders deflated, but she didn't even try to lie. "He had a black eye today. And the gash on his head was re-opened. He probably should've had stitches the first time. Now it's worse, and it looks infected."

"I love how much you care. I really do. But you need to let the police do their job."

Wrong thing to say. "Do their job? That's the problem. They don't think keeping homeless people safe is part of their job at all. The only time they pay attention to them is if they sit down in a neighborhood that's too nice. Seriously, I wouldn't be surprised if the Upper West Side installed metal spikes up against buildings, like they do on train trestles to keep pigeons from making nests."

"I don't want you following homeless people to parks where it's dangerous at night."

She huffed. "I only wanted to find out where he was going so I can go back down to the police station tomorrow and ask them to patrol the area better."

"What park did you follow him to?"

"You know that old bridge they restored uptown? The one people walk across up near 155th Street?"

"You went all the way up to Washington Heights?"

"It might look nice from the bridge, but underneath hasn't been cleaned up. I guess the politicians just shook hands and took pictures on the top while underneath it was filled like a junkyard. Did you know there's a whole little city of people under that viaduct?"

"Peyton, you gotta cut this shit out. I know you want to help, but it's dangerous in those places."

"It was still light out, and I didn't actually go into the camp."

"Peyton..."

"Seriously. Everything is going to be fine. I'm going to stop in at the precinct closest to the park tomorrow. Hopefully the cops up there remember their job is to serve and protect *all* the citizens of this city."

"Promise me you won't pull shit like this again."

She smiled and leaned over to wrap her hand around the back of my neck. Gently grazing her fingers on my skin, she said, "I promise."

CHAPTER
15

Reese

The office wasn't the same when Chase wasn't there. Sure, I was busy and had enough work to do for a month—work that I loved doing—but the anticipation of seeing him throughout the day was missing. He'd only been gone two days on his business trip, but I'd missed him since day one.

I was up to my eyeballs in drafting presentations for an eventual focus group—a cross-section of women who we would try out some branding slogans and product-packaging mockups on—when my phone buzzed late on Thursday. Seeing Chase's name made me smile.

Chase: *Miss me?*

I did, but he certainly didn't need any encouragement.

Reese: *Did you go somewhere?*

Chase: *Cute.*

Reese: *I thought so.*

Chase: *I've been thinking about our little deal.*

Reese: *What deal? I don't recall agreeing to anything.*

Chase: *Exactly. Which is why we need a sit-down. To negotiate our terms.*

The man made caterpillars turn into butterflies that fluttered around in my stomach. I leaned back in my seat and rotated so the back of my chair was facing my open office door. It was late, and there were only a few people still milling around the floor, but I sought privacy as I typed with a smile.

Reese: *Terms? Are we discussing a business deal?*

I slipped my right shoe off and dangled it from my toe as I watched the three little dots jump around. It was pitiful that I was growing antsy waiting.

Chase: *Is spending time in my bed still off limits because I'm your boss?*

Reese: *It is.*

Chase: *Then I want time outside of the bedroom.*

Reese: *I see you at the office all the time.*

Chase: *I want more.*

My heart did a pathetic pitter-patter. *I want more, too.*

Reese: *More how?*

Chase: *I think this requires a face-to-face, sit-down conversation.*

Reese: *Like a date?*

Chase: *Don't think of it as a date. Think of it as a business meeting where we negotiate terms that lead to full performance of the contract in the future.*

Reese: *And that full performance would be...*

I nearly fell over in my seat, hearing Chase's voice behind me. "You in my bed, of course."

I whipped my chair around. "I thought you were away until tomorrow."

"Came back early. Had some pressing business."

"How long have you been standing there?"

"Not long." He pointed to the window. "But I could see your reflection in the glass, and I liked watching your face as you texted."

"Voyeur."

"If I can't have, I'm not above watching. Is that an offer?"

Chase looked like he hadn't shaved in a day or two. I wondered what that stubble would feel like rubbing against my cheek...and against the inside of my thighs. His tie was loose, his suit jacket draped over one arm, and his shirtsleeves were rolled up, revealing muscular forearms. I definitely had a thing for forearms. When I finally pulled my gaze back up to his eyes, he looked pleased at my being flustered.

"What did you ask?" I managed.

With a knowing grin, he said, "How about dinner? Did you eat yet?"

I picked up the protein bar on my desk that I hadn't gotten around to. "Not yet."

He tilted his head toward the hallway. "Come on, let me buy you some dinner. I can't have my employees working twelve hours a day and starving."

When I didn't immediately agree, he sighed. "It's not a date. We're sharing a meal. Business associates do it all the time."

I pulled my purse out of the drawer and pressed the button to put my laptop to sleep. "Okay. But this isn't a date."

"Of course not."

"All right then."

He winked. "It's a negotiation."

Apparently, I'd decided to take this negotiation thing very seriously, because I didn't even wait until we got to the elevator before I started being difficult.

"Have you ever been to Gotham in Union Square?" Chase asked.

"That's a date place. Too romantic. How about Legends in Midtown?"

"Do we have to eat at a dive bar for it to not qualify as a date? We'll go to Elm Café, down the block."

"Bossy," I said under my breath.

Because it was after regular building hours, we rode the service elevator down to the back entrance and exited the building on 73rd Street. Elm Café was only two blocks away.

Of course, when we passed by Iron Horse Gym, Bryant happened to be walking toward the door at that very moment. Because that was just my luck.

He looked at me, then at the man standing next to me, and stopped.

"Reese. Hey. Are you coming to Iron Horse?"

I wasn't sure if it was just me, or if everyone felt awkward. Perhaps it was guilt over running into my recent ex while standing next to my current...something. "Umm...no. We were just heading down the street to grab a bite to eat. You remember Chase?"

Bryant extended his hand. "Cousin, right?"

"Second cousin," Chase shook. "By marriage. We're not blood related."

Of course Bryant didn't understand the insinuation. But I did.

"Yes," I gave Chase the evil eye. "Second cousin Chase."

Bryant looked like he was going to say something, but changed his mind. "Well...I'm going to hit the gym. Guess I'll see you around?"

"Sure. Take care, Bryant."

Surprising me, Chase didn't question the odd exchange or my status with Bryant as we continued on to the restaurant. In fact, he was relatively quiet while we walked the block and a half.

Once we arrived at Elm Café, he asked for a table for two, then added, "Something quiet and romantic, if you have it."

The host sat us at a table off in the corner, and Chase pulled out my chair.

"Is this table romantic enough for you?" I asked sarcastically.

He sat. "I'll just have to tell you all the things I'd like to do to you to make up for the lack of romance in the setting."

I swallowed my sarcastic comeback, knowing better than to challenge him. If I was truly going to keep this a platonic relationship, it was best to limit the visuals. I was pretty good at imagining what I'd like him to do to me on my own. If I heard it from him—well, a girl has only so much willpower.

Luckily the waitress came over to take our drink order.

"I'll have a Jack and Coke, and she'll have a Peppermint Schnapps martini."

I glared at him and spoke to the waitress. "*She'll* just take a water. Thank you."

When the waitress walked away, Chase was grinning. "What? It worked at the office Christmas party. Can't blame me for trying."

"I think rule number one is I'll be staying sober if we're alone."

"Can't trust yourself, huh?"

Totally. "You're so full of yourself."

After the waitress brought our drinks, Chase wasted no time telling me what had been on his mind the last few days.

"So sleeping with me is off the table, but what about sharing a meal occasionally?"

"You mean like dating?"

"No. You said dating was off the table, too."

"So what would be the difference between sharing a meal and dating, then?"

"You wouldn't come home with me after the meal."

I laughed. "You say that as if *all* of your dates end up going home with you."

He gave me a look that didn't need to be accompanied by words.

Of course they all do. What am I thinking?

"God, you're an ass." I rolled my eyes.

"Is that a yes to twice-weekly meals together?"

"Do you have meals with all of your employees?"

"Does that matter?"

"It does, yes."

"Well, I have dinner with Sam occasionally."

I leaned back in my chair and folded my arms over my chest. "But not twice weekly."

"No. Not that often."

"Well, then I'm not sure it would be appropriate. We should probably stick to no more than what you do with other employees."

Chase squinted, then gave me a sly grin and held up one finger. He proceeded to whip out his phone and make a call. I listened to half the conversation.

"Sam, can you have dinner with me twice a week?...Does it matter what it's for?...Okay, then. I want to run things by you

for the new rebranding campaign. I like your perspective...."
He sighed. "Yes, fine. But we'll order in on the night we eat at
your place. I almost choked on that dry-as-shit chicken you
forced me to eat last time."

I couldn't make out everything, but I heard Sam's voice
rise and a string of words yelled through the phone. When
she took a breath, Chase forced the end of the conversation.

"Whatever you want. 'Night, Sam." He looked delighted
with himself when he hung up. "Yes, I do have twice-weekly
dinners with other employees."

I was in the mood to screw with him some more. "That's
different. Sam is your friend outside of the office. You two
have been friends longer than she's worked for you."

"And we've known each other since you bled all over me
in middle school."

"I think you're a little insane."

"I'm starting to agree with you." He sipped his Jack and
Coke.

Chase's cell phone buzzed, and a photo of a woman
flashed on the screen. I saw it, and Chase knew I did.

"You can take it," I told him. "I don't mind."

He hit reject, and then locked eyes with me. "That brings
me to my next negotiation point."

"There's more? Maybe I should be having something
stronger than water after all."

Chase extended his Jack and Coke to me. I took it and
sipped.

"I take it from the exchange you just had with Becker that
you're no longer a couple."

"We weren't really ever a couple. But yes, you're correct.
Bryant and I aren't dating anymore."

"He looked wounded. Did you tell him you were hot for
your cousin/boss when you broke his heart?"

"Is there a point you're trying to make buried under all the self-adulation?"

"There is. One of the things I had planned to negotiate in our deal was that you would break it off with Bryant."

He'd taken the Jack and Coke back from me, and I swiped it from his hands again.

Bringing it to my lips, I said, "And he finally gets the name correct."

Chase, of course, ignored me. "So we have an understanding, then? Until you quit or get fired—or sooner if you break—you won't be dating other men."

"And I won't be dating you, so basically I'll be dateless and abstinent?"

"I'm sure you have a vibrator. If not, I'll pick one up for you."

"You'll go to the store and buy me a vibrator?" I asked incredulously.

Chase abruptly grabbed our shared Jack and Coke from my hand and gulped down the remainder.

His voice was a groan. "I'm jealous of a goddamn vibrator now."

The strain in his voice made me feel empowered. It also gave me confidence to share things I might not normally have shared.

"Nothing to be jealous about." I leaned in. "My vibrator and I have already enjoyed a vivid three-way with you."

The look on Chase's face was priceless. I'd made his jaw go slack. The waitress was a few tables over, and he raised his hand to get her attention.

When she arrived at our table, he said, "Can we get a double Jack and Coke and two Peppermint Schnapps martinis, please?"

We spent the next two hours laughing and sharing drinks. In between, we set some ground rules. We'd have a meal together twice a week, outside of the office, but not in an overtly romantic place. Thanks to me, he'd also be sharing frequent meals with Sam in the upcoming months. Neither of us would be dating anyone else, and there would be no kissing or fooling around of any kind. If and when my tenure at Parker Industries ended, we'd give a real date a try and see where things led. In the office, we'd never refer to any private time we spent together outside of the office, and he would show me zero favoritism.

That last part I was passionate about. The entire reason for denying my attraction to Chase was to keep things professional in the office. There was no way I wanted anyone to even think there was something going on between us.

With the basics established, it had only taken me two hours to break my self-imposed inebriation ban. I was not off to a good start, yet I was feeling good (and tipsy) by the time we got up to leave.

"So how do we do this?" I asked. "How do we end our evenings together?"

"Fuck if I know. We've already established the way my evenings generally conclude." Chase steered me out of the restaurant with his hand on my lower back. As we walked onto the street, his hand dipped lower.

"Ummm...your hand is on my ass."

His eyes gleamed. "Is it? It must have a mind of its own."

He didn't move it, though, even while he hailed a cab. When one pulled to the curb, he informed me we would be sharing it.

"We'll drop you first, so I can make sure you get in safely."

"I'm perfectly capable of getting home myself."

"I've bent on everything you asked, but taking you home at night isn't negotiable."

I really loved his chivalry; it was myself I didn't trust. Chase held the cab door open and waited. Before slipping inside, I turned to face him and stepped into his personal space.

"Okay. I'll give you that. But you need to promise me something in return."

"And that is?"

"That even if *I beg,* you won't come inside."

CHAPTER
16

Reese

Friday afternoon, a few of us from the marketing department had ordered in lunch and were sitting around the break room eating while we talked about our plans for the weekend.

"Do you think we'll work again this weekend?" I asked Lindsey.

"I don't think so. Josh is going away on that Pre-Cana retreat weekend his fiancée is making him do. And I think Bossman has a hot date Saturday night."

"Hot date?"

"City Harvest Gala. A bunch of rich people throw a big party to raise millions for food for the homeless. It's at some swanky hotel this year, and Chase is being honored. I heard him tell his secretary to book a suite with a fancy name. The last two years he's gone with models from our ad campaigns. Life must be rough when you're rich and gorgeous."

Of course, Chase walked in right at that moment. I looked away but felt his eyes on me as he went to the coffee machine. He'd spent so much time and effort getting me to agree to not date other people—I couldn't imagine he would already be violating his own terms. But I also couldn't stop a pang of jealousy from creeping up inside of me.

"Hey, boss," Lindsey called. "We're not working this weekend, are we?"

"No. Not this weekend. I have some things I need to take care of."

"I was sort of hoping we would be. It's supposed to be nice, and Eddie wants to head down to the Jersey Shore to visit his mother."

"And that's not a good thing, I take it?"

"She runs around doting on him like he's royalty—always makes me feel inadequate."

Chase smirked. "You could always do some doting of your own to get rid of that feeling."

"Are you crazy? It took me fifteen years to get the man to lower his expectations. Why would I screw that up now?"

Chase smirked. "What about you, Reese? Plans this weekend?"

Jules had been bugging me to go to some new club for the last month. I had no desire to go. Until that moment. "Girls' night on Saturday. My friend Jules and I are going to check out Harper's downtown."

I caught the slight flex of his jaw, but he answered unaffected. "Sounds like fun."

"And what about you? Hot date?"

It wasn't exactly an appropriate question to ask your new boss. But Chase was not a traditional boss anyway. He was connected to his employees and knew what was going on in their lives. So my nosey question didn't raise any suspicion.

"Just a fundraiser we donate to. I'd prefer to just write the check, but somehow they talk me into showing up every year."

I smiled. It was completely fake, but no one really knew me well enough to notice. Except Chase. "Well, enjoy *your date."* I forked a piece of chicken from my Caesar salad and shoved it into my mouth.

I avoided Chase for the afternoon after that. At one point, he came down the hall toward my office, and I quickly popped into Josh's so we wouldn't be alone. Part of me knew I was being silly. Surely tomorrow night wasn't a real date, and I was building something in my head that didn't exist. This was *exactly* the reason I avoided office romance. Work needed to be about work, instead of letting my personal life interfere in places it didn't belong.

So when Chase showed up at my office door at six o'clock, I was determined to keep things strictly professional.

"Share a meal together Sunday night?"

"I don't think so. I'm going out clubbing Saturday and you—" I waved my hand as if saying *whatever*. "—have your date Saturday night. I'm sure we'll both need Sunday to recover."

He looked confused by my response. "Is everything okay, Reese?"

"It's fine. Why wouldn't it be?"

"I don't know. You seem like something's bothering you."

"Nope," I answered, fast and curt.

Maybe too curt. Chase studied me with his lips pressed together. He was looking for clues, but I wasn't giving any.

"I feel like it's about Saturday night. But I figured you'd never go for a night when you had to wear a gown as our non-date, casual sharing of a meal."

I cocked my head. "I'm sure you'll have a better time with a real date anyway."

His brows gathered again, and then his face transformed with a smug smile. "I wouldn't exactly call Sam a real date."

"Sam?"

"That's who I'm taking. Who did you think I was going with?" He moved closer.

"I don't know."

"Did you think I was taking a date? After what we'd discussed the other night at dinner?"

"Someone might have mentioned that you usually took a model and were staying overnight at the hotel this weekend."

"I'm taking Sam. To network. I booked a suite for her and *her husband* to stay afterward. It was part of the deal I made with her."

"Oh."

He edged closer again. "You were jealous."

"I was not."

"Bullshit."

"Whatever. It doesn't matter."

"It does to me."

"Why?"

"Because if you're jealous that means you *want* to be with me as much as I want to be with you. You like to leave me out there dangling, not knowing what you're thinking."

He closed in on me as I sat in my chair. Placing one hand on each armrest, he lowered his face to mine. "I'm glad it's mutual."

I rolled my eyes. "Whatever."

"Sunday night? Share a meal with me."

"Lunch."

"Dinner."

"Lunch. It's more casual."

He held my stare, trying to pull off serious, but I saw the corner of his mouth hint at a smile. "Fine. But I'm taking you someplace romantic for lunch."

I was never into clubbing to begin with, but I really put in the extra effort Saturday night. Jules and I didn't get to spend much time together, and I missed her and thought if there was ever a time I needed to cut loose, this was is it. Between my change of jobs and ever-growing addiction to thinking about Chase Parker, I needed to feel young and free again.

We bounced around early in the night, dancing at places before they became so packed that it was impossible to do anything but rub up against sweaty people on the dance floor. By the time we arrived at Harper's, I was beginning to regret wearing five-inch heels. When I saw the line to get in—the one that extended almost a full city block—I decided the little half-empty Irish pub we'd just passed wasn't looking half bad.

"Look at that line," I groaned.

Jules grinned and grabbed my hand, pulling me toward the door. "What line?"

A Herculean bouncer wrapped one arm around Jules and lifted her off the ground. "You showed up!"

"How could I resist free drinks and no line?"

"And here I thought you came for me."

"Maybe a little of that, too." She bumped her tiny shoulder into his chest. "What time do you get off?"

He looked at his phone. "About an hour."

Jules remembered me standing next to her. "This is Reese. Reese, this is my little brother's best friend, Christian."

"Nice to meet you, Reese." He nodded to me and turned his attention right back to Jules. "How about you drop the introduction as your little brother's best friend now?"

"But you are."

"Been trying to get you to see me as something different the last month." He leaned down. "In case you hadn't noticed."

Jules waved him off, but I could tell there was a reason we were at Harper's tonight, and it didn't have anything to do with being able to skip the line. "Any chance you can get us a table? Reese needs to rest her dogs or we won't make it an hour."

"You going to have a drink with me when I get off?"

"If you're buying."

He chuckled and shook his head. Lifting a walkie-talkie, he called to someone inside and said he had VIPs who needed taking care of. A minute later, a woman who had to be six feet tall *without* her gargantuan heels came to greet us.

"Jesus," Jules mumbled.

Christian smiled. "Kiki, this is Jules and Reese. Could you find them some seating on the second floor and hook them up with some drinks for me?"

"Sure thing, sweetie."

The statuesque hostess led us to the second floor and opened a roped-off reserved table that overlooked a packed dance floor below. "What can I have sent over for you ladies?"

We ordered extra-dirty martinis and looked around in awe. The club was massive, and everything from the velvet seats to the shiny, black granite bars was top of the line.

"I feel like a celebrity," I said. "And you're fooling around with your brother's best friend? How does Kenny feel about that?"

"I'm not fooling around with Christian. *Yet*. And Kenny doesn't know."

"How will that go over?"

"We're all adults. He can't tell me who I should go out with."

I smirked. "So he's gonna have a shit fit, huh?"

A grin spread across her face. "Pretty much."

"Give me the backstory."

"Kenny and Christian have been friends since pee-wee football. When I was thirteen, and Christian was eleven, he was big, but not huge like he is now. One afternoon, I walked in on him changing, and the thing was enormous, even back then. I mean, dangling enormous."

"And?"

The waitress brought our drinks. "And what?"

"What's the rest of the story?"

She shrugged. "That's it."

"So you've been pining to see his junk again for fifteen years."

She sipped her drink with a wicked smile. "Pretty much. He stayed in California for a few years after college, then came back for the NYPD."

"He's a cop?"

"Yep. I ran into him on the street a few weeks ago, and we started texting. He looks so good in his uniform—the shirt, the pants. I'm totally making him cuff me and play cops and robbers."

"Good for you. He seems into you—couldn't keep his eyes off of you even when hot Amazonian woman was standing next to us."

"What about you? How is that delicious boss of yours?"

I lifted the plastic toothpick from my martini and slipped off an olive using my teeth. "Even more delicious than this olive, and you know how I love my martini condiments." I sighed. "But...he's still my boss."

"I absolutely get the reason you've put up the wall at work to separate business and pleasure. Not having one cost you a job you loved. I'd probably do the same thing. But damn...I might consider making an exception for that man."

"Well, he's definitely trying to get me to make an exception. Somehow he got me to agree to twice-a-week meal sharing."

"Meal sharing? Like a date?"

"Nope. Sharing a meal in a non-dating capacity?"

"Let me get this straight...you're sharing a meal twice a week, alone with him?"

"That's right. In a non-dating capacity."

"Which means what? You won't be fucking at the end of the night?"

I sipped my drink. "Exactly."

Jules cracked up. "He talked you into this crap?"

"What do you mean?"

"You're dating him and don't even know it. I might love this man."

I wasn't dating him. *Was I?* We were just sharing a meal twice a week. Getting to know each other. Not seeing other people. And thinking of each other while we took care of ourselves. *OMG. I am dating him!*

Jules sipped her drink and watched me, amused, as I came around to the same conclusion she'd gotten to in two seconds flat.

"Holy shit. Am I really this big of an idiot?"

"Sweetheart, I know you. You didn't put up that wall to keep him out. You put it up to watch him break it down to get to you."

I absolutely needed another drink. Make that a double.

For the next hour and a half, Jules and I took advantage of the free drinks. We were in a fifteen-dollar-martini bar, and I was glad we didn't have to pay the bill. Sometime after midnight, we'd reached the giggle stage of our inebriation. We were mid-way between sober and slurring, settling nicely into what I liked to call the confessional stage, where everything seemed crystal clear, and sharing it seemed liberating.

Jules's well-hung bouncer hadn't yet joined us, so we had frequent visitors offering to buy us drinks or asking us to dance. Two clean-cut guys stopped by our table.

"Can we buy you ladies a drink?" The broader one smiled confidently.

Dimples. Damn. I was pretty sure he didn't get turned down often.

"Thanks, but our drinks are on the house tonight, and I have a massive crush on my boss."

One eyebrow perked. "Lucky boss. How about a dance then?"

I looked to Jules.

"Not me," she said. "I've been waiting fifteen years, remember? Christian is going to be off soon."

Politely, I declined. "No, thanks. Not tonight."

After they'd walked away, Jules said, "The tall one was hot. Why didn't you dance with him?"

"What's the point?" I brought my drink to my lips to sip, only to discover after tilting my head back that my glass was empty.

"Of dancing or of men in general? Because my answers would be pretty different."

"Of dancing with him. I'm just going to compare."

Jules gave me a funny smile. "Tell me what you like about Bossman."

"He's smart, cocky, hard, but sort of soft at the same time. Does that make sense?" I *thought* she was distracted looking for Christian when I caught her eyes over my head. "Are you even paying attention to me?"

"I am." She tossed back the rest of the liquid in her fancy glass. "So what were you saying? You liked his persistence? That it was a turn-on?"

I hadn't said that, but she wasn't wrong. "I swear, if he pushed me up against the door of my office, I'd have no willpower. Him being the boss is why I'm keeping away from him, yet his bossiness totally does it for me."

Jules was grinning like a Cheshire cat.

"What the hell is wrong with you?" When she just kept on smiling, I knew. *I knew.* "He's standing right behind me, isn't he?"

A warm hand touched my bare shoulder.

I closed my eyes and mumbled to my best friend, "I'm going to kill you."

She shimmied out of the booth and kissed me on the cheek. "I should check and see if my Hulk is off work yet. Be back in a bit." She wiggled her fingers in a cute wave. "Hey, Bossman." Then she disappeared.

Chase didn't even have the decency to feign modesty. He slipped into the seat next to me, rather than sitting across the table as Jules had been. God, I wanted to smack that cocky, full-of-himself smile off his face. His gorgeous, perfectly chiseled, *God, I want to kiss you even more now that I'm drunk* face.

"What are you doing here, Chase?"

"Making your dreams come true, apparently."

I turned, facing him head on for the first time, which was probably a mistake. He was too good-looking for my sober thoughts; alcohol could only make things less bearable. Tonight he wore a tuxedo. Or more properly described, he had on a crisp white shirt unbuttoned at the collar, and a bow tie hung loosely around his neck. The sleeves of his shirt were rolled up, revealing tanned, toned forearms. He really had *great* forearms. I was a sucker for forearms. Had I said that already? Even if I had, it warranted repeating.

But the thing that did me in was, surprisingly, his hair. Normally unruly, tonight it was parted dramatically at the side and slicked back. Couple that with his flawless, tan skin, clean-shaven face, and a carved, masculine jawline, and he could have just walked out of *The Great Gatsby*. It totally threw me off.

"You look...so different."

"Different bad or different good?"

I couldn't lie. I'd had too much truth serum. "You look like an old-time movie star, very classically handsome. I like it."

"I'll be investing in additional hair gel first thing tomorrow morning."

A little smile I'd tried to hold back escaped. Chase ran his thumb down my cheek, then traced the corner of my lips.

"Maybe a case, if it brings out that smile," he added.

"What are you doing here?"

"You said you were coming here the other day."

I had but... "Shouldn't you be at the charity event?"

"It's almost over. Besides, I couldn't stop thinking about you all night." His arm was slung casually over the back of the bench seat we shared, and his fingers began to caress the exposed skin of my shoulders. "I wasn't sure if I should come, and now I'm glad I did."

"Why is that?"

"You like my persistence. What was that you said? My bossiness turns you on?"

I rolled my eyes. "I need another drink."

"Yes, let's both. Triple Peppermint Schnapps?"

Chase flagged down the waitress and ordered us both drinks. Looking around the busy club, he asked, "So do you do this often? Go out clubbing with your friends?"

"Not much anymore. I like to dance, but it's kind of a meat market."

His finger stopped tracing. "Is that what you were doing tonight? Shopping for meat?"

"Nope. Just enjoying a night out with my friend."

"Because if meat is what you're looking for..."

I smacked his abs playfully, but I could feel how hard his body was underneath his shirt. *Note to self, keep your hands at your sides at all times, for your own safety.*

"Is this how you meet women? You go stalking at clubs looking all sexy at midnight?"

"Not generally. This is the first time I've been inside a club—unless it was for an event I had to attend—in years."

"Where do you meet women then?"

"Various places."

"That's specific." I lifted a brow.

"Okay. Let's see... The last woman I went out with I met on a flight from California."

"Was that Bridget?"

"No."

"Where did you meet Bridget?"

"A party."

"Work party?"

The waitress brought our drinks, and Chase gulped half his glass.

"Thirsty?"

"Just trying to take the edge off."

"So...Bridget. What kind of a party?"

"I'd prefer not to talk about other women when I'm sitting here with you."

"Okay. What would you like to talk about then?"

"Why don't we start with all the things I thought about doing to you tonight?" His gaze slid down my face and took its time as it appreciated my body in the form-fitting little black dress I wore.

Watching him look at me with all that hunger weakened my resistance.

I swallowed. "Chase..."

He responded by lifting my hand and bringing it to his lips for a gentle kiss. "How much have you had to drink tonight?"

"Enough."

"That's a shame."

"Why?"

"Because I'm not a man who takes advantage only because Peppermint Schnapps has relaxed a woman's uncertainty."

It was my turn to gulp from my glass. I was feeling lightheaded, and it had nothing to do with the alcohol. "So are you saying that no matter *what* I say or do, you won't be sleeping with me tonight""

The heat in his eyes said otherwise. "That's right."

I smiled devilishly. "That sounds like a challenge. Dance with me."

CHAPTER
17

Reese

I woke to a nibble on the shell of my ear. *What the...*

Last night. Last night. Oh my God. Did I? Panicked, I momentarily froze in bed as I wracked my hungover brain, trying to remember the end of the evening. I was never so relieved when a paw smacked me in the jaw.

"Jesus..." I grumbled, turning to find Tallulah licking my ear and swatting my face. I pulled the sheet over my head, blocking Ugly Kitty access. Undeterred, she climbed on top of me and settled my chest.

"Meow." She nuzzled at the sheet hiding me.

I attempted to lift my head, but it hurt too much. "What? What do you want?"

"Meow."

"Ugh." Even her tiny cry hurt. I would have sworn there was a little drummer getting warmed up inside my skull. There was no rhythm to the pounding, just a hammer whaling against the bass, then the snare, followed by a few slams of the symbols. *Ugh.*

What the hell did I drink last night?

I remembered Chase showing up, and dragging him out onto the dance floor so I could rub my body against his and tempt his willpower. *Oh God*. I'd made it a game—see if I could get Chase to give in.

We'd laughed over shots of disgusting Peppermint Schnapps, and Christian and Jules had eventually joined in. The two of them were looking mighty cozy, I remembered. Things got a bit fuzzier after that.

There was the cab ride home.

I remembered being tired.

So tired.

I just needed to close my eyes for a bit, put my head down to rest while we drove across town.

My head.

So sleepy.

I'd rested it all right. *In Chase's lap.*

I remembered he'd woken me. When I'd lifted my sleepy head, I'd brushed against the crotch of his pants.

Oh God.

He was hard. *And I made a comment about it. Awesome.*

Chase had helped me out of the car and told the cabbie to keep the meter running.

The elevator had taken forever. When we stepped inside, I leaned against his chest and took a deep breath, smelling him up close.

Oh God.

I told him he smelled good enough to eat.

I suggested he purchase a cabin in the woods and chop wood shirtless.

His arms were wrapped tight around me as we walked toward my apartment. In hindsight, I might have actually needed the support to walk.

We'd arrived at my door.

I vaguely remembered wrapping my arms around his neck and inviting him in. He smiled and shook his head.

"There's nothing I'd like more than to come inside. And I mean that in more ways than one." He'd kissed the top of my head.

The top of my head!

"But not this way. Get some sleep." Taking my keys from my hand, he'd opened all of my locks and waited for me to go inside.

The last things I remembered were his arms over his head as he leaned against the doorframe and him saying, "We'll finish this game next week. Things are going to be a lot more fun around the office, that's for damn sure."

I'd canceled my lunch date with Chase a little later that morning, too hungover to get out of bed. When he tried to push me into rescheduling for Monday, I was noncommittal and eventually stopped responding to his texts.

A line had been crossed, and I didn't know how to back up other than cut myself off completely. It was my own fault, and Monday morning I was adamant about fixing what I'd screwed up.

"Morning." Chase stood in the doorway of my office with the exact same stance he'd had the other night at my apartment door.

I had psyched myself up all day yesterday—I was a professional, I could put what happened Saturday night behind me and work around Chase like nothing had happened. I glanced at my phone...7:05 on Monday morning, and I'd already failed. *Great. Just great, Reese.*

Chase grinned like he knew I was thinking unprofessional thoughts.

I folded my hands on my desk. "Good morning, Mr. Parker."

His brows jumped. "Is that how we're going to play this?"

"I have no idea what you're talking about, Mr. Parker."

Chase walked to my desk. "I like the sound of you calling me Mr. Parker. You'll have to keep it up."

I swallowed as he moved even closer. My voice showed signs of weakening. "No problem, Mr. Parker."

"How about, *please*, Mr. Parker?"

"Please, Mr. Parker, what?"

"Just wanted to hear how good it will sound coming from your lips." He closed the distance between us, coming around to the other side of my desk and leaning his hip casually against it. He reached out and rubbed my bottom lip with his thumb, speaking directly to my mouth. "*Please,* Mr. Parker. It will be coming from these lips...mark my words."

What the hell did I get myself into?

It was ironic that I was supposed to be preparing for a focus group, when I was completely unable to focus. The morning blown by my wandering mind, I was glad Monday afternoon was tightly scheduled so there would be no more room for screwing around.

The first of two meetings was at one o'clock in the large conference room on the east side of the building. It was next to Chase's office, and I couldn't stop myself from peeking inside as I passed. With the blinds open, his office was a virtual fishbowl. He sat at his desk, leaning back in his leather executive chair with one hand behind his head; the other held his corded desk phone while he talked, looking up at the ceiling.

Momentarily distracted, I stopped paying attention to where I was going and walked straight into Josh. Upon impact, I squeezed the tall coffee in my hand, causing the lid to pop off. I then bobbled the laptop and notepad in my other hand. As I leaned forward in a fruitless attempt to stop everything from falling, I proceeded to pour the entire contents of my coffee all over the front of my blouse, and everything fell to the ground—followed by my empty cup.

"*Shit!*"

"I'm sorry. I walk too fast," Josh said.

"No. It's my fault. I wasn't paying attention."

He looked at my shirt. There was steam coming off of it. "That must have been pretty hot coffee. Are you burned?"

Chase came out of his office with some paper towels, handed them to me, and bent to pick up my laptop and notepad. Handing the dripping equipment to Josh, he said, "Why don't you dry off the laptop, and I'll take care of Reese."

I blotted at my blouse, but it wasn't much use—I'd spilled a forty-ounce coffee, and the skin underneath was almost as soaked as the fabric of my sheer shirt.

"You need more than a handful of paper towels. Come with me." Chase guided me into his office. I was hyper-aware of his hand splayed out at the small of my back, a few of his fingers fanning to that place that isn't quite ass, but no longer back either. I was pretty sure it was innocent, but my thoughts were anything but.

I was pissed at myself, at how unprofessional I was, and I projected my frustration at Chase. "This is all your fault, you know."

"My fault?"

"You have me distracted today."

Instead of feeling bad that he was the cause of my mess, Chase looked pleased. "I can't wait to see the mess you make when I actually *try* to distract you." He reached into a closet and pulled out a white dress shirt. "Here. Put this on."

"I can't wear your shirt."

"Why not?" He flashed a dirty grin. "It'll be practice for when you're making me pancakes the morning after."

I hated that I visualized myself standing in front of that big, stainless steel, double-oven stove I knew he had in his house, wearing one of his dress shirts. I'd gone from acting bothered, to hot and bothered in less than ten seconds.

Chase caught the look on my face and chuckled. "There're towels in my private bathroom." His eyes dropped to my chest, where my nipples stood up proudly through my soaked shirt, and grumbled, "Get out of that wet shirt, before I help you out of it right in the middle of my office with the blinds open."

I didn't doubt he would do it for a minute, so I quickly trudged to the bathroom, hoping I'd also find my wit there, along with a clean shirt.

A minute later, I looked in the mirror, happy with my reflection. I must say, I totally rocked a man's shirt. Even though it was ten sizes too big, with a few buttons left open at the top and a knot at the waist, Chase's dress shirt actually looked kind of cute with my black pencil skirt. I was rolling up the sleeves when there was a light knock at the door.

"You decent?"

Except for my thoughts about you. "Yes."

When Chase opened the door, he had a folded T-shirt in his hand and was looking down at it. "I have this old Brown

T-shirt that was stuffed in my gym bag if you want to try—
" He paused, stopping in his tracks as he looked up at me.
"Wow. Looks better on you."

Earlier in the day, the man had told me he was going to
make me beg, and that hadn't made me blush. Yet something
as simple as *looks better on you* had my cheeks heating. It
wasn't so much the words as the intimacy with which he said
them.

He stepped into the bathroom and took over the rolling
of the sleeves. "Let me."

We exchanged a few silent smiles as he worked on the
shirt.

"How are you feeling today?" he asked.

"Better."

"Glad to hear it. We're sharing a meal tomorrow tonight."

"Are you telling me or asking me?"

He finished rolling and waited until I looked up. "Telling.
You owe me, considering what a gentleman I was the other
night."

He *had* been gallant. "Thank you for that, by the way.
You were very respectful, and I didn't make it easy for you."

"No. You definitely made it *hard*."

I shoved his shoulder playfully. "Come on, Bossman.
We're already late to the meeting."

Elaine Dennis, the VP of Advance Focus Market Research,
had just started her presentation when we walked into the
conference room a few minutes late. Her pitch detailed
her company's experience moderating focus groups in the
women's industry, and she spoke a lot about the importance
of running groups in different geographic areas.

"The women's products industry is very different in New
York and the Midwest. Most women want the same things—

smooth skin, to feel beautiful and pampered, to look attractive to the opposite sex—but what works for selling beauty can be quite disparate in various geographic areas."

Getting comfortable in my seat, I attempted to put the last fifteen minutes behind me and took notes as she worked through her presentation. I'd done plenty of marketing focus groups during my years with Fresh Look, but there was always something new to learn. The ad world changed by the minute, and advertising to women was even more of a challenge. Let's face it, we women wear our right to change our minds like a badge of honor—what we want today could be passé by tomorrow.

I was sitting two seats away from the presenter on the right side of the long conference table. Chase sat a half dozen chairs away from her on the far end of the opposite side of the table. It wasn't the first time I'd noticed he didn't sit at the open head of the table during marketing meetings. He was the kind of boss who had his eye on everything, and participated, but didn't feel the need to constantly remind people he was in charge. Holding my pen to my lips, I wondered if he did it on purpose.

When my eyes flicked back to him, he was watching me intently. I looked away, but two seconds later, I glanced back again. He looked around the room to see if anyone was paying attention to him. Of course everyone else was watching the presentation, as we both should have been.

Then he mouthed to me, *I really love that you read lips.*

I smiled coyly and scanned the room before looking back.

It felt like we were in middle school, trying not to be caught passing notes. His gaze was glued to my lips as his mouth formed soundless words. *I also really love your lips.*

Flustered, I shifted in my chair to face the woman giving the presentation. I managed to hold out for less than five minutes before my eyes wandered back. This time, Chase didn't even bother to see whether anyone was watching. He mouthed, *I really like my shirt on you.*

I shot him a look of warning. It didn't scare him one bit. He continued—and like an ass, I couldn't look away.

I can't wait to see what's underneath it.

I wanted to kill him. I also wanted to hear what he was going to do once he saw what was underneath. Luckily, my focus was forced to return to the room when I heard my name spoken.

Josh had opened a discussion on in-store product placement testing vs. focus groups and asked me to share my experience from Fresh Look. It took a minute to regain my footing, but marketing wasn't just my job, it was a passion. Once I began talking, that passion took over. Over the next hour and a half, I did my best not to fidget when I found Chase watching me.

At one point I was putting on Chapstick—something I did a dozen times a day—and Chase was mesmerized watching me line my lips. It made between my legs tingle, and I squirmed in my seat.

When it was Chase's turn to speak, I admired how he dominated the room with his thoughts and ideas. He was so different than my boss at Fresh Look—a typical CEO whose presence had been felt in almost a bullying kind of a way. There was no way Scott Eikman was *not* sitting at the head of the table during a meeting like this. My old boss would have been there with his arms folded over his chest, making everyone around him sit up straighter.

Chase's style was understated, and he captured the room with brains and natural charisma. He caught me watching him while he spoke, and the corner of his mouth twitched up.

Luckily, unlike me, he didn't become tongue-tied when being watched so closely.

After all the questions had been answered, Elaine went in to close the deal. "I know you said your timeline was evolving, but we have two focus groups available this week, if you'd like to jump in. One is in Kansas and one here in New York City."

Of course, she'd also spent a good deal of her presentation speaking about the importance of collecting feedback from the Midwest, in addition to both the coasts. And she just happened to have two such groups available for us to join in the next few days. I had to hand it to her, though—she gave a good sales pitch.

Josh told her we'd get back to her quickly, and the projector had not even cooled down from her presentation when the second appointment was escorted into the room. I was disappointed that Chase had said he wouldn't be able to sit in on the second focus group presentation, but also relieved I'd have nothing to distract me.

When the meetings finally ended at six, we sat around the conference room discussing the two companies. We agreed unanimously that Elaine's Advance Focus was the better firm to handle our focus groups. Josh looked to Lindsey and me.

"Think we can pull together the rest of the samples and presentations in time to join the groups Elaine has running this week in Kansas and here in the city?" he asked.

"We can," Lindsey said. "It'll be close, but we can pull it together tomorrow, I think."

Josh nodded. "I need to be here for a photo shoot we have going on the rest of the week uptown. So which one of you is staying in New York and which is heading to Kansas?"

Lindsey looked to me, and I said, "I'll do whatever you don't want to do."

"Good. Because I hate to fly. I'd rather cover the New York focus group."

"Well, that was easy," Josh said. "Chase may want to join you for some of the focus group here, Lindsey. Let him know when you're confirmed with the details."

She nodded. "Will do."

While I was going to miss out on spending time with Chase, I knew deep down that I needed some distance between us. A few thousand miles might be the only thing that could separate us enough to let me clear my head.

CHAPTER
18

Reese

My flight was booked for early on Wednesday so I'd have the afternoon to set up at Advanced Focus's Kansas City consumer research office for the first focus group session on Thursday morning. Chase had been out of the office all Tuesday afternoon, so I'd texted him that I wouldn't be able to have dinner. He had responded with one word. *Fine.* He probably thought I was trying to blow him off again after I'd let things—let myself—get out of hand this weekend.

Now it was nearly six-thirty Wednesday morning, and I was getting ready to head to the airport when he finally expanded on his previous text.

Chase: *I'll take a rain check. But this time I'm collecting it.*

There wasn't time to text back. The car service was coming at six-thirty, and my elevator could sometimes take a few minutes. I zipped my suitcase closed, tossed my phone in my purse, and gave Ugly Kitty a quick pet.

"Your real owner is going to take care of you while I'm gone. Make sure she doesn't go through my shit." I stroked Tallulah's head. "You be a good little Ugly Kitty and claw my mom's ankles when she starts rummaging through my underwear drawer. Okay?"

A dark town car was waiting in front of my building when I got downstairs. Even though my flight wasn't for two and a half hours, I began to stress when we hit a dead stop on our way to the Tunnel. Taking a deep breath, I began to relax when we finally made it out of Manhattan, only to panic again when the other side of the Tunnel was worse than the city.

"What's going on?" I asked the driver. "This is bad even for rush hour traffic."

"Construction. Supposed to end by six each morning, but the laborers must want the overtime." He shrugged and pointed to the road ahead of us, which was a sea of brake lights as three lanes attempted to converge into one.

As we inched our way forward over the next hour, it killed me to discover that although the cones were out for miles, there wasn't actually any construction going on anymore. Checking my watch, I realized there was a distinct possibility I could miss my flight if traffic didn't clear soon.

On a good day, I was a nervous flyer. The added stress of possibly being late caused my heart to accelerate even more. Needing to distract myself, I took out my phone. A new text had just arrived.

Mom: *You need to clean out your refrigerator more often. You have expired pickles.*

Really? Was she hiding outside in an alleyway when I left? Just couldn't wait to go in and start her investigation? I'd left Ugly Kitty with a full dish of food. It wasn't even necessary for her to stop by until tomorrow. I'd fix her. Screwing with her would take my mind off of my upcoming flight.

Reese: *Don't throw it out. I keep the expired stuff to feed to Tallulah.*

Moving on, the next text was the one I hadn't answered yet from Chase—about the rain check for the dinner I'd canceled last night.

Reese: *Won't be back until the weekend. My boss wanted to get rid of me, so he sent me to Kansas.*

After responding to a few more texts and emails, I successfully took my mind off how late I was running. I arrived at JFK with thirty-five minutes before takeoff and hauled ass to a kiosk for check-in. When I spotted the length of the security line up ahead, I almost broke down and cried.

Desperate, I walked over to a TSA agent. "There's no way I'm going to make my flight if I wait in this line. The Tunnel took forever to get through, and there was construction on the LIE. Any chance I can cut ahead? I'm traveling for business, and I really can't miss my flight."

"Ticket." She held out a plastic-glove-covered hand and looked at me like she heard the same sob story a hundred times a day. Handing it back to me, she pointed over her shoulder. "First-class line to the left."

I let out a breath when I saw there was no line where she was sending me. "Thank you so much!"

Of course, my gate was at the other end of the terminal, but I managed to get through security and down to the boarding area just as they announced last call. Since there was a small line to board, I caught my breath and walked up to the ticket counter to see about changing the middle seat I'd been issued when I purchased.

"Is there any chance I could switch my middle seat? I know I'm late and the last to board, but I figured it couldn't hurt to ask."

"We're pretty full...but let me check." The attendant took my ticket and punched a bunch of numbers into the computer. Furrowing her brow, she said, "You actually don't have a middle seat. You have an aisle." She slid the ticket back to me and pointed. "Row two."

That made no sense. "I was in row thirty-something when I bought the ticket."

"Not anymore. You're in an aisle seat in first class. You must have been upgraded."

The line to board had dwindled, and who was I to argue about being in first class anyway? When I reached row two, I pulled my purse from my shoulder and shoved it under the aisle seat. The window seat was empty, but I noticed the *New York Times* folded in half atop where there was no passenger. I opened the overhead compartment and checked for room to store my bag before reaching down to grab my suitcase handle.

A large hand startled me when it covered mine. "Here. Let me."

My head whipped toward the man standing next to me, but I already knew whom I'd find.

"What's going on in that head of yours?" Chase asked.

I'd been quiet since finding him on the plane. I was a nervous flyer to begin with, and having Chase surprise me the way he did had thrown me for a loop. My heart was beating out of control as we began to barrel down the runway. I gripped the armrest between us and gave him a curt answer.

"I hate takeoff. And landing. All the stuff in the middle is fine."

Chase covered my hand with his and squeezed. He didn't let go when we were in the air. Once our altitude leveled, I let out a deep breath, and my shoulders relaxed.

"Why didn't you tell me you were taking this trip?"

"It was a last-minute thing."

I squinted, wondering if he had planned this all along. "How last minute?"

He looked me straight in the eyes, and I could see his apprehension. "I don't even have an overnight bag."

"What do you mean, you don't have a bag?"

"I left my house this morning with every intention of going to the office." He paused and ran a hand through his hair, muttering the rest. "Not even sure how I got here anymore."

"Are you serious?"

Shaking his head, he said, "You'll be the one sharing your shirt with me this time."

"I don't think my shirt would fit you."

"So you want me shirtless, then? I knew it."

The flight attendant came by and gave us menus. "Can I get you something to drink?"

Chase answered without looking at his menu. "We'll take two mimosas."

I looked at him. "It's barely nine in the morning."

"It's a special occasion."

The flight attendant smiled and took the menus. "Are you celebrating something?"

Chase's hand still covered mine on the armrest. He lifted them, linked my fingers with his, and brought my hand to his mouth for a kiss. "It's our honeymoon."

"Wow. Congratulations! That's wonderful. Are you connecting through Kansas or is that your final destination today?"

"We're staying in Kansas. The new Mrs. is a huge *Wizard of Oz* fan and wants to hit the museum." He pointed with his chin down to our feet. I *happened* to be dressed in all black and wearing red heels. "She gets a little carried away sometimes."

The flight attendant managed to keep her smile, but I could see she thought I was a little nutty. I mean, who the hell in their right mind would go to a museum when they'd just married a man who looked like the one I was sitting next to?

After she walked away, I turned to Chase. "A *Wizard of Oz* fan?"

Chase grinned. "It's more of a fetish, but whatever you're into."

"And who would you be? The scarecrow with no brain? Where do you come up with this stuff?"

"Was coming out of the bathroom when you walked onto the plane. Saw those sexy-as-shit red shoes, and I might have had a little role-play fantasy."

"I really think you need help."

"You might be right." He leaned close and lowered his voice. "But if you wanted to wear those shoes, pigtails, and nothing else, I'd be one happy Tin Man."

After the flight attendant had brought our drinks (and called me *the bride*), Chase and I had a moment of honesty.

"How long are you staying in Kansas?" I asked, reaching down into my purse to grab my Chapstick for a quick freshen up.

His eyes followed along as I lined my lips. "You use that stuff a lot, huh?"

"What, Chapstick?"

"Yeah. I've noticed you putting it on a few times."

"I'm kind of addicted to it."

"I don't like the waxy feel on my lips. You're going to have to stop using it soon."

"Let me guess—because my lips will be smearing it on yours?"

"Exactly."

"Yet another reason why we could never work," I teased.

"One of us will get over it."

I shook my head at his persistence. "So how long did you say you're staying in Kansas?"

"That's up to you."

"Up to me?"

"I didn't lie when I said I tried to not come. The minute I heard you were going out of town, I wanted to join you. Thought about telling you I wanted to sit in on the sessions, but figured you'd see right through that."

"So you're saying you came for no other reason but me?"

He nodded seriously. "Just you."

"Is this your normal style? Stalkerish chic?"

"Not exactly...which is probably why I have no idea what to do. Avoiding it hasn't really been working."

"So what is your style then when you date?"

"How's this honesty thing working for me?"

I laughed. "Pretty good so far. Go ahead, I won't judge."

Chase gulped back the rest of his mimosa. "I haven't had to work too hard for a woman's attention."

"I would have guessed that. Is that what the intrigue is here, then? A man who wants what he can't have? That's not a novel concept."

His eyes went back and forth, searching mine, and I knew he was deliberating saying something. Eventually, he said, "You're right. I do want what I don't have. That's part of it. But not in the way you think. Don't ask me to explain it, but when I'm around you, I'm happy. That's all I'm after."

His answer caught me totally off guard. "Wow. That's... that's...incredibly sweet."

Chase took my half-full mimosa from my hand and chugged it before speaking again. "Now don't get me wrong, I'd be way fucking happy if you were beneath me at night. But you want to keep some distance between us physically? I respect that. Although, I'm going to be right here…making it hard for you."

It was my turn to lean in. "Is that in the literal or figurative sense?"

Chase still had my hand entwined with his. He pulled it to his chest and lowered it down his abs, stopping just above the top of his pants. "Keep it up—I'm going to demonstrate."

After landing, we caught a cab to the focus group offices and spent a few hours working with the facilitator who would run things the next day. Chase helped set up, but he deferred to me for decisions that needed to be made where I had more expertise. I liked that in a boss…and a man.

After we'd finished, we stopped by a mall on the way to our hotel since Chase really hadn't brought an overnight bag and had nothing to wear. Inside Nordstrom's, I helped him pick out some casual clothes. While he was in the fitting room, I continued to shop on some of the nearby racks. He walked out wearing a pair of jeans and a simple navy polo that fit perfectly across his wide chest. His feet were bare and his hair even more mussed than usual from changing.

I walked over with a button-up I'd picked out, and Chase held out his arms and did a little spin circle. "Good?"

"I seriously doubt there's anything that looks bad on you." I held out the other shirt for him to try on.

He reached up over his head, tugged at the yoke of the polo, and pulled it off in that way that only boys remove their shirts. It was impossible not to stare. His body was just so incredibly perfect. Tanned and lean, every muscle seemed carved into his body. The jeans were a bit loose at the waist and hung low, showcasing his deep-set V. I was pretty sure he had the best body I'd ever seen up close.

I had inadvertently licked my lips, and Chase noticed. "You keep looking at me like that, we're going to wind up in the fitting room."

A vision of the two of us in the fitting room, up against the mirror, flashed in my head. When I didn't respond, Chase knew—*he knew*—what I was visualizing. My arm was still extended, holding the shirt. Chase reached out, but instead of taking it, he tugged my hand and pulled me close.

"You're fired," he groaned as he buried his face in my hair. "So fucking fired."

I was one exhale away from giving in when a woman's voice brought me back to my senses.

She cleared her throat. "Is there anything I can help you find?"

I jumped back, putting space between the two of us. But I was still unable to speak. Chase answered her, speaking into my eyes.

"No, thanks. I think I have everything I need." Our gaze held until he finally said, "Let me go get dressed."

"Ummm...yeah...right...okay. I'll grab you a few T-shirts while you change."

When he turned to walk away, still shirtless, for the first time I noticed a tattoo on his side. I couldn't make out what it said, but it looked like a bunch of writing going up his ribs.

Shaking my head as I walked away, still feeling hot and bothered, I thought to myself what an enigma my boss was. A smart CEO with custom-tailored suits, a nipple ring, and tattoo—a man who gets on a plane without luggage and admits he tried to keep away but couldn't stop himself. The only thing holding all those distinctively different traits together was that they all said the man had passion. I could feel that in the way he looked at me. And as much as it turned me on to no end, it also scared the living crap out of me.

We were quiet for a while after that. Chase reappeared fully clothed, and it took us another half hour in Nordstrom's to grab T-shirts, boxers, and sneakers. When we were finally done, the sun was beginning to set outside, and I yawned on the walk to the rental car in the parking lot.

"Tired?"

"A little. It's been a long day."

Chase opened my car door, waited for me to get in, then tossed his purchases in the backseat.

Before pulling out, he turned to me. "How about dinner at our hotel, then? The website said there's a steakhouse. We can get you fed and into bed."

"Into bed?"

"I meant for some rest. But if you've got something else in mind…"

Oh, I had something else on my mind all right. And it was getting harder by the moment to think of anything else.

CHAPTER 19

Reese

The hotel gave us rooms right next to each other. After hanging my dresses in the closet, I stripped out of my clothes, pulled my hair up in a ponytail, and took a quick shower. Letting hot water massage my shoulders, I relaxed and thought about how much I'd loved spending the day with Chase. Working side by side, shopping together, sitting in the car as we drove to our hotel—everything just felt natural. What *didn't* feel natural anymore was pushing the man away from me. Instead, it felt like I was depriving myself of something that could possibly be really special.

Bill and Melinda Gates had started out working together. He was her boss even.

Michelle Obama was Barack's mentor at the law firm where they both worked.

Celine Dion married her manager—who was more than twenty-five years older.

Some things worked. Some things didn't. There were more consequences when things didn't last and you worked together, but sometimes the possibilities outweighed the consequences.

Possibilities.

When Chase knocked a little while later, I had just finished getting dressed. My hair was up in a messy bun, and I'd traded my sleek black suit in favor of a simple jersey wrap dress with a lively print of greens and blues. My red heels were now open-toe sandals.

His eyes slid over me. "We could skip dinner…"

I shoved at his chest and exited my room without putting on the necklace I was going to wear because I didn't trust myself to invite him inside while I finished getting ready. The way Chase looked at me while we waited for the hostess to seat us—his eyes dropping to my cleavage—I don't think he missed the diamond pendant I hadn't had a chance to fasten around my neck.

During appetizers, we talked about the focus group and plans for tomorrow before moving on to more intimate conversation. I was mindlessly tracing my finger through the condensation on the base of my wine glass when Chase reached over and traced the scar on my hand.

"It almost looks like a tattoo. Even your scars are beautiful."

I remembered what I'd noticed on Chase's body earlier. "Speaking of tattoos…I couldn't help but see yours this afternoon. Is it your only one?"

Chase leaned back in his chair. "Yes."

The fact that he didn't offer more and seemed anxious to move on from the subject made me pry even further. "What does it say? They're words, right?"

He looked around the room, then lifted his drink and took a healthy gulp. "It says *Fear does not stop death. It stops life.*"

I waited until his eyes finally settled on me to speak. "Well, I can certainly relate to that."

We stared at each other. I struggled to find the right words of encouragement to get him to open up as his eyes left mine and went back to my scar. I hadn't found those words yet when he unexpectedly continued.

"Peyton and I went to high school together. We were friends—didn't get together until my last semester of college. My life was moving really fast by then. I had patents, office space...I was hiring staff." He paused. "A year after we graduated, I proposed. She died two days later."

My heart practically leaped into my throat. There was pain in his voice, and I literally felt tightness in my chest. "I'm sorry."

He nodded and again took a minute before continuing. "I was pretty screwed up afterward for a long time. It's why I initially licensed most of my products. I was drinking heavily and knew I wasn't in the right frame of mind to do everything it would take to bring new products into the marketplace myself. Luckily, my lawyers *were* in the right frame of mind. They negotiated deals where I got a generous royalty just for letting companies use my patents for a few years. I kept my research team, so I had something to focus on, but there wasn't much else I had to do."

"Sounds like you did the right thing."

"Yeah. In hindsight, I did."

I was dying to ask the question but wasn't sure what words to use. "How did...your fiancée...I mean...was she... sick?"

He shook his head. "No. She was assaulted. Seven years ago next week. Never caught the guy who did it."

I reached out and took his hand. "God, I don't know what to say. I'm so sorry."

"Thank you." He paused then said, "It was a rough few years. Even when I began to date again, I don't know that I was capable of doing anything more than...you know—" He gave me a sexy half smile. "—dating."

"You mean having sex."

He nodded. "Don't get me wrong—I don't want to sound like a total asshole. I never led women on. I just wasn't interested in more than a physical connection. It wasn't intentional. At least I don't think it was. I don't know. Maybe I wasn't ready to move on. Or maybe I just hadn't met the right person to move on with."

"That makes sense." My stomach was in knots. It wasn't lost on me that he'd said he *wasn't* ready and he *hadn't* met the right person, as if those things were past tense. He'd made it clear he wanted me physically almost from the beginning— that was never a question in my mind. I wanted so much to ask if he thought more was possible now, but I was afraid of the answer. I mean, how do you move on—fall in love with another woman—when you've never stopped loving someone else?

When I said nothing, Chase reached over and put his hand on my chin, gently lifting until our eyes met. "I want more with you. I can't promise you what that is or where it will go, but it's more than just physical. I'm attracted to everything about you—you're smart, honest, funny, brave, a little nutty—and you make me smile for no reason. There's no denying I want you in my bed. I think you've caught on to that part by now. But I want this, too. I'm tired of looking back. It's been a long time since I've wanted to live in the moment."

"Wow. I don't know what to say. Thank you. Thank you for being so honest."

Just then, the waiter came with our dinner. The air was heavy, and I had no idea how to lighten the mood, yet I felt like we needed it. If there was one thing I knew, it was that talking about sex usually made Chase playful.

I cut a bite of my steak and brought the fork to my lips. "Have you ever played Would You Rather?"

His brows drew down. "When I was a kid."

"My friend Jules and I play it all the time—usually after a few drinks."

"Okay..."

I sipped my wine and held his gaze. "Would you rather pay for sex or be paid for sex?"

He cocked a brow. "Be paid. You?"

"I think I'd rather pay for it."

"I like this game." Chase leaned back in his chair and scratched his chin. "Top or bottom?"

"Bottom." I paused. "You?"

"Top." He pointed his fork at me. "See how compatible we are. Lights on or off?"

"On. You?"

"On. So I can watch your face while I sink inside of you."

Warmth prickled my skin. I gulped. "You're not supposed to elaborate. You're only supposed to say your pick."

"Why would I do that, when giving a more descriptive answer makes your skin turn such a sexy shade of pink?"

We went back and forth like that for the rest of our meal, sharing snippets of both sexy and not-so-sexy preferences. It did what I'd intended it to do—lightened the mood—but it also had desire fighting the voice of reason inside of me.

And, at the moment, desire was kicking reason's ass.

After dinner, when Chase and I arrived at our adjoining suites, I felt like I was ending a first date in high school.

He took both my hands in his, keeping a few feet between us as he spoke. "Thank you for having dinner with me. And for letting me crash your trip."

"You were on the plane when I got on. It's not like I had much of a choice." I was joking, of course.

"I'm going to take off after the morning focus group, head back to New York on an afternoon flight."

"You're leaving? Why?"

"Because I keep pushing, hoping you'll break. And tonight I realized you need to get there on your own. I'll be waiting when you do." He pulled me to him and planted a kiss on my forehead.

"Now go inside before I change my mind and you're up against the door instead of behind it safely."

I leaned my head against the door for a solid ten minutes once I was inside. After five, I'd heard Chase's door click open and close, and I wondered if he'd been standing on the other side struggling like I was.

I couldn't remember ever wanting another man as badly as I wanted Chase. For a while, I'd thought it was because he was my boss—that exciting feeling of being tempted by the forbidden. But I knew it was more than that. So much more, it scared the hell out of me. I'd been using the fact that he was my boss as an excuse to keep distance. But the truth was, the things I felt around the man terrified me. I hadn't exactly been lucky in love. Neither had my parents. Could I find true love in the shadow of another woman?

I was afraid—and I was also tired of *being* afraid. That realization made me think of his tattoo.

Fear does not stop death. It stops life.

Eight little words, yet it held the story of both of our lives.

As I took a deep breath, it hit me that I hadn't turned on the lights in my room yet. *That* was totally unusual for me. Ordinarily, I'd have performed my sweep of the room within ten seconds of entering—checking in the closet and shower, looking under the ever-intimidating bed. Sighing, I forced myself not to look, even though it was now gnawing at me since I'd mentally acknowledged I'd been remiss. At least there was *one* fear I wasn't going to allow to control me tonight.

Lying on the floor of my hotel room in the dark, I felt dizzy from my mind spinning. I kept replaying bits and pieces of the conversations we'd had over the last month in my head.

At his house: "If you weren't seeing someone, I'd have you up on that kitchen island *showing you* what I want to do to you, rather than telling you."

I wanted him to show me in the worst way.

In the cab after too much to drink at the club, my sleepy head resting on his warm thighs and brushing against his erection as I sat up when we arrived at my building.

I wanted to feel him. Wrap my fingers around his hard-on and watch his face as I slid my hand up and down.

In his office… "Get out of that wet shirt before I help you out of it right in the middle of my office with the blinds open."

God, I wanted him to rip my damn shirt off.

Closing my eyes, my hand slid down my body. He was right on the other side of that door. Would he hear me if I brought myself to orgasm? A part of me hoped he would. My hand skimmed over the lace of my underwear once, then a second time, lingering over the sensitive front before slipping inside. My clit was already swollen just thinking about Chase. It was definitely not going to take long. Two fingers gently circled, massaging. Imagining it was Chase's hand instead of my own, I quickly increased pressure as I found my rhythm.

Images swept through my head.

Chase finally looking up at me that first night in the hallway of the restaurant. *God, he is gorgeous.*

Shirtless at the gym, beads of water trickling down his carved chest.

My breathing sped up.

Today outside the fitting room. The way he looked at me, his eyes stripping away anything in his way. His words—"I'm attracted to everything about you."

God.

Oh God.

So close. So fast.

Until...

A loud knock made me jump.

Jesus.

I sprang upright, my breathing erratic like I'd just sprinted a marathon.

"Reese?" Chase's voice called. He'd knocked on the interior door between our rooms.

I cleared my throat. "Yes?"

"Can I borrow your iPhone charger? I forgot to pick one up today."

"Ummm...sure. Give me a minute to find it."

My hands were shaking as I turned on the light and began to rip apart my overnight bag in search of my charger. *What the hell am I doing?*

Finding it, I took a deep breath and steadied myself for thirty seconds before opening the door between us. I couldn't look him in the eye.

"Here you go," I said to his shoulder.

"Thanks."

My voice sounded odd, even to me. The pitch was high and...I was talking way too fast in one long run-on, unpunctuated sentence. "You're welcome you can keep it I won't need it until the morning I was just going to go to bed anyway."

Chase's brow was furrowed when I glanced up. "Are you okay?"

"I'm fine. Why wouldn't I be?"

He wasn't buying it. "I don't know." Looking over my shoulder, he checked out my room. "What were you doing?"

"Nothing," I responded *way* too fast.

"Nothing, huh?"

My face was flushed, and I could feel a sheen of perspiration on my forehead and cheeks, but damn if I wasn't going to try to lie my way right through it.

Chase's eyes trailed down the length of my body, and then our gazes locked.

And I knew.

He knew.

He knew.

I could actually see his pupils dilate when he realized it. After an intense stare-off, during which I thought it was entirely possible I might melt from the heat, he simply said, "Goodnight, Reese."

I'd just begun to breathe again when he stopped the door from closing at the last second. Reaching down, he took my hand and cupped it in his. Then he slowly brought it to his face and closed his eyes. When he inhaled deeply, *smelling* the hand I'd just touched myself with, I wanted to die.

I wanted to die.

It was the most embarrassing, yet most erotic thing I'd ever seen in my life.

My body shook, the ache between my legs unbearable. I couldn't move, I couldn't say a word. I just stood there, watching him breathe my scent in and out. When he finally opened his eyes, and a groan came from his lips, I was done. *So done.*

I launched myself at him, throwing my arms around his neck. "I quit."

He wrapped his arm around my waist, and with one quick hitch, he lifted me up. "It's about damn time."

My legs wrapped around him, and he turned, backing me into the open door between our rooms. One of his hands unraveled my tied-up hair so it fell loose, only to have Chase wrap it around his hand, closing his fist tightly around it. He gave it a good strong yank so my head bent back, and then his mouth crashed down on mine.

I swear I almost came right there. Our mouths opened, and tongues frantically collided. He tasted insanely good, and I never wanted to come up for air. I didn't care if I died of asphyxiation—I'd die deliriously happy.

He pressed himself harder into me, his erection straining through his pants. Since I was still wearing a dress and my legs were wrapped around him, I was effectively wide open— spread-eagled as he pushed harder against me. I moaned when he rubbed himself up and down. The sheer fabric of my panties allowed the friction of his zipper to spark like a rock to flint, and my body ignited.

Chase mumbled into my mouth, "Do you feel what you do to me? What you've done to me since that first night?"

He made a low, husky sound that came from deep in his throat and bit down on my bottom lip, tugging at it before he released my mouth. Reaching behind his neck, he took one of my hands, sliding it between us until I covered the top of his cock. When my fingers tightened around it, he growled and deepened the kiss.

I loved how needy he sounded, as if he had been waiting for this moment forever. Lord knows, it felt like I had waited an eternity.

Eventually—I'm not even really sure how—we made our way into my bedroom. Chase laid me down gently on the bed and hovered over me. When I reached up and touched his cheek, he turned and kissed the inside of my palm.

"You're so beautiful. I can't wait to see all of you." He buried his nose in my hair and whispered in my ear, "Can't wait to taste all of you."

I held my breath as he kissed his way from my neck down the exposed skin on my chest and stopped at my cleavage. My wrap dress had a tie at the right side. Chase leaned to his left, trailing his hand down my body to tug at the bow. He spread the fabric open and pulled his head back to take a good look at my body. Focusing on my breasts, he leaned in and licked a line from the top of my breastbone down into my cleavage. Shivers spilled over me, and goosebumps littered my skin. My nipples hardened and pushed through the lace of my bra, begging for attention. *God, I want his mouth on me.*

Using his thumb, he pushed down the cup of my bra and sucked in my left nipple. *Hard.* His eyes watched me constantly, taking in my response to his touches. When my eyes flitted closed, he did it a second time before turning his attention to my other breast. After a few minutes, he continued his exploring, his mouth lowering to trail a string of kisses over my stomach.

Lower.

Then lower.

He placed a gentle kiss on my panties and spoke with his lips vibrating right on my clit. "Were you thinking of me when your fingers were inside of you?" He hooked a thumb under the side of my panties and began to slide my underwear off. "Say it. Tell me you thought of me while your fingers were in this pussy."

Settling between my legs, he sucked my clit into his mouth, swirling his tongue while applying the perfect amount of pressure. It felt heavenly, and my hands dug into his hair, never wanting him to stop.

Then suddenly, he did. "Tell me."

I would have sworn I was Queen Elizabeth if it meant his mouth was back on me. Admitting the truth felt like a small price to pay. "You're the only person I've thought about while I've touched myself since the day I met you."

Chase's eyes blazed triumphantly and his mouth returned. He didn't tease this time. No. He sucked and licked until I was sufficiently wet and then added his fingers. It all built so fast, so furiously. Fingers pumping in and out, tongue sucking and swirling—my body began to tremble and tighten, my heels digging into the mattress, fingers pulling at his hair. The steep climb up the roller coaster was quick, and I felt the anticipation *everywhere*. God, it felt good. So good. I let out a sound that was a cross between a moan and a chant of his name.

My back arched off the bed, and Chase used one hand to hold me down as he pushed his mouth farther into me.

It's all too much.

Not nearly enough.

Oh God.

Oh God.

I reached the top of the roller coaster and teetered briefly for a second before...

I was free falling.

Sliding.

Barreling uncontrollably.

I didn't feel my legs. I didn't feel anything in the moment except pure, unadulterated ecstasy. It was so good, so breathtaking, that my eyes actually started to well a little.

My breathing was still erratic when Chase climbed back up my body and took my mouth again. The kiss was so different from the frenzy of a few minutes ago. Beautiful, languid, gentle. He stroked my hair as our tongues twined and cupped my face as he broke the kiss. "I'll be right back."

He disappeared for a moment and then returned with his wallet, pulling out a strip of condoms and tossing them on the nightstand.

I eyed them. "Big plans?"

He started to undress. "You have no fucking idea."

The way he looked at me while he shed his clothes—determination on his beautiful face—made my sated body spring to life again. He wasn't my first, wasn't even my second or third, but something about the way he looked at me made me feel like he was—like it was going to be my first real time, and I had no idea why.

Chase was a beautiful man...that much anyone could see. But when he stripped out of his clothes, I realized just how crazy perfect he really was. His chest was chiseled, pecs firm above a deeply carved six-pack, and his thighs were thick and powerful. *And that nipple ring.* I couldn't wait to have it between my teeth. As he stood there in tight, black boxer briefs, I was glad he'd given me a minute to prepare myself before he unveiled what was beneath.

He hooked his thumbs into the waistband of his briefs and bent to step out of them. When he stood, my mouth hung open. *Lord have mercy.* The man truly had the full package. And by that, I didn't mean good looks, charm, and money...

No, Chase had a damn *full package*. His cock was ridiculously thick and rigid. Already fully erect, it bobbed flush against him, reaching almost to his navel.

I licked my lips as he tore a condom from the strip, grasping it between his teeth and ripping the foil open.

Watching my face, he said, "You're going to be the death of me, aren't you?"

He took my hands in his as he climbed over me, weaving our fingers together and pulling them up over my head. He kissed my lips gently and then lifted his head to look into my eyes. Our gaze held for the longest time, even as he slowly pushed into me. I was wet, soaked even—as ready as I could be for him.

"Fuck," Chase muttered, and his eyes briefly closed. "You're so wet." He eased in and out a few times, being cautious and relaxing me enough to accept his girth without hurting.

Once he'd sufficiently broken me in, he began to move in and out rhythmically, with more intensity. Gentle thrusts became hard. Easing became rooting deep into my body. The only thing that didn't change was the way Chase looked at me. He stared into my eyes like he could see inside me. It made me feel exposed, yet beautifully accepted.

Everything in the background faded away except the sound of our breathing. When I moaned, he smashed his lips to mine, seeming to need to swallow the sound of my coming undone. I pulled at his hair as I climbed closer, and his breathing became short, shallow spurts.

"I'm gonna..." I started, but my body beat me to the finish. "Oh God."

Chase bit down on my shoulder, sending my slowly building orgasm into overdrive. It came over me like a tsunami, grabbing me and pulling me under. My muscles began pulsating, and my hooded eyes looked up at Chase.

He saw it on my face, felt it inside my body, and quickened his pace, working toward his own release. Finally, he ground down one last time, burying himself as deeply as he possibly could, and let out a groan as he released.

Unlike my previous lovers, he didn't collapse and roll over abruptly after his finish. Instead, he kissed me softly until he had to pull out, then got up to dispose of the condom. When he came back, he had a warm facecloth, which he used to wash me. Then he grabbed a bottle of water from the mini-fridge, and we shared it—passing it back and forth—both of us still naked.

After all of the adrenaline running high for so long, suddenly I started to crash. I yawned, and Chase tossed the empty bottle on the nightstand. He lifted me on top of him and lay back, positioning me over his body, my head on his heart. His heartbeat was soothing as he stroked my hair.

"Get some sleep," he said softly. "We have a long day tomorrow, and we have to be up early."

I liked the idea of getting some sleep. It had been so long since I'd felt this relaxed. This *safe*.

Already groggy, I said, "Okay. But we don't have to be at the focus group until ten."

He kissed the top of my head. "I know, but we're going to need a few hours for round two."

CHAPTER
20

Reese

I woke to movement in the bed. The room was dark, and my innate reaction was fear—until my eyes began to focus, and I remembered where I was.

Chase was flailing around and mumbling something in his sleep. The only other person I'd ever witnessed having nightmares was my brother, Owen, after the break-in. He would cry in his sleep. Some nights it became too much, and my mother would wake him and console him. I wasn't sure if I should let Chase sleep through this or not. He was so restless and seemed so tormented.

It was hard to watch him suffer, so I decided to try nudging him a little. Maybe just enough to bring him out of whatever was going on in his head.

Reaching for his shoulder, I gently tapped. "Chase?"

I almost jumped off the bed when he abruptly bolted upright.

He seemed confused at first. "What? What? Are you okay?" He was breathing heavy, his chest heaving.

With my hand still clutched over my rapidly beating heart, I said, "Yes! Yes...I'm fine. I think you were having a nightmare."

Chase raked his fingers through his hair. "I'm sorry. You're sure you're okay?"

"I'm perfectly fine."

Appeased, he blew out a deep breath and slipped from the bed, heading to the bathroom. He stayed in there a long time before the door opened again. The bed dipped when he returned, but he didn't immediately lie down. Instead, he sat on the edge of the mattress with his elbows on his knees, head hanging low, and his back to me.

I reached out and touched his bare skin. "Do you want to talk about it?"

"Not really. I've just started having them again. Hadn't had one in a few years before that. Not that I was aware of anyway."

"Are they...about your fiancée?"

He nodded. "I'm sorry."

"There's nothing to be sorry about. My brother had them for a while after the break-in. I don't want to push, but...but maybe it will help if you talk about it."

Chase was quiet for a long moment. "I finally got you into my bed. The last thing I want to do is talk to you about another woman while we're in it."

I sat up and crawled to where he was sitting. Wearing only the panties I'd put on while he was in the bathroom, I straddled him from behind, wrapping my arms around his waist. My cheek pressed to his shoulder, and my bare breasts smooshed against his back. He still smelled so good—woodsy with a delicious masculinity.

"We're not in your bed," I told him. "We're in my hotel room."

"There's no room for anyone else when it's me, you, and any bed."

My arms squeezed around his waist. "Well, I'm here if you want to talk."

Chase twisted his body to face me. One large hand wrapped around my throat while his thumb stroked the hollow of my neck. He leaned in to run his tongue over a pulsating vein. "I don't want to talk."

"But..." I tried to argue, but his lips were already at my ear.

"Shh," he whispered. "No talking. My mouth has other plans."

Before I'd realized he was moving, he dropped to his knees and pulled my ass to the edge of the bed. What he did with his mouth after that was far better than talking anyway.

We arrived at the focus group ahead of schedule and worked together setting up the display. Earlier, we'd eaten eggs and fruit naked in bed while discussing some questions I'd been considering adding to the moderator's list.

Elaine came to greet us, and even though I'd been the one to give her the list of things we'd decided to change, she still addressed her questions to Chase.

"What do you think about modifying question eleven to make it a yes-no response and then having the moderator talk about the question in group discussion to get oral feedback?"

I loved that Chase directed her to me for an answer. "Whatever Reese thinks. She's the boss. Only brought me to carry her bags."

While we worked through finalizing the changes, Chase's cell rang, and he excused himself, leaving just Elaine and me in the room.

"Can I ask you a personal question, Reese?" she said.

"Umm...sure."

"Are you seeing anyone?"

I had no idea how to answer. I mean, *was* I seeing someone? Chase and I had had sex three times since last night, but we hadn't exactly put a label on it.

"Sort of. I mean...I recently met someone."

"So it's not serious?"

"It's still very new."

"Well...my brother just moved to New York, and I was hoping it would be okay to give him your number. Maybe let him buy you a drink or something? I don't usually fix people up, but I think you two would get along."

Luckily, the moderator came in and interrupted Elaine's attempt at matchmaking. The participants for the focus groups had started arriving, and things got busy after that. I spent all morning on the other side of the one-way glass, listening, watching, and taking notes. Chase alternated between business phone calls, catching up on emails, and taking in bits and pieces of the study. At one point we were alone in the room, and I sat on a stool near the window.

Chase walked up behind me and cupped one of my breasts. Kneading it, he said, "I love one-way mirrors."

I elbowed him. "Stop it. Someone might walk in."

He wound my hair around his hand and tugged my head back to expose my neck. I'd noticed that seemed to be *his thing*. It was also fast becoming *my thing,* too. "I'll lock the door."

My eyes closed, succumbing against my better judgment. "We're at work."

"That'll make it more exciting."

A knock on the other side of the glass startled me, and I almost fell off the stool. Luckily, Chase steadied me, his hands catching my shoulders and keeping me upright as I bobbled. He chuckled behind me as Elaine held up five fingers, letting us know we would break for lunch in a few.

"No problem, Elaine," he said, even though she couldn't hear him. "I can be done in five minutes. I'm pretty sure Reese is wet already, anyway."

"You're such a perv."

He spun my stool around to face him and took my face in his hands. "What do you say we go back to the hotel for lunch?"

I squinted. "To eat?"

"Pussy, yes."

I squirmed a little. "All this time I've been worried about what would happen at work when things end. I should have been worried about what would happen at work when things got started."

"I see nothing but good things happening at work in our future."

"Is that so?"

"It is. The first night we get back to the office, I'm going to bend you over my desk and fuck you from behind while you watch the city light up in the dark."

I swallowed. "That's probably a no-no in the employee handbook."

"I'll have to fix that promptly. You know what else I can't wait to do with you?"

"What?"

"I want you on your knees while I sit at my desk."

"While you...sit at your desk?"

He nodded slowly. "I want to look down and watch your head rise and fall as you take my cock into your throat." He tugged my hair. "I'm going to hold a fistful of your hair and keep you there until you swallow every last drop of my come."

184

What probably should have been concerning to me about the state of my future employment was, instead, totally working for me. His *dirty mouth* totally worked for me.

"What else?" I breathed.

"The conference room table. I want to spread you on the top of the glass and lick your juicy little cunt until the entire office hears you moaning the boss's name."

I let out a shaky laugh. "I think you've lost it, Bossman."

Chase's back was to the door when it opened, blocking the view of anything going on between us. He leisurely unwound his hand from my hair.

"You two want to grab a bite to eat or order in?" Elaine asked.

Chase looked to me. I tried to hide my coquettish smile as I lied.

"Actually, Chase has a telephone conference he needs to do at lunch, so we're going to head back to the hotel for an hour."

"Do you want me to order you something for when you get back?"

"No, but thank you. I'll make sure he gets something to eat at the hotel while he's busy playing boss."

For the rest of the day, Chase and I were busy but exchanged flirtatious glances all afternoon. Even though a part of me still worried it was stupid to get involved, I was starting to not give a damn about the consequences if it meant spending my days feeling like this. I honestly couldn't remember the last time I'd been this giddy over a guy, and it felt good. *Really good.*

At the end of the sessions, Elaine schmoozed us into having dinner with her. She was pushy and made it hard to say no. During drinks we sat around in the bar and talked shop, but then things turned personal.

"So are you single, Chase?" she asked.

My eyes immediately jumped to his. He responded to her while looking at me. "I'm not married, no. But I'm seeing someone."

She nodded. "I swear I never play matchmaker, but I had a friend in mind for you, too."

"Too?"

She had his attention now.

"Yes. I'm going to fix Reese up. My brother recently moved to the city, and I think they'll hit it off."

Chase's eyebrows raised, and he looked at me. I had no idea what to say, so I just sat there. I couldn't backtrack now without sounding like an idiot. I'd just figured I'd blow her brother off if she did have him contact me.

Chase had a different idea on the approach. He took a long draw on his beer and said, "I thought you were seeing someone, Reese?"

"Umm...I am...well, sort of. It's new."

"This new guy...he doesn't mind you going out with other people?"

I wanted to smack him. He was enjoying how uncomfortable the conversation made me. "I don't know, actually. We haven't discussed it."

He finished his beer. "I'd put my money on him having no plans to share you."

His comment made me feel warm, though I should have known better than to expect him to stop there.

He spoke to Elaine with a straight face. "She's dating her cousin."

"Her cousin?"

"They're second cousins. Met at her great-uncle's funeral last week."

Elaine had no idea what to say. When she looked at me, she must have mistaken bewilderment for grief. "I'm sorry for your loss."

I caught Chase's grin as he pulled his ringing cell from his pocket. "Excuse me for a minute."

When he came back, he was less playful, quiet even. I wasn't sure if the call he'd received was on his mind or if Elaine fixing me up with her brother had actually bothered him more than he let on. But something was off. Elaine didn't seem to notice it, though. We talked about marketing for most of the rest of the evening, which was usually one of my favorite things to discuss, yet I found myself preoccupied with Chase's lack of participation.

At the hotel, things were pretty much the same. It was late, and we'd had one hell of a long day—beginning at four o'clock this morning. Chase took a shower in his room while I washed up and changed. He came into my bathroom while I was brushing my teeth. "Can I borrow your charger again?"

I spit out a mouthful of toothpaste. "Sure. It should be plugged in on the desk."

I don't know why, but I assumed when he asked me for the charger, he meant he was taking it to his room, not spending the night in mine again. So I was surprised when I found him plugging it in on his side of the bed. *His side of the bed. Well, that happened awfully quick.*

Grabbing my moisturizer, I sat on the chair at the desk and pumped it a few times, squirting the white cream into my hand.

I'd begun to rub it into my legs when Chase said, "Come here. Let me do that."

I handed him the lotion and sat at the bottom of the bed, extending my legs in his direction. He stared at them while he rubbed, his fingers massaging more than needed to work in the lotion.

"Is everything okay?" I asked.

He nodded. It wasn't very convincing.

"Are you upset because of the thing with Elaine's brother? Because she just caught me unexpectedly. I wasn't really planning on going out with him. I would at least be up front if I was planning on dating someone else."

He'd been working his thumb into my calf, kneading a muscle that was cramped from twelve hours in high heels, when his hand abruptly stopped, and he looked up at me. "You're planning on dating someone else?"

"No. Well...I know we talked about not dating other people. But I wasn't sure—"

"I'm sure," he interrupted.

"You are?"

"I'm not sure how we got here or where we're going. But I'm damn sure I don't want to share you."

He'd said exactly what I felt. "I don't want to share you either."

"Good. Then it's settled?"

"It is." I smiled and then motioned to my legs. "Now rub more...that feels good."

"Yes, ma'am."

Although the air between us was clear, I suspected something was still on Chase's mind when he turned off the light. Pulling me onto his chest, he stroked my hair in the dark.

"The call at dinner tonight? It was the detective from Peyton's case."

I turned, propping my head atop my hands on his chest and looking up at him. "Everything okay?"

"Yeah. Since it's technically an open case, she still comes around once a year and touches base. Told her I'd see her next week."

"That must be hard on you."

"Just odd timing. It had been a few years since I'd had a nightmare. Started happening again a few weeks ago. And then tonight she called."

"Do they check in with you at the same time every year? Maybe it's been in the back of your mind that it's coming up, and that prompted your subconscious back into action."

He nodded like it made sense. "Maybe."

I crawled up his body and planted a kiss on his lips. "Thank you for sharing that with me. It means a lot."

CHAPTER
21

Chase – Seven years ago

My phone buzzed on my desk. I picked it up and barked without saying hello. "You're late."

"Did you really expect me early?" Peyton asked. I knew she was smiling from her voice.

I shook my head and smiled back even though I wasn't happy she was late. *Again.* "Where are you?"

"I got out later than I thought and had to make a stop. Go on without me. I'll meet you at the restaurant instead of your office."

For an actress, she really needed to work on being less transparent. "Where you heading, Peyton?"

"Just running an errand for Little East."

"Running an errand or following Eddie?"

"Aren't they the same thing?"

"No, they're not. Please tell me you're not heading uptown again to that homeless camp."

She was quiet.

"Damn it, Peyton. I thought we agreed you weren't going to do this shit anymore."

"No, you told me I wasn't going to. That's not the same as agreeing."

I dragged my fingers through my hair. "Wait for me at the coffee shop on 151st Street when you get off the subway."

"I'm fine."

"Peyton..."

"You're being overprotective. Is this what it's going to be like when we're married? Are you going to expect me barefoot and pregnant, waiting with your slippers at the door?"

I'd proposed two days ago. It was probably not a good idea to tell her I'd love exactly that. At least then I'd know what the hell she was up to. I grabbed my suit jacket from the closet in my office and headed for the elevator.

"I'm on my way, you pain in the ass."

Out on the sidewalk, I called my sister as I trekked to the subway to tell her we would be late.

"You're going to be late to your own engagement celebration?"

"This thing was your idea, not mine. You look for any excuse to throw a party."

"My little brother is getting married. It's a big deal, not an excuse. God knows we all thought you'd die from some STD before Peyton came along."

"This is not a discussion we're having. We're going to be late because my bride-to-be thinks she's Columbo. I gotta go."

"Who?"

"Forget it. I'll see you in a bit. And thanks, Anna."

By the time I exited the subway up on 151st Street, it had started pouring. As soon as I could get cell service, I called Peyton's phone. She didn't answer.

"Fuck," I grumbled to myself and went to stand against the nearest building. Rain pelted down diagonally, and I had to cover my phone with one hand just to keep it dry. I hit redial and waited for Peyton to answer. She didn't.

"Goddamn it." I knew the makeshift homeless community wasn't far, and I assumed Peyton hadn't bothered to wait. Pulling up Google maps on my phone, I found the area of the park with the trestle. It was only three blocks away, so I started to walk in the rain. Every thirty seconds, I hit redial. I grew more and more anxious each time the ringing went to voicemail. There was a strange feeling in the pit of my stomach, and after the third unanswered call, something made me start to jog.

Another redial.

Another voicemail.

I turned the corner and saw the area under the trestle that Peyton had described off in the distance.

Another redial.

Peyton's voice came on, telling me to leave a message at the tone.

Something felt off. *Horribly off.* My jog turned into a run.

By the time my phone vibrated in my pocket, my heart was pounding in my chest. Seeing Peyton's face flash on the screen should have calmed me, but for some reason, it didn't.

"Chase, where are you?" Her voice was shaky; I could tell she was scared.

"Where are you?

She didn't answer.

"Peyton? *Goddamn it.* Where are you?"

The clank of the cell phone tumbling to the ground was loud in my ear. But it was what came next that would haunt me for years to come.

CHAPTER
22

Reese

I woke to the sound of Chase gasping for air. It was a gritty, raw, ear-splitting noise that felt like it should come after being pummeled in the gut. There was no hesitation before I woke him this time.

"Chase...wake up." I shook him vigorously.

His eyes flew open, and he stared at me, yet I could tell he didn't actually see me.

"You were having another nightmare."

He blinked a few times, and his vision came into focus. "Are you okay?" he asked.

"I'm fine. But you...sounded like you couldn't breathe. I wasn't sure if it was a nightmare or you were really having some sort of respiratory distress."

Chase sat up. His face was damp with sweat, and he wiped his forehead with the back of his hand. "Sorry I woke you."

Just like yesterday, he got out of bed and spent ten minutes in the bathroom with the water running. When he returned, he sat on the edge of the bed again, so I followed suit and straddled him from behind—only this morning I was wearing a T-shirt.

"You okay?" I asked.

He nodded.

"Anything I can do?"

"You could take off the shirt. Your tits pressed up against my back does a lot to stop the nightmares."

I pointed out the obvious. "Umm...you're already awake. I don't think that would help with this morning's nightmares."

"Maybe not, but there's always tomorrow."

I smiled, leaned back, and lifted my shirt over my head. Pressing my bare skin to his, I asked, "Better?"

"Sure is."

We stayed like that for a good ten minutes, our breaths synchronizing in the quiet, dark room.

"Peyton's dad took off when she was little, and her, her mother, and her two sisters ate all their meals in a shelter for a while. When Peyton got older, she wanted to give back, so she volunteered at a few local soup kitchens. She made friends with this one guy, Eddie. He had issues with people coming too close to him, so he refused to sleep in the shelters. Eddie was being harassed by a group of teenagers. They'd show up at night at a homeless camp—where a lot of people who had nowhere else to go slept—and start trouble. It was a game they played. Every few days he'd come in with a gash on his head or bruises."

"That's horrible."

"Yeah. Peyton went to the police, but they didn't do much. Eddie didn't speak more than a word or two here and there, and Peyton couldn't let it go. She started following him at night to see where he was staying, thinking if she gave the police more specifics they might look into it further. I told her it wasn't safe, but she didn't listen. The day of our engagement party, Eddie showed up at the shelter with a broken nose and two black eyes. Peyton had figured out where he was staying, and went down there that night to see if she could pry more information out of others since Eddie didn't talk much. She was supposed to wait for me at the train station."

"Oh God."

"I found her a few minutes too late. Eddie was cradling her and rocking back and forth, sitting in a pool of her blood. Knife wound. She must have gotten in the way of their game of beating up homeless people." He took a deep breath in and out. "She was gone before they got her in the ambulance."

My throat burned, and tears stung my eyes as they slid down my face.

Chase must have felt the wetness on his back. "Are you crying?"

The passage from my chest to my lips was clogged. It was hard to speak. "I'm so sorry that happened to you, Chase. I can't even imagine what you went through."

"I didn't tell you to get you upset. I wanted you to know so there's nothing between us. I hate that the nightmares came back at all, but this is the first time I've felt anything more than physical for someone since Peyton, and I don't want to screw it up before it even has a chance to get started."

"You're not screwing things up—just the opposite."

Chase turned, pulling me from behind him onto his lap. Pushing a piece of hair behind my ear, he said, "I'm not the hero your brother is."

My eyebrows drew together. "What are you talking about?"

He shook his head. "I didn't keep Peyton safe."

"Keep her safe? What happened wasn't your fault. How could it be?"

"I should have been there with her."

"Chase, that's crazy. You can't be with someone twenty-four hours a day to protect them. It's not like you put the knife in the killer's hand. People need to take responsibility for their own protection. That's why I'm the way I am. My own experiences have made me even more aware of that. "

Chase looked into my eyes, like he was searching for sincerity. When he found it, which of course he did because I'd meant every word I said from the bottom of my heart, he nodded and kissed my lips gently.

He exhaled, and I actually felt the tension leave his body. Checking the bedside alarm clock, he said, "It's not even five o'clock. Why don't we try to get some sleep?"

I wasn't sure if it was appropriate or not, but I wanted to make him feel better, get his mind off of the sadness of the past. Neither one of us could change what had happened in our lives, but we could leave it there and move forward and continue to live. My eyelashes fluttered before I spoke from beneath them. "I'm not sleepy."

"No?"

I shook my head back and forth slowly.

The timbre of his voice dropped. "What did you have in mind?"

"Maybe a little of this." Dipping my head, I kissed his pectoral muscle. Working my way up, I alternated between gentle licking and sucking until I reached his jaw. My tongue trailed from one end of his beautiful mouth to the other, planting a soft kiss at the corner of his lips.

Turning his head to catch my lips with his, Chase kissed me deeply. The kiss felt different than the others we'd shared—more intense, more passionate, more meaningful. If our kisses were each a story, this was the one where the hero got the girl, and they rode off into the sunset.

For the next hour, we shared more than just our bodies. The sun had begun to rise, casting a golden hue across the room as Chase slowly moved in and out of me. It was beautiful and tender, and I felt it in a place I never knew another human being could touch—my soul.

We had an evening flight home after the second day of focus groups wrapped. After working side by side during the day and sleeping wrapped in each other's arms, a feeling of melancholy washed over me as we drove to the airport. I looked out the town car window, lost in thought, as Chase spoke on an overseas conference call with one of his manufacturers.

He covered the phone and leaned toward me, pointing to a large billboard up ahead. "You want to go, don't you?"

It was an advertisement for the Wizard of Oz Museum.

After he hung up, he surprised me by reaching over and hauling me snugly against him. "You're awfully quiet."

"You were on the phone."

"You've been sitting as far away from me as you can possibly get and staring out the window. What's on your mind, Buttercup?"

"Nothing. Just a long day."

"You sure?"

I thought for a minute. I wasn't the least bit tired; that's not what was casting a shadow of gloom over me. So why was I lying? Why hide what I was thinking about?

I turned to face him. "Actually, no. I'm lying. Something's been on my mind all day."

He nodded. "Okay. Lay it on me."

"Well...I enjoyed my time here with you."

"I enjoyed my time inside of you as well."

I laughed. "Not exactly what I said, but let's go with it. I guess...I'm concerned about what happens when we go back to reality."

"I thought we'd already discussed that. Bending you over my desk, underneath it on your knees, conference room table—you have a *full* schedule once we're back in the office." He tugged at the material of his slacks. "Fuck. I can't wait to get back to work. Maybe we should go in when we land tonight."

I playfully nudged his shoulder. "I'm serious."

"So am I. I treat fucking you with the utmost sincerity."

"Well, utmost sincerity or not, I don't think any of it should be happening in the office."

His face fell as if I'd just told him there was no Easter bunny. "No office sex?"

"I'm not sure it's a good idea that anyone finds out."

"I'll close the blinds."

"It would probably be safer if we kept our distance at work. Obviously, we'll be in meetings together at times, but no inappropriate touching."

"Safer for whom?"

That was a pretty damn good question. "Me?"

"Are you asking me or telling me?"

"I'm new. I want to earn people listening to what I have to say, not have them nod their head because I'm screwing the boss. And...when...you know, we aren't together anymore, it's going to be weird enough between the two of us. Having the entire office watching our interactions would just make it worse."

Chase grew quiet. He looked out the window, and the

distance between us widened, even though we were sitting side by side. "Whatever you want."

Arriving at the airport, we breezed through security and had more than an hour to kill before we boarded our nine p.m. flight, so we went to the first-class lounge. Chase had gone to the men's room while I ordered us drinks at the complimentary bar. A nice looking, young guy walked up next to me as the bartender opened a new bottle of Pinot noir.

"Can I buy you a drink?"

I smiled politely. "They're free."

"Damn. I forgot. I'll buy you two then."

I laughed. "I'm good. But thanks anyway, big spender."

The bartender set my glass of wine on the bar and went to work making Chase's drink. I studied the electronic flight board hanging above the bar to check that ours was still on time.

Watching me scrutinize the chart, the guy next to me said, "My flight's been delayed twice already. Where you heading tonight?"

I was about to respond when a deep voice behind me beat me to it. "My house."

The guy took one look at Chase, who stood close at my back, his hand wrapped possessively around my waist, and nodded. "Got it."

Taking our drinks, we sat at a quiet booth in the corner.

"I didn't take you for the possessive type."

Chase looked at me over his drink as he sipped. "I'm not usually. Yet I feel very greedy when I look at you. I don't want any other man to even come close."

Our eyes met. "Is that why you're upset with me? Because you're feeling territorial, and I don't want anyone in the office to know about us?"

"No."

"Then what is it? You've been quiet for the last half hour, ever since we talked in the car."

Chase looked away, his eyes roaming the room as he collected his thoughts before he looked back. "You said *when*, not *if*."

I furrowed my brow.

"In the car. When you were talking about how you didn't want things uncomfortable in the office, you said *when* we aren't together anymore...not *if* we aren't together anymore. You've already planned our breakup in your head *and* how it will impact you at work."

"I did n—" *Oh my God. He's right.*

I'd skipped right past the relationship part and was already worried about how our demise was going to affect me. Talk about not giving something new a chance.

"You're right. I'm sorry. It's just that I don't exactly have a good track record with relationships. And I left a job I loved over my last office romance. I guess I'm using my past to set expectations about the future."

Chase watched me intently. "No expectations, no disappointment?"

I don't know why, but admitting that as the truth made me embarrassed. I looked down. "I guess."

Chase leaned in. Touching my chin, he gently lifted. "Give it a chance. I might be the one who doesn't disappoint you."

CHAPTER
23

Reese

Predatory. That was the only way to describe how Chase looked at me when I walked into his office. We'd been back at work for a week, and he'd been good about keeping his distance, keeping things professional during the day like I'd asked. But the butterflies in my stomach as I watched his heated eyes follow me told me that was all about to go to shit. Evidently five days was his limit.

Thank God there were other people in the room. Josh was talking as he flipped through blown-up glossies from last week's photo shoot. The woman in the shots wore sexy, white, lacy lingerie with garters and stockings, yet Chase wasn't paying one bit of attention. Lindsey, who sat to the left of Josh, pointed to one photo and compared it to another while Chase tracked my every move. I set a binder his secretary had handed me down on the glass table at the other side of the room and put some distance between us by sitting on the adjoining couch.

Chase's eyes were mischievous when he casually got up from his desk, walked to the little refrigerator built into the credenza, and pulled out a few water bottles. He placed one each in front of Josh and Lindsey as they continued to speak, and then walked over to hand one to me. His eyes blazed as our fingers brushed. He leaned in, clearly not caring if anyone was paying attention.

"Saw this in the hallway outside of your office. Figured you dropped it." He handed me a Chapstick.

The glimmer in his eye told me to take a closer look, so I did. He'd handed me a *Dr. Pepper*-flavored Chapstick, and his eyes dipped to my mouth. I smiled like a schoolgirl at how sweet he was—finding a workaround for his not liking my lip addiction.

My answer was to wait until he sat back down behind his desk and then open the tube and slowly line my mouth. *Very slowly*. When I licked my lips with as much obscenity as I could possibly ooze, Chase looked like he was a few breaths away from clearing the room.

His stare turned feral. I'd just prodded a bull, and I happened to be wearing a red dress. I squirmed in my seat and attempted to avoid his ferocious gaze. But it was impossible. He was just too irresistible, and when he had that dominating glimmer in his eye, he ambushed all of my senses. That was most likely why when no one else was looking and he mouthed *Go into my bathroom and take off your panties*, I was even considering it.

But these were my rules—if anyone had to abide by them, it should be me. I sat farther back on the couch and continued to listen from a distance, rather than pull a chair up to his desk and join the three of them. Last night Chase had a business dinner, the night before that I'd had dinner with my mother, and earlier in the week one or the other of us had needed to work late each night to catch up from being gone. Because of our schedules, we hadn't been together since our trip—hadn't even so much as touched—and I was feeling as needy as Chase looked.

After a while, Chase glanced at the clock and asked if we'd like to order in lunch with him.

"Can't. Meeting Bridezilla for lunch so she can show me swatches of something I don't care about," Josh said.

Lindsey declined, too. "I brought lunch."

Chase looked to me. "Hungry? How about I order us the same thing we had in Kansas for lunch both days?"

Josh and Lindsey turned in my direction. I smiled at Chase and willed my blush to stay at bay as I remembered what he'd eaten for lunch. *Me.*

"Sure, that sounds good." I offered the first explanation that came to mind. "I have a thing for Kentucky Fried Chicken."

As Josh and Chase finished talking about mocking up some photo ads, Chase walked to his wall of glass and pressed the button for the blinds, concealing his office from the outside hallway.

Even though no one asked, when they were fully closed, Chase said, "Sam would chew my ear off if she walked by and we were holding up glossies of a half-naked model." He paused and looked at me. "Plus, I like to eat without being watched."

A few minutes later, we broke for lunch. Chase shut the door behind Josh and Lindsey. When he stared at me and locked the door, I felt the sound of the audible clank between my legs. *This is not going to be easy.*

Chase had told Josh to leave the glossies so we could look at them over lunch, and I tried to busy myself examining them as I stood at his desk. My eyes closed when he came up behind me, close enough that I could feel the heat from his body and his breath on my neck, but not touching.

"You didn't take off your panties like I asked."

"Is that what you mouthed? I couldn't make out the words."

He inched closer. "Liar." Grabbing one of my hips, he pulled me against him. "You want to know what I think?" he whispered. "I think you kept them on because you're wet, and you're trying to hide it from me."

"I am not."

"Only one way to find out." Before I could respond, he'd lifted the back of my dress, and pressed his hand against the damp lace of my underwear.

My eyes closed. "Chase..."

He buried his face in my hair from behind, inhaling deeply, then wrapped it around his hand and tugged my head back. "You're soaked. How long will you stay mad at me for bending you over this desk and fucking you, Buttercup?"

"We shouldn't."

"Your mouth says no, but your body is screaming yes." Shoving everything on his desk to one end, Chase gently guided me down until my chest pressed against the cold wood. Following, he covered my back with his front, and his erection pressed against my ass.

I was fighting a losing battle, but wasn't going down without at least one more feeble attempt. "What if someone comes?"

"That's the point." His teeth found my earlobe and bit down. At the same time, he lifted my hands over my head and wrapped my fingers around the other side of the desk, guiding me to hold on.

I tried again. "I don't think I can be quiet."

"I'll cover your mouth with mine before you come." Cool air replaced his body as he stood and unzipped his pants. One of his hands tore at my panties, and he hiked my dress up to expose my bare ass. He palmed it in his hand. "This ass. I can't wait to take it. But not here. I won't be able to keep you quiet when you have my cock in your ass and my fingers in your pussy at the same time."

My eyes rolled into the back of my head as his fingers pressed down on my swollen clit. He turned my head to the side, leaning down for a kiss, and I sighed into his mouth, murmuring his name as he rubbed his erection against my ass.

"Chase..." I was already on the verge of coming, and there was no way in hell it was going to be quiet.

"Okay." He abruptly stood, and for a second I wanted to kill him—until I heard the loud tear of the foil packet. I looked back over my shoulder, and, I swear, if I hadn't already been wet, I would have been after catching a glimpse of Chase. The condom package he'd ripped open was still between his teeth, and he was sheathing his fully hard cock using both hands. I was already weakened and shaky...it was a good thing I was leaning on the desk because my knees almost buckled at the erotic sight.

He wasted no time as he lined up the wide head of his cock and sunk into me.

"Fuuuck," he groaned as he leaned over and again found my mouth. He kissed me long and hard without moving. Now that he was inside of me—that he'd brought me to the brink of orgasm with his fingers but not finished me off—I needed him to move. The feeling of him filling me from behind was incredible, but I needed that friction.

"Chase...can you...."

"Spread your legs wider. I need to be deep inside of you."

I didn't question him. I just widened my stance, opening myself up to whatever it was he needed. In that moment, I no longer cared that we were in his office, that he was my boss, what other people thought of me. The only thing I cared about was him. Him inside of me, moving the way I knew he could to make me feel...

"Chase—"

"Say it. Tell me you want me here. Right now."

"I do. I want you. Please. Please move."

I whimpered as he reared back and thrust deep. Pulling almost all the way out, he leaned down and angled himself to stroke upward, hitting just the spot, reaching new depths inside of my body. My orgasm didn't take long to build again, and the second time it came at me with a vengeance—almost as if the first time I'd pissed it off not allowing it to thrum its way through my body. This time, it was going to make sure it was unstoppable.

My body began to shake as he pumped harder, faster, deeper.

"Come, Reese."

His voice was so strained and gruff, it was enough to push me over the edge. Just as I began to cry out his name, he smothered my sound with a kiss. By the time the last quake had wracked through my body, I felt as if he'd swallowed my orgasm whole...swallowed *me* whole.

Eventually, my pants became breaths, and the rise and fall of Chase's chest, plastered to my back, slowed in unison. He kissed my lips gently before going to his en suite bathroom to clean up and bring me a warm washcloth. I breathed out a sigh of contentment, feeling sated and relaxed.

But all that changed when a knock came at the door.

CHAPTER
24

Reese

My cheeks were flushed, my hair was a disheveled mess, and I looked exactly what I was. *Fucked.* I'd scurried into the bathroom so Chase could answer the door to his office. Looking in the mirror now, there was no doubt I'd made the right choice. I was even more certain of that when I heard Samantha's voice. *Great,* the VP of human resources had just walked into Chase's office, and it probably still reeked of sex.

The serenity I'd felt not three minutes ago was long gone—replaced by its evil friend, paranoia.

Were we loud?

Was I loud?

Did the whole office hear?

What was I doing? I'd set ground rules and promptly broken them the first time Chase pushed a little. Had I learned nothing from my mistakes?

Feeling vulnerable, I tiptoed to the door and pressed my ear against it.

"What were you doing in here?" Samantha asked.

"I was on the phone."

Her voice sounded suspicious. I pictured her squinting her eyes as she spoke. "With whom?"

"A supplier. Not that it's any of your business. What do you need, Sam?"

Her voice became more distant, and I had to strain to hear. She must have walked to the windows or the seating area on the other side of the room. "Detective Balsamo called me this morning. She said she's been trying to reach you."

"I've been busy."

"That's why I'm here asking the question. It's not like you to blow off anything related to Peyton. There was a time when they couldn't get you out of the police station, you were so involved."

"That was the same time when I blew off my work and spent most nights drunk. Not sure I want to go back to those days."

"I get that. I do. But I wanted to make sure nothing else was going on. You seem...different lately."

"Different? How?"

"I don't know. More jovial, I suppose."

"Jovial? What am I? A jolly old fat guy who rides around in a sleigh?"

"Something's going on with you. I can tell. Are you seeing someone new?"

The room went quiet for a minute, and I wondered how he was going to respond. A part of me wanted him to say he was seeing someone, just to hear him declare it out loud to one of his closest friends. Then again, he was talking to the vice president of human resources at my place of employment—probably not the best person to make that declaration to.

"Not that it's any of your business, but yes, I am seeing someone."

"Someone you've gone out with more than once?"

"I'm not talking about this with you."

"When do I get to meet her?"

"When I'm ready."

"So that means you expect her to be around a while?"

Chase huffed. "Did you have any actual business you came here to discuss? Because I was in the middle of something important when you interrupted."

"Fine. But you love my interruptions, and you know it."

I heard footsteps move closer followed by the click of the doorknob, but then it went quiet again without the door closing. Samantha's voice was serious the next time she spoke, and for some reason, I visualized her stopping and looking back over her shoulder.

"I'm glad you're moving on, Chase. I hope it works out and I get to meet her." She paused for a second and then spoke softly. "Maybe it's time you take down the shrine, too."

I waited a few minutes before hesitantly cracking opening the door. Chase had opened his windows to the outside and was staring at the advertisement on the building across the street.

He didn't turn to face me when he spoke. "Sorry about that."

"Things went too far today. We shouldn't have…" I trailed off.

He was quiet. I assumed his mood shift was because of what I'd overheard. Even though I'd never had one, I imagined talking about a dead ex-fiancée was kind of a buzz kill. So he surprised me when he turned and said, "I want this."

"Sex in the office?"

The corner of his lip twitched. "That, too. But that's not what I meant."

"No?"

He shook his head. "I want this. Me and you. Sam just came in here to talk about Peyton. The lead detective on the case called her, too. It's time for her annual call where she tells me they're still working the case but nothing new has come up."

"I'm sorry. She called you last week, right? That must be hard."

He nodded. "It was always hard. I'm not saying it's easy now. But normally I go to a dark place after the mention of Peyton's case. I pretty much expected to feel miserable after Sam walked out the door—waited for it to hit me even. Took a deep breath while I was waiting, and you know what happened?"

"What?"

"I smelled you on me."

I blinked a few times. "I don't understand."

He shrugged. "Neither do I. But I fucking love smelling you on me."

He looked so sincere, even though it was a bizarre thing to say.

"And smelling me made you feel better?"

His grin was lopsided. "Uh-huh."

"Okay then." I fought a blush. "I really should get back to work."

"Dinner tonight?"

"I'd like that. How about if I make you something at my place?"

"Even better. Then I don't have to wait to get you home to get you naked."

Over the years, I'd learned to accept my neuroses. Checking under the bed, behind the shower curtain, and inside every closet had become part of my daily routine. I didn't try to change it. I'd let it become part of who I was instead of letting it define me. Plenty of women were extra precautious... especially living in New York City. Yet, as I was about to enter my apartment with Chase right behind me, I wished like hell that my compulsions could take the night off. I unlocked the top lock, and my key hovered at the next one. Deciding to just get it over with before going inside, I spun around and confessed right there in the hallway.

"I have a routine when I get home."

Chase's eyebrows drew together. "Okay..."

"I told you I have issues with safety. I check behind the shower curtain, open all the closet doors, check under the bed and couch." I paused and chewed on the nail of my pointer finger. "I have a routine, and I do it in a certain order. And I do it at least twice—sometimes more if I don't feel calm after the second time. Although most days it's only two passes."

He said nothing for a few seconds, his eyes questioning. Finding I was dead serious, he nodded. "Show me the routine, and after you're finished with the first pass, I'll take the second."

I had no idea what I'd expected him to say, but that answer couldn't have made me happier. He didn't poke fun or belittle my safety concerns. Instead he was going to pitch in. Pushing up on my tippy toes, I planted a sweet kiss on his lips.

"Thank you."

Tallulah, of course, was waiting with green eyes glowing in the dark. If I ever had a house, I could put the beast in the window to scare away children at Halloween. I flicked on the lights, and Ugly Kitty stared at Chase as she licked her lips.

I know, Ugly Kitty, I know. He's pretty delectable.

"Jesus, she's even uglier in person," he said.

I scooped Tallulah from the top of the couch and kneeled down to check beneath it, beginning my rounds. Chase followed quietly along. After my last checkpoint, I turned to him. "That's it."

He set the bottle of wine he was holding down on the kitchen counter and took Kitty from my arms.

"I'll be back."

Watching him go through my routine was comical. He must have thought holding the kitty was part of it. I didn't bother to tell him because...well, because oddly, I really liked watching the oversized man walk around and check my closets for prospective intruders while holding a hairless cat. It certainly wasn't a sight you see every day.

Finishing, he bent down, let Tallulah go, and walked into the kitchen where he began to open my drawers, looking for something. Finding a bottle opener, he spoke as he unscrewed the cork. "How'd I do?"

"Perfect. You're hired. You can come sweep my apartment for criminals every night, if you like."

He pulled the cork from the bottle with a loud pop. "Be careful. I might take you up on that."

Since my refrigerator was even emptier than I'd thought, we ordered in Chinese food. I got the kung pao chicken, and Chase chose shrimp lo mein. We sat on the floor in the living room, eating out of containers with chopsticks and swapping meals from time to time.

"Do you think Sam knows?" I asked.

"About us?"

"Yes."

"No. She's not subtle. If she knew, she'd say it."

"How do you think she would feel if she did know? Considering I'm an employee and all."

"Doesn't matter. She doesn't like it, I'll make her change the policy."

"From prohibited relationships to screwing in the office strongly encouraged?"

He grinned. "Absolutely."

I'd been thinking about the things I overhead in the bathroom all afternoon. While the conversation was obviously not meant for my ears, I couldn't unhear it. Part of my hesitancy with jumping into this relationship full force with Chase—even aside from him being my boss—was wondering where his relationship with Peyton had left him. Whether he could *truly* move on. What shrine had Sam been referring to? I'd been in his house, and nothing had struck me as unusual.

I looked into Chase's eyes when I spoke. "I overheard some of your conversation with Sam today from the bathroom."

He swallowed his mouthful of food. "Okay."

"Can I ask you something that's probably none of my business?"

He set down his carton on the coffee table. "What's on your mind?"

"Are you...able to move on?"

He'd told me he wanted to try. But trying and actually putting the past behind you were two very different things. I should know.

"To be honest, the last seven years, I had no idea I *wasn't* moving on. Thought what I was doing *was* moving on."

"You mean sleeping with women?"

He shook his head. "Yeah. I was standing in place a long time. Not letting go."

"But you think you're ready to move on now?"

"I think it took me this long to realize what moving on meant. It doesn't mean forgetting what you've left behind. It means making her a memory and deciding to have a future without her in it."

"Wow. That's sad and beautiful at the same time."

He took my hand. "*This* feels right. So, to answer your question...am I able to move on now? It feels like I already have."

Chase was sitting on the floor with his back against the couch. Setting my container down on the table next to his, I climbed over him, straddling his hips, and gently kissed his lips.

"That was a really good answer," I whispered.

"Oh yeah? Do I get a prize for the right answer?" Chase's thumb brushed gently along my jaw.

"You do. You get your pick of rewards. Tell me how you'd like to receive yours, and your wish is my command."

I felt his cock harden beneath me. "Any way I want?"

I nuzzled into him. "Any way you want."

He grabbed a fistful of my hair and pulled hard, gaining access to my neck. Leaning in, his tongue licked its way from the top of my throat down to my collarbone. Reaching the soft spot between my neck and shoulder, his teeth sunk in, not breaking the skin but strong enough that I suspected I'd have a mark tomorrow.

I moaned, and Chase ground up, pushing his erection into me with a groan.

"Does any way I want include tying you to the bed for days?"

Just as he pulled me down to him again, sealing his mouth over mine, his cell phone began to ring.

"That's you," I mumbled into our joined mouths.

"Ignore it."

His hand slipped under my blouse and found my pert nipples, which made ignoring the ringing cell easy. But then thirty seconds after it stopped, it started again. Someone really wanted to reach Chase.

"Don't you even want to see who it is?"

His dexterous fingers unhooked my bra. "Don't care."

But when his phone stopped and started a third time, even Chase couldn't ignore it any more. He groaned and reached into his pocket to dig his cell out.

"Shit. It's my brother-in-law. He never calls. I need to take it."

I leaned back and gave him room.

"What's up?"

I heard a man's voice, but couldn't make out the words.

"Isn't it too early?" And then, "Yeah. Okay. I'm on my way."

He swiped to end the call.

"What's going on?"

"My sister's in labor. She's a month early, but her water broke, and they said the baby is far enough along that it's safe to deliver. Sounds like she's going to have him really soon."

"Wow. That's exciting."

Even though it had sounded like he was going to leave right away, Chase made no immediate attempt to move. So I prodded him.

"Go. I'll take a rain check on tonight. Besides..." I teased. "I didn't have any rope anyway."

"Will you come with me? Keep me company. Meet my new nephew?"

"Sure. I'd like that. Let me quick clean up so Ugly Kitty doesn't polish off the rest of the Chinese food, and we'll go."

Evan, Chase's brother-in-law, had just given us an update and gone back in to his wife. He'd been dressed in blue scrubs and a hat with matching blue paper booties over his shoes.

"How is what he was wearing any different than street clothes?" Chase asked. "He just walked through the hospital and out into the waiting room wearing that outfit. It's not like it's any more sterile than what I'm wearing now."

"You have a point," I said. "Maybe they just make the father wear it so he feels like he's part of the team."

"Maybe. But if I know my sister, Evan's the only teammate she's berating right now while she's in labor."

I shrugged. "That seems fair, if you ask me. He didn't have to walk around carrying a bowling ball for nine months, and doesn't have to suffer through labor. The least he can do is take some abuse."

Chase smiled at me. "Is that so?"

"It is."

We were the only two in the waiting room, so I pulled my legs up and snuggled into him. Chase pulled me closer and wrapped an arm around me.

"You want to berate your husband some day?"

That was a strange question. "Not on a daily basis, I hope."

He chuckled. "I meant in the delivery room. I was asking you if you wanted to have kids some day?"

"Oh." I laughed. "I totally missed that."

"Kinda figured that from your answer."

I thought for a minute before responding. "I never really thought I'd get married, much less have kids. I guess my parents didn't give us the best example. Even before everything happened with Owen, all they did was fight all the time. I remember playing house with my friend Allison when we were in elementary school. She'd pretend to be the mom and be baking a cake in the fake oven, and I'd be the dad and come home and pick a fight. Her mom overheard us play-arguing one day and thought we'd gotten into a real fight. When we told her we were playing house, she asked why we were yelling, and I said because the daddy came home. I remember her just staring at me, not knowing what to say."

Chase squeezed me.

"I started to see things a little clearer as I grew older, realizing not all families were as dysfunctional as mine. But by then, I was already checking under the bed two and three times when I walked in the door. I guess I just couldn't imagine having a family of my own when I was afraid of imaginary things that lurked in my apartment."

"Sounds like what you really need is someone to make you feel safe. The rest will just fall into place."

I pulled my head out from its comfy place in the crook of his shoulder and looked up at him. "You might be right."

If only it were that easy.

It was after five in the morning when a booming voice woke us. Evan looked exhausted, stunned, and out-of-his-mind happy when he announced he had a son. He and Chase exchanged hugs and talked for a few minutes before Evan said he'd better go check on his wife.

"Room 210. I have to get back before she convinces the doctor to give me a vasectomy without anesthesia. But they said she'll probably be in her room within the hour."

Chase headed to the lobby to get us some coffees while I went to the bathroom to wash up. I had some dried drool on my cheek, and my hair looked like a giant rat's nest, even though I'd slept sitting up in one position. Splashing some water on my face, I realized I was about to meet Chase's sister for the first time.

Over the last few days, it felt like our relationship had changed. It wasn't just physical anymore. Chase and I had shared a lot about our lives and the things that made us who we were, and now I was already about to meet some of his family. Things moving this fast would normally scare the crap out of me. Yet I found I was more anxious and excited than nervous.

Anna was the spitting image of Chase—only somehow his rough edges were smoothed out, and his masculinity had been replaced with feminine beauty. I smiled at the way his sister lit up when she saw him.

"You're here?"

He pecked her cheek. "I couldn't listen to you complain about missing it for the next fifty years. Of course I'm here."

Evan slapped Chase on the back. "Come on, walk with me to the nursery. They should be finished cleaning him up by now."

Chase did a quick introduction for Anna and me before leaving the room with his brother-in-law.

"I had a feeling I'd meet you eventually," she said.

I was surprised she knew anything about me—even that I existed.

"Congratulations. I'm sorry if I'm intruding. I wanted to keep Chase company while he waited. I can wait outside and give you some privacy."

"I just had half the hospital staring up my gown. Getting to shut my legs feels like privacy at this point." Her smile was genuine.

I laughed. "Did you pick out a name for your son yet?"

"Sawyer. We're naming him after my Dad. Sawyer Evan."

"That's beautiful."

"Thank you. I'm glad Chase brought you. He talks about you at our weekly dinners. I'll admit, I was curious."

"Curious? Why?"

"He doesn't usually talk about women, doesn't bring them to any family events, and definitely doesn't leave them alone around me."

I smiled. "He's afraid you'll tell all his secrets?"

"Yep. And I better hurry and do it because the nursery is only down the hall."

I thought she was kidding, but then her face turned serious.

"My brother is a great guy—ask him, he'll tell you," she joked. "But the thing is...underneath all that cocky arrogance, I think he's afraid of a relationship."

"Because of Peyton, you mean?"

Anna looked surprised. "You know the whole story?"

"I think so. Can't say I blame him for being nervous about getting close to anyone after what happened. People are afraid for much less than that." *Like me, for example.*

She nodded like we were on the same page. "Just don't let him fool you. He walks around like he's wearing a coat of armor, but the truth is, there're some chinks in that protective shield."

"Maybe that's why we get along so well. My armor has some pretty big bullet holes. But thank you. I'll try to remember mine are just more noticeable than his."

Chase walked in behind Evan, who was wheeling a plastic baby carrier. In the center of the translucent tray lay a tiny bundle swaddled in blue hospital blankets.

"Didn't even have to look at him to know which one was yours," Chase teased his sister. "He was screaming so loud. Kid's got your lungs already."

Her husband gently lifted the baby and placed him in Anna's arms. She cooed to him and then lifted him up so we could see his sweet little face.

"This is your Uncle Chase. I hope you got your brains from him, but your looks from me."

Chase leaned closer. "Considering you look just like me, that's a smart wish."

Anna rocked the baby in her arms when he started to fuss. "Have you talked to Mom and Dad yet? I told Evan not to call since it was so late."

"I haven't. But they wouldn't have been able to get a flight up from Florida until this morning anyway."

We stayed with Anna and Evan another half hour until Anna yawned. She must have been exhausted after being in labor all night. Hell, I was exhausted just from napping in the waiting room.

Traffic was light in the city as we pulled out of the lot around the corner from the hospital. "Your place or mine?"

"That's presumptuous of you," I teased.

"You make me keep my distance at the office during the week. It's Saturday. I figure the weekend is mine."

I thought back to what had transpired yesterday, what we were almost caught doing. "You didn't seem to be keeping your distance yesterday when you had me pinned down face-first on your desk."

He groaned and adjusted himself in his seat. "Your place. It's closer. And now that you just reminded me of how spectacular your ass looked raised in the air, that's the way I'm going to take you the first time when we get home."

It was just a figure of speech, I knew, but I loved the sound of Chase saying *when we get home.*

Although, what I loved even more was what he did when we arrived at my place. Taking the keys from my hand, he unlocked my bevy of locks on the front door and walked inside first. He then completed my ritualistic entry sweep. Twice. In my exact neurotic order, all while holding Tallulah.

After he finished, he kissed my forehead. "Good?"

Nodding, I pushed up on my toes and kissed him on the lips. "Thank you."

"Anytime. By the way, I called the guy who did the security at the office. They're going to install a monitoring system here. I've referred a lot of business his way. He owed me a favor, so he's doing the install free, and the monthly cost will be absorbed into the office bill."

"What? No."

"Too late—it's being installed next week. He's going to get back to me with which day he can get here. I'll need a key to let them in, or you'll need to be here."

"Chase, I don't need an alarm."

"You're right, you don't. But it will make me feel better, especially when I'm traveling and out of town."

"But..."

He lowered his head and silenced me by pressing his lips to mine. "Please. Let me do this. It will make *me* feel better."

I huffed and stared at him. Eventually, I gave. "Fine."

"Thank you."

I dug my extra set of keys out of a drawer for him, told him to relax, and went into the kitchen to make us some omelets for breakfast. We ate in the living room in front of the TV, watching *Good Morning America*, and then snuggled on the couch, him lying behind me. Although we'd slept for a little while at the hospital, both of us had been sitting up in chairs, which wasn't productive sleep at all.

I yawned. "Your sister seems great."

"She's a pain in the ass. But she's good people."

He took a deep breath in and out, and I felt his breathing begin to slow. After only a few minutes, I thought he might have fallen asleep, but then he spoke, his voice groggy. "She's going to make a good mom. So will you someday."

CHAPTER
25

Chase – Seven years ago

I couldn't smile at another person.

"Thank you for coming." I shook another faceless hand. *Next.*

"Yes. She was a beautiful woman." *Next.*

"I'll be okay. Thank you." *Next.*

It just needed to be over.

I was supposed to ride with Peyton's mother and her sisters from the funeral service over to the cemetery, but when the back door of the limousine closed, my lungs suddenly felt deprived of air. I couldn't breathe. *Couldn't fucking breathe.* My chest burned, and I knew I was two seconds away from gasping for air. Flinging the door back open, I gulped fresh breaths before excusing myself with a lie that I needed to escort my parents.

A light, misting rain had just begun, and everyone hurried from the church to their parked cars. Tucking my head down, I walked past the row of waiting stretches without anyone noticing. So I just kept on walking. Four or five blocks later, the mist had turned to pouring rain. I was soaked, yet didn't feel anything. Not a damn thing. Inside and out, I was bone dry.

My judgment wasn't the best, which was probably why I decided to walk into a seedy bar a half-mile in the opposite direction of the cemetery and plant myself on a stool.

"Jack and Coke with an extra shot of Jack on the side."

The old bartender looked me over and nodded. I peeled off my drenched, dark suit jacket and tossed it on the empty chair beside me.

There was only one other person in the bar—an old man who had his head down on the bar and an empty pint glass gripped in his hand.

"What's up with him?" I asked the bartender when he brought my drinks. He looked over his shoulder.

He shrugged. "That's Barney."

He said it like that would explain everything. I nodded and picked up my shot, sucking it back. The liquid singed my throat the same way the air had in the limousine. I slid the empty shot glass back over to the bartender and pointed my eyes down to it with a nod.

He spoke as he poured. "Only ten-thirty in the morning."

My phone started to ring, so I slipped it from my pocket and tossed it on the bar, hitting ignore without even looking at the name of the caller. Picking up the full shot glass, I again tossed back the liquid. It burned less going down the second time. I liked the way it felt.

"Keep 'em coming."

The bartender hesitated. "Got a problem you wanna talk about?"

Looking over at Barney, I shook my head. "I'm Chase."

A big mound of dirt was covered with a green tarp. The tents set up to shelter the mourners were still standing, but the people were long gone. Well, all except one lone man standing by himself. I'd missed the beginning of the graveside service and spent the part I did see standing off in the distance where the taxi had dropped me off. Preferring to say my goodbyes in private, I figured I'd wait for whomever the latecomer was to take off.

The alcohol had slowed my responses, so it took almost a full minute for the face to register when the man turned around. *Chester Morris.* Peyton's goddamned father. I'd never met him myself, only seen him in pictures, yet I was positive it was him—mostly because Peyton looked just like the man. My heart, which had been beating listlessly in my chest, suddenly hammered inside of my rib cage.

How dare he show up here?

This was all his fault.

All his fucking fault.

Without thinking it through, I trudged through the wet grass toward the grave. He was looking down and didn't see me coming.

"She was following a homeless person."

He turned around, having no idea who I was, and hung his head, nodding. "I read it in the paper."

"Do you know why she was following him?" My voice rose. "Why she took it upon herself to try to help every *fucking* homeless person in this city?"

"Who are you?"

I ignored him. "Because after *you* walked out on her mother and sisters, she practically lived in a shelter for years."

I needed someone to blame, and her useless, piece of shit of a father was as good as anyone. In fact, the more I thought about it, the more I realized it wasn't just a drunken thought that had popped into my intoxicated mind. Her father *really was* to blame.

At least he had the decency to look hurt. "That's not fair."

"Really? I think it's more than fair. A man's choices are his own. You think you can just walk away from your family and not be responsible for your own actions? For the consequences left behind in your wake?" I stepped closer, jabbing my finger into his chest as I spoke. "You left them. They ate in a fucking shelter every night. She died trying to help someone who ate in one. That's no fucking coincidence."

His eyes narrowed. "You're that rich fiancé she had, aren't you?"

I didn't give an answer because he didn't deserve one. Disgusted, I shook my head. "Just leave."

He made the sign of the cross, took one last look at me, and started to walk away. Turning back, he stopped. "Where were *you* when she was being attacked? You're so quick to point the finger at me for something that happened twenty years ago. If you're looking for a person to hold accountable, maybe you should look in the mirror."

CHAPTER
26

Reese

Travis was perched at the front desk flirting with the receptionist when I walked in on Monday morning. I'd slept at Chase's last night, and we'd come to the office early together. Well, not actually to the office. We'd gone as far as Starbucks walking side by side. Chase wasn't happy when I made him give me a minute's head start after we picked up our coffee, but I didn't want to stroll in together and raise suspicions. Finding Travis at the front desk, I was glad I'd forced the issue.

"You look especially smoking hot this morning." He fell in step with me, draping his arm around my shoulder. "When are you going to let me take you out to dinner?"

"Never."

Travis and I had become friends. His flirting was over the top but harmless and more of an ongoing joke than anything.

"Come on. Never is a long time."

"You probably shouldn't hold your breath."

He laughed. "Lunch, then?"

"I told you, Travis. I don't date people I work with." Was that even a lie? More like a technicality. I don't work *with* Chase, I work *for* him.

"Ah...read your email." He winked. "You *are* having lunch with me today."

"What are you talking about?"

"We're having a team meeting at noon. Josh is bringing in lunch. So you're having a hot lunch date with me whether you like it or not."

Arriving at my office with Travis still in tow, I flicked on the lights and walked to my desk. "If the entire team is there, it's not really a date, is it, Travis?"

"Maybe not. But I'm going to pretend it's a date. I bet you secretly will, too. I think underneath all that negative vibing you're throwing my way, you're really into me."

I was busy powering up my laptop, so the voice that came next surprised me.

"I believe we have a no fraternization policy." Chase's voice was terse. He stood in the doorway, a full head taller than Travis.

Because of the casual nature of the office, Travis probably assumed Chase was joking. But I saw the tick of Bossman's jaw. There was an element of something else there. Jealousy, maybe?

Whether or not Travis thought Chase was serious, he took the hint to disappear when the boss stepped into my office.

But not before saying, "See you at our lunch date."

Chase raised an eyebrow once it was just the two of us.

Instead of answering, I had a little fun. "I thought you were getting rid of that pesky fraternization policy, Mr. Parker?"

"I'll get rid of it if you let me mark my territory here in the office."

"Mark your territory? Is that like bite marks or a hickey?"

He stalked closer to my desk. "I was thinking more along the lines of you screaming my name while I bury my face in your pussy right there on that desk. But if you'd like a few bite marks, I'm happy to oblige."

Chase inched closer to me. I put a hand to his chest, stopping him. "Keep it right there, Bossman. It's only Monday. We're not starting off our week like we ended it on Friday."

Just at that moment, in my peripheral vision I caught Samantha walking by. Unfortunately, she'd seen us, before I saw her. Stopping in my doorway, she looked at us funny. I pulled my hand away, but we were still standing close. Too close. Chase was in my personal space, and he didn't back up.

Her brows were slightly drawn as she read the unspoken clues. "Morning."

"Hey, Sam," Chase said.

I pulled my chair out and sat, anxious to put some breathing room between us. "Good morning."

She spoke to Chase. "You have some time to chat this morning? I have some things I want to go over with you."

"Calendar is open until afternoon," he told her. Then turned to me with a twinkle in his eye. "Unless you were ready to pick up where we left off on Friday?"

I spoke through a forced smile. "No. Definitely not ready for that."

Chase turned to Sam. "It's your lucky day. I'm all yours, then."

She rolled her eyes. "I'll come by in a half hour." Sam was about to walk away until Chase stopped her.

"Oh! I forgot to text you. Anna had her baby on Saturday."

"She did? Wow. Congratulations. Almost a month early. How is she?"

"She's good."

"A boy, right? Everything good?"

"Yep. Sawyer Evan. Ten fingers and toes and the lungs of his mother."

She smiled warmly. "That's great. I'm happy for them. I'll give her a call next week. Did the Parker genetics dominate as usual? Sawyer looks like you and Anna?"

Chase looked to me for confirmation. "I think he does?"

Considering they were both staring at me, I had no choice but to answer. I wanted to kill Chase for what he'd just revealed.

I nodded. "Yes, he looks exactly like the two of you."

Sam looked back and forth between us and nodded with a measured smile. "I'll let you get settled in. See you in a bit."

As soon as she was out of earshot, I whacked Chase with my notebook. "Are you kidding me?"

"What?" He almost looked like he didn't know what I was talking about.

"You're standing in my office, in my personal space, and just told the vice president of human resources that I went with you to the hospital to see your sister. Why don't you just send out an email to the company announcing that we're sleeping together?"

"I wasn't thinking. Sorry."

"No, you're not. You did that intentionally," I snapped.

He frowned. "I actually didn't. But what's the big deal? Sam and I are friends. She's not going to care."

"It's not about her, Chase. It's about me. *I* care. I don't want people to know because it will make it really uncomfortable for me when we *aren't* seeing each other anymore."

Chase's jaw flexed. He was obviously annoyed. "Wouldn't want to screw up something you're so sure will happen."

"Chase..."

"I'll let you get to work."

The rest of the day I felt like shit. Chase passed by our lunch marketing meeting, eyed Travis sitting next to me through the glass conference room windows, and didn't bother to stop.

By late afternoon, I was unable to focus. After Chase exposed our relationship as something more than boss-employee to Sam this morning, I'd been intentionally hurtful. I knew saying *when* we broke up would piss him off. It had upset him the first time, when I'd said it without realizing.

I tried to put myself in his position. What if he'd said something similar in a different context? How would I feel if I overheard a friend asking him if he wanted to try out a new singles bar and Chase responded, *"I'm seeing someone, but maybe after we break up."* Ooh.

For the past few weeks, I'd been worried about the fallout from something I felt was inevitable, based on my track record. I was afraid to believe that maybe, just maybe, us ending *wasn't* the foregone conclusion to our story.

But I certainly didn't want us to end. Chase had never even hinted that he wanted us to end. Just the opposite, he'd been confident and sure about us since things began— nothing like my previous office romance. So why was I so hell bent on convincing myself it would end badly?

I was staring at the screen on my laptop when the answer came to me. It was so clear that I realized there's a reason *obvious* and *oblivious* are so close in spelling.

I'd been absolutely *oblivious* to not see it sooner.

Because it was *obvious* I was falling in love with Chase.

The thought terrified me, yet acknowledging it also brought new perspective. And I owed Chase both an apology and an adult conversation on the subject of making things public between us. I wasn't sure I was ready for that, but at the very least, we should discuss it rather than going with my one-sided decision stemming from my own insecurities.

Holding a file so it would appear my visit was business-related, I walked over to Chase's office. His secretary was coming out.

"Is Chase gone for the day?"

"No. He just stepped out for a while." She looked at her watch. "He should be back soon, though. Want me to tell him you stopped by?"

"Umm...actually...I'm just going to leave this file and a note for him, if you don't mind?"

"Go right ahead." Smiling, she walked back to her desk where her phone was already ringing. Inside Chase's empty office, I jotted a quick note and was about to walk back out when I changed my mind about my approach.

A half-hour later, I sat in my office responding to an email from Josh when I decided to click on Chase's name. The light that had been red a little while ago— indicating he was not currently online—was now green. My nails clicked away on the keyboard.

To: *Chase Parker*
From: *Reese Annesley*
Subject: *Lost and found*
Do we have one here?
By the way, I'm sorry for being a jerk this morning.

I waited a few minutes until my laptop pinged, notifying me that a new email had arrived.

To: *Reese Annesley*
From: *Chase Parker*
Subject: *Come here*
Not that I'm aware of.
Apology accepted. Took you long enough. Get your ass to my office.

Fidgeting in my seat at just the dominating tone of his email, I typed back.

To: *Chase Parker*
From: *Reese Annesley*
Subject: *You really need one*
Without a lost and found, misplaced items can wind up anywhere.
Your office? Is there something you need from me?

I pictured Chase's chocolaty eyes darkening as he thought about his response.

To: *Reese Annesley*
From: *Chase Parker*
Subject: *What I need*
What did you lose?
I need lots of things from you, starting with your mouth wrapped around my cock.

The sensible side of me should probably have been worried about whether the IT department scanned or read emails. But the part of me that was falling for the boss had lost her senses about a half hour ago. I responded with five words in the subject field.

Check your top left drawer.

My office door was closed, and I half expected it to fly

open once Chase found my underwear in his desk. Instead my email pinged.

To: *Reese Annesley*
From: *Chase Parker*
Subject: *Hard*
They smell incredible. Get. Your. Ass. In here. Now.

I stopped in the bathroom on the way to Chase's office to freshen up. I'd decided he was going to get exactly what he'd said he needed in his office—my mouth wrapped around his gloriously thick cock. Looking in the mirror, I found my cheeks already flushed with anticipation. I gave my hair a good fluff, unbuttoned the top button of my blouse to show a hint of cleavage, lined my lips with Dr. Pepper-flavored Chapstick, and popped a Listerine breath strip in my mouth before heading to the Bossman's office.

Chase was on the phone when I walked in, but he didn't need to say anything to me to reveal what he was thinking. His eyes followed my every step. Even though he didn't move, I felt like prey being hunted.

My nipples hardened. What an extraordinary talent for a man to have—the ability to incite with only a look.

I walked to the concealed control panel and pressed the button to sheath the glass with the electronic blinds. Chase's eyes blazed as he continued his conversation, his voice growing thicker and deeper as the blinds moved across their track, each inch blocking out more of the outside world. When I shut and locked the door, he rushed whoever was on the line off the phone.

Call ended, I took slow, deliberate steps toward his desk, one heel-clad foot in front of the other. Just as I reached the corner, there were two quick raps on the door, and someone attempted to open it.

I looked to Chase. Neither of us said a word, both hoping whoever was on other side of the door would disappear.

"Chase?" Samantha called as she knocked a second time. No such luck.

He dropped his head and groaned before getting up. "Don't move. I'll get rid of her."

That task didn't prove as easy as he'd thought. Chase opened the door, but attempted to block the entrance to his office. That only made Sam more interested in what was inside.

"What are you doing in there?"

"Working."

"Are you alone?"

"None of your business."

She ducked under Chase's arm and saw me inside.

Chase's voice indicated that his patience was wearing thin. "What did you need, Sam?"

"I was going to see if you wanted to grab a bite to eat tonight instead of tomorrow night."

"I have plans tonight."

"With Reese?"

He hesitated, and Sam decided his response for him.

"That's what I thought. I'll join you. How about six?"

Chase grumbled something and let out a frustrated sigh. "Fine."

Shutting the door, he turned back to me, shaking his head. "I'm sorry."

I tried not to look panicked. "She knows. What are we going to say?"

He was suddenly serious as he gazed into my eyes. "You tell me."

CHAPTER 27

Reese

I had no idea what I was going to say if Samantha asked point blank.

We were meeting her at the restaurant, a small Italian place a few blocks from the office that I'd never been to before. Clearly Chase had. The manager, Benito, greeted him by name and showed us to "Chase's special *romantica* table." It was in the back, in a dark corner by a large, rustic brick fireplace.

Chase pulled out my chair.

"I take it you've been here before."

He sat while the busboy set up a third place setting. We were a few minutes early, and Samantha hadn't arrived yet.

"Sam loves this place. Pretty sure Benito thinks we're a couple. She likes to sit by the fireplace."

I was quiet, and I'm certain doubt registered on my face.

Chase sat back in his chair. "She's my friend. And there's not much she can do about it if she doesn't like it anyway."

I frowned. "It's so much easier for you."

He leaned in. "Is that what you think?"

"You're the boss. No one is going to look at you differently or think your ideas were accepted because of who you slept with."

"I get that. I can even understand it. So if you decide you'd rather keep things between us secret, I'll accept that." Chase edged closer. "But don't think this is easy for me. You're the first woman who's been anything more to me than a casual f—"

He caught himself, stopping short of painting the visual he'd been about to throw out. "Anything more than a casual *relationship* in *seven years*. And we're sitting down at a restaurant, about to have dinner with my dead ex-fiancée's best friend, who is also the vice president of human resources for the company I own. A company where I entrust her to write policies such as the *no fucking in the office* policy I want to violate every goddamn time I look at you."

Chase looked away. I stared at him. It had never occurred to me how difficult it would be for him to come clean with Samantha. For me, it was a job and stupid mistakes from my past that formed my fears. For him, it was so much more. He just made everything *seem* so easy to do. *God,* sometimes I was a giant, selfish idiot.

Before I could apologize and clear the air that hung heavy between us, Samantha was at our table. Chase stood until she sat.

"Nice to see you, Reese." Her face was friendly and warm when she greeted me.

"You too."

The waiter quickly appeared to take our drink orders. Samantha glanced at the wine list and asked some questions about their selections. I looked from her to Chase and was caught in his troubled gaze. He looked hurt, angry, and deflated. And I hated that I'd made him feel that way.

Our eyes stayed locked as Samantha finished talking to the waiter, and then she looked between us. "So, what's new with the two of you?"

Making my decision, I extended my hand across the table to her. "Not much, other than Chase and I are a couple."

Sam took our news better than I had expected, and once dinner finished, Chase and I decided to stay at my place that night. When we arrived, I was surprised to find the new alarm system had been installed. Apparently, while I was busy being a vindictive bitch and stewing in my office half the day, Chase had been at my apartment having an added measure of security installed because he wanted to do something to quell my fears. My apology earlier in the day hadn't been enough to make it up to him.

I went into the bathroom to wash up and came out to find Chase sitting in my bed with his back against the headboard. Pulling a knee up, I crawled to him, planting a kiss on his lips. When I moved to pull back, he stopped me by taking my face between his hands.

Looking directly into my eyes, he said, "Thank you."

I knew what he meant, but pretended I didn't. "I haven't even given you anything to be thankful for. *Yet.*"

He smiled but continued with a serious tone. "It means a lot to me that you decided to tell Sam tonight."

"You know. I realized tonight that it wasn't Sam I was afraid to tell, really."

"No?"

I shook my head. "After the dumb mistakes I've made in the past, of course the thought of a relationship with someone at work scares me. But I think what I've really been afraid of was feeling strongly enough about someone to be willing to *purposely* take a risk." I grinned. "I tend to be risk averse, in case you hadn't noticed."

He attempted to conceal his smile. "I hadn't noticed."

"Thank you again for having the alarm installed. It was really sweet of you." I kissed him again. Leaning my forehead against his, I whispered, "We're really doing this, huh? Going to be a couple out in the open with my long-lost, middle school, second-cousin boyfriend who is also the bossman?"

He pushed a lock of hair behind my ear. "That's a mouthful. How about if we just call you my woman?"

"Your woman, huh?"

His gaze roamed over my face. "It's the truth. We've both been fighting it for different reasons. But you've been mine since I saw you in that dark restaurant hallway."

"You mean when you called me a bitch? I don't think that's quite how you won me over. It was a little after that, I'd say."

"Maybe for you. But you were under my skin from the first minute I laid eyes on you. I wanted to know what made you tick."

I cocked my head. "And have you figured that out? What makes me tick?"

He flipped me on my back and braced himself over me. One hand trailed down my side, causing my skin to prickle.

"I'm still learning. Maybe we should play that little game you had me play once before."

"What game?"

"Be watched masturbating or watch someone masturbating?"

"Ah...we're playing Would You Rather?"

Chase answered by rubbing his nose along my neck.

"Are we talking about you I'm watching, or someone else?"

He stiffened and pulled back to look at me.

"Kidding. I was kidding." I pecked his lips. "Watch you. I think I'd actually enjoy that."

His face relaxed somewhat. So I continued the game with a real question. Lightly scratching my nails down his back, I said, "Office memo or PDA?"

His response was quick. "PDA."

"What kind?"

He brushed his lips sweetly against mine. "Like this."

"Mmm...show me again."

"This is fast becoming my favorite game."

"Mine too."

I could spend all day doing this, but there were more pressing *would you rather* questions to attend to.

When our kiss broke, I asked, "Give or receive first?"

He grinned, but I didn't give him a chance to respond. Instead, I lowered my head down his body.

Receive.

CHAPTER
28

Reese

Chase wasn't exactly good at following the script.

The next day we traveled to the office together early, as had become our habit lately. Only this time, after picking up our coffee, we rode the elevator together up to Parker Industries. I was acutely aware of his hand on my back as we exited. Even thought it felt comfortable and natural to have him touching me, doing it in the office felt strange. And it wasn't a monumental gesture, by any means. In fact, this morning we'd discussed that were going to avoid any public displays of affection until after I spoke to Josh. So I was pretty sure Chase wasn't doing it intentionally.

I owed my boss a certain amount of respect and wanted to let him know what was going on before Chase and I completely came out of the closet, so to speak. The plan was that I would talk to Josh this morning, and then Chase and I would go out to lunch together alone. We could be touchy-friendly, in a way more than a typical boss-employee relationship, but there would be no *statement* PDA. Or so I thought.

After I'd settled into my office, Travis found me in the break room making my oatmeal for breakfast.

"Morning, sexy," he flirted.

I opened the microwave, removed my bowl, and stirred the oats. "Hi, Travis."

"When are you going to let me make you breakfast?"

I extended the bowl in his direction. "You want to stir my Quaker Oats?"

"At my place. The morning after. I make a mean eggs over easy."

"I think your pickup lines need some work."

Travis leaned his hip against the counter next to me. "Oh yeah? Tell me what you like. I'll work on my game."

"Well, for starters, we don't like you to assume we want to have sex with you. So opening with a line regarding the morning after is definitely a no-no."

"So what's a good opening line?"

"How about something real? Complimenting something you actually like about the person."

Travis's eyes dropped to my breasts, and he grinned. "I can do that."

I rolled my eyes. "No. Not like that. A compliment of a non-sexual nature."

"That doesn't leave me with many body parts." He looked me up and down, then pushed off the counter and stood tall. "Your toes always match your outfit. I like that."

"Very good. Shows you're paying attention to details and doesn't make you sound like a pervert right off the bat."

"Got it. So I'll leave off that I really want to suck on them."

Of course, Chase walked in right at that moment. From the look on his face, I gathered he'd caught at least the last part of Travis's sentence. "*I really want to suck on them.*"

"Travis..." Chase warned.

Travis raised his hands in surrender. "I know, I know... no fraternization."

Chase grabbed two bottles of water from the refrigerator. "Actually, we're rewriting that policy."

"Really? Have I mentioned how much I love working here?" Travis mused.

Chase's eyes narrowed on Travis as he walked to me, offering a bottle of cold water. I took it, but Chase didn't let go as he spoke to Travis while looking at me.

"If you love working here so much, perhaps you should spend more time working and less time harassing women who are taken."

"Taken? Who's taken?" Travis muttered.

Rather than answer his question, Chase leaned in and kissed me on the lips. With a cheeky grin, he added, "Twelve for lunch good, Buttercup?"

So much for subtlety and avoiding PDAs.

I had thought Sam would be the person who wouldn't take the news well. I wasn't expecting it to be Josh.

"This puts me in a very uncomfortable position, you realize." He looked at me sternly.

"I'm...I'm sorry. I didn't intend for anything to happen between us. In fact, it was the last thing I wanted to happen at my new job. I really like working here. I like working for you."

Josh sighed. "I've been with Parker Industries for five years. I started where you are and worked my way up. Chase is a very intelligent man. I'm sure you know that. He questions everything and has a strong hand in managing this business at every facet. It took me a long time to build a relationship of trust with him—one where he'll rely on my expertise, even if he doesn't necessarily agree with my direction. I won't have you undermine that."

I was completely shocked. "I won't. I *wouldn't*."

He frowned. "I hope not."

We stared at each other awkwardly. "Does Sam know?"

I nodded. "She does."

After a few seconds, Josh nodded hesitantly. "I appreciate you coming to me at least."

"Of course."

He put his reading glasses back on, signaling that our conversation was over. "Why don't you finish compiling the focus group results, and we'll discuss them over lunch. My assistant will order us something in."

There was no way in the world I was going to mention that I already had lunch plans. Plans with *his boss*. I'd be canceling with a certain someone else.

My text letting Chase know things didn't go as well as I expected with Josh went unanswered, as did the follow-up one I sent letting him know I needed to cancel lunch. I could see it had been read, but not even a quick *K* came back in response. I chalked it up to him being busy and dove into compiling the last of the data Josh and I were going to review over lunch.

It was clear that I'd damaged my relationship with my immediate boss, and it was going to take some time to repair. Although we worked together right through lunch and for hours into the afternoon, things between Josh and me felt strained. It was as if he'd put up a wall of professionalism that wasn't there before. I hoped time would chip away at that wall once he realized I had no intention of undermining him in any way.

As we cleaned up the paperwork we'd spread all over the table in his office, Josh said, "Why don't you update the PowerPoint with our final slogans and packaging picks and email it to me." He caught my eye. "I'll forward it on to Chase to take a look at."

I nodded.

Just before I walked out of his office, he added, "I'd like to keep communications through the proper chain of command in the future. I spoke to Chase about it as well this morning."

I nodded again.

Although I thought it unnecessary, I couldn't blame him for feeling the way he did. And I was curious at how his conversation with Chase had gone this morning. Normally, I heard or saw Chase around the office a few times during the day. But his blinds and door had been closed whenever I passed by today. His absence was noticeable, and by the time the end of the day rolled around, it had started to make me feel anxious.

I waited until after the office began to empty out—after Josh, specifically, had left for the day—before making another trip down the boss's hall. Just as I rounded the corner, Chase's door opened, and he walked out with a woman. I'd never seen her in the office before. She was attractive, with blonde hair pulled back in a neat ponytail that worked with her business-casual look. They shook hands, and I assumed it had been some sort of a business meeting...until she put her other hand on top of their joined hands. It was a small, yet intimate gesture. She said something I couldn't hear, and I suddenly felt like I was intruding as I walked up to them, but I couldn't very well back up.

They both looked over at me, realizing in unison that someone else was in the hallway. My heart started to beat a little faster.

"Hi...umm...I thought I'd stop by before I left since I haven't seen you all day."

The woman looked back and forth between the two of us. "I better run anyway. It was good to see you, again."

Chase nodded.

Oddly, I felt even more uncomfortable after the woman left. Yet in my internal battle between uncomfortable and curious, curiosity won out.

"Who was that?" I asked, trying to sound casual.

Instead of answering my question, Chase spoke curtly. "I have a lot of work to get back to."

My uneasiness grew. "Okay. I'll talk to you tomorrow, then? I guess?"

He didn't look at me as he nodded, and I jumped at the sound of his office door slamming behind him. *What the hell is going on?*

I had a sinking feeling in the pit of my stomach that whatever it was, I was about to get hurt.

CHAPTER
29

Reese

Chase didn't show up at work the next day. My uneasiness had worked its way into an overall sinking feeling, and my stomach was upset because I knew something had changed. I had no idea if it had something to do with the woman coming out of Chase's office last night, or maybe with the reaction Josh had had to our couple-status news, but my anxiety over the unknown was killing me.

There had been no response to my text checking in on him either. Even though my phone was set to make a sound whenever a new text arrived, I found myself checking it every two minutes.

I was fast losing the little focus I'd brought with me to work. A tiny voice in my head whispered, *See? This is what you get for having an affair at the office. Don't you ever learn your lesson?*

I tried to ignore it. Toward the end of the day, I stopped by Chase's secretary's desk and attempted to sound casual. "Do you know when the boss will be back?"

"He didn't say. Just received a one-line email saying he wouldn't be in." Her brows drew together, and she shrugged. "Not really like him."

I stayed at the office until after seven. Still not hearing anything from Chase, I picked up the phone and called before I left. Voicemail answered on the first ring. Moving from anxious to worried, I sent another text. The second one never even showed delivered. Whatever was going on, his phone was off, and he didn't want to be reached. I struggled with what to do next.

Show up at his house unannounced? We were in a relationship; it was normal for me to be concerned that I hadn't heard from him, right?

Then again, if he'd wanted to hear from me, I would have spoken to him by now. Unlike him, I was exactly where I was supposed to be. And completely accessible in any number of ways—text, voice, email, office phone. He could certainly reach me.

Unless.

Unless something was wrong.

Oh my God. Something was wrong.

What the hell was I doing sitting in the office?

Practically sprinting to the subway, I hopped on the first train and traveled uptown. I rang the bell, but Chase's brownstone was dark. The mail hadn't been taken in for a day... maybe even two. Not knowing what else to do, I reluctantly went home after a while. First thing in the morning, I'd go see Sam if I still hadn't heard from him.

I tossed and turned the entire night. Eventually, I took a shower and got myself ready even though it was barely five a.m. I'd had my phone on the charger, and when I opened the text string I had with Chase, I noticed my messages from last night had been recently read. Yet there was no response. He must have plugged his phone in somewhere. Possibly home?

My emotions swung back and forth like the pendulum on a grandfather clock. He was obviously somewhere that he could plug in his phone, so he could've called to let me know he was all right. Yet...maybe he wasn't okay. Maybe he needed someone. Maybe that someone was meant to be me.

And so back uptown I went. The sun had just started to rise as I reached Chase's stop. This time, when I reached his brownstone, there was a light on inside. And mail no longer stuck out of the box hanging next to the door.

I ran the bell and waited anxiously. After a few minutes, the door opened. I sucked in a breath and waited for Chase to speak.

But he didn't. Even more heartbreaking, though, was that he also didn't open the door and invite me in. Instead, he stepped outside onto the stoop. Keeping distance between us, he stared off somewhere down the block, no place in particular.

"Chase?" I took a step forward but stopped when I smelled him. Alcohol teemed from his pores. It was then I realized he was wearing the same shirt and slacks he'd been wearing the last time I saw him in the office. They were a crumpled mess now, and his tie was missing, but it was definitely the same clothing.

He still hadn't responded or looked at me.

"Chase? What's going on? Are you okay?"

The silence was painful. It felt like someone had died, and he couldn't say it out loud, couldn't face it.

Oh my God. Has someone died? "Is Anna okay? The baby?"

He closed his eyes. "They're fine."

"What's going on? Where have you been?"

"I needed some time alone."

"Does this have something to do with the woman who was at your office the other night?"

"It has nothing to do with you."

"Then what does it have to do with?" My voice came out high and reedy, and it broke on a whisper. "I don't understand."

For the first time, Chase finally looked my way. When our gazes met, I saw so much in his eyes—hurt, pain, sadness, anger. I gasped. Not so much because it scared me, but because I could feel the pain he was experiencing for whatever reason. My chest tightened, and a knot swelled in my throat, making it difficult to swallow.

Even though his body language was anything but welcoming, I reached out, wanting to offer him comfort. He pulled back as if my touch was fire.

"Chase?"

He shook his head. "I'm sorry."

I furrowed my brow, refusing to understand. "You're sorry? For what? What's going on?"

"You were right. We work together. Nothing should have happened between us."

It felt like someone had backhanded me across the face. "What?"

He looked down at me again, his eyes meeting mine, yet I felt like he still couldn't *see* me. Why did he look so *lost*?

"I hope you'll stay on. Josh thinks very highly of your work."

"Is this a joke? What happened? I don't understand."

Chase's expression went from blank to hurt, and I suddenly wanted to see more of that on his face. I felt used and insignificant. *Ashamed.* And I hated that he'd made me feel like that. It was him who should be ashamed at how he was acting.

He hung his head, not facing me—like a coward. "I'm sorry."

"You're sorry? I don't even understand whatever it is you're sorry for."

"I'm not the right man for you."

I took a step closer, forcing him to look at me. "You know what? You're right. Because the right man for me would have the balls to at least give me the truth. I have no idea what happened, but I don't deserve this."

I saw a flash of something in his eyes, and for a half of a second, it looked like he was going to reach out to me. But he didn't. Instead, he took a full step back, almost as if he needed distance to keep himself from touching me.

I began to turn around—wanting to get the hell out of there so I could disappear with some shred of my dignity intact—but then turned back.

"You know the worst part of this? You were the first person who'd made me feel safe since I was a kid."

CHAPTER
30

Chase – Two days ago

"There's a Detective Balsamo here to see you."

My secretary's face was wary when she came into my office. I had an eleven o'clock meeting I was already running late for after my director of marketing had interrupted my morning to tell me what he thought of my new relationship.

This day was getting better by the fucking minute.

"Can you call R&D and tell them I'm going to need to reschedule?"

"For later today?"

"No. Leave it open as of now."

She nodded. "Should I send the detective in?"

"Give me five minutes, and then she can come on back."

I drew the electronic blinds and opened a text message from Reese canceling our lunch date. Could this day get any shittier?

Perhaps I shouldn't have challenged the powers that be with that question.

Nora Balsamo was the lead detective on Peyton's case. She was early thirties, slim, attractive, with blonde hair that was always pulled back in a ponytail. The first time we met, I'd looked right past her—literally over her head—and asked her captain for a more experienced detective. I never even gave her a chance.

Those early days were definitely not my best. Looking back, I'd wanted everyone around me to pay—especially the cops. I blamed them for not doing more to help Eddie. Early intervention could have changed everything. Today, however, even though Peyton would never be an easy subject to speak of, I was in a better place, more accepting of how the past had shaped who I was today. I was pretty sure my therapist was driving around in a Range Rover from her hours spent making that acceptance happen a few years back.

I stood when Detective Balsamo entered and walked around my desk to greet her. "Nice to see you, Detective."

She smiled. "Is it? I'm pretty sure you've been avoiding me the last two weeks."

I'd forgotten she called bullshit as sport.

I chuckled. "Maybe I was. I'm sure you're a great person, so don't take this the wrong way, but I never look forward to your visits."

She smiled, and I motioned to the seating area near the windows.

"Can I get you something to drink? A bottle of water?"

"I'm good. Thank you." She sat on the couch. "How've you been?"

"Good. Really good, actually."

I took the chair across from her and caught her looking over my shoulder out the window. It was impossible to miss Peyton's giant-sized face still painted on the building across the way. Her eyes returned to me without her asking a question, verbally at least. The woman had a stealth ability to make me offer more than I ever wanted to.

"We're actually in the process of planning a new marketing campaign," I said.

She nodded and kept looking at me pensively. It was probably my own paranoia, but I always felt like I was being observed around cops.

"So, to what do I owe this in-person visit, Detective?"

She took a deep breath. "I have some news about Ms. Morris's investigation."

At first, after Peyton was killed, I'd *needed* to talk about her case. So much so that I'd frequently shown up at the police station to run through things I'd remembered or to demand an update. After I started drinking heavily, those visits became daily and were more like the tirades of an angry person. I didn't sleep, didn't eat, drank alcohol in my Cheerios for breakfast, and often forgot to add the cereal.

Eventually, Detective Balsamo showed up at my house at five in the morning one day, hoping to catch me sober, she'd said, and told me to stop coming down to the station.

I didn't listen to her for a very long time.

When I finally did, she promised if she ever had news about Peyton's case, she'd make sure I was the first to know. This morning was the first time I'd ever heard her say those words.

Detective Balsamo cleared her throat. "Two weeks ago, a woman was assaulted pretty badly. Stab wound to the chest." Our eyes locked. "Happened at a homeless camp uptown."

"The same one?"

"No, it was a different one. Different precinct, too. That's why the detectives who caught the case didn't make the connection at first. The woman was out for a few days, but when she woke up, we found out she was a waitress. Turned out she used to stop at the makeshift camp after her shift and bring the day's leftovers from the place she worked. She was a do-gooder."

"Like Peyton."

She nodded. "When I heard that during our morning briefing, something clicked for some reason. So I had the medical examiner compare photos of the wound from the new case to the ones in Ms. Morris's case file."

"And it was a match?"

"It was. The knife blade had a small nick in it, so it made a pretty distinct mark."

"So these kids are still at it? It's been seven years."

"That was our original assumption. The same gang of kids we've been looking for for seven years was still terrorizing homeless camps, and another bystander victim was caught in the crossfire. But then we got to talk to the victim, and we found out it wasn't a gang of kids that attacked her."

This was what she needed to tell me in person, what was so important she had to show up at my office unannounced. She knew it was something I wanted to hear. Needed to hear. The rage I'd felt for so long after losing Peyton was back and coursing through my veins.

My hand shook, and I clenched my fist to steady it. "Who was it?"

She took a deep breath. "I'm sorry to have to tell you this, Chase. But it was...Eddie."

It had been more than two hours—I'd made the detective go through all of it with me, again and again. I paced back and forth like a caged lion trying to figure out my attack.

Somehow it had been easier to imagine that a group of drug-addicted teenagers from screwed-up homes was responsible for something so violent. The world was a much more fucked-up place when a homeless man people had spent years trying to help was guilty. I didn't want to believe it was true.

"Where is he?" I demanded.

"Who? Eddie? He's in custody."

"I need to see him."

"That's not a good idea. I knew this wasn't going to be easy for you to hear. But I'm hoping that eventually, knowing the case is closed and her killer will be locked away for the rest of his life will help you move on."

But I *had* begun to move on. This...this felt like I was being robbed of light I'd only just begun to see after *years* of walking in a dark place.

I scoffed and then began to laugh maniacally. "Move on. I *was* moving on."

Detective Balsamo's jaw dropped. "I...I didn't know. I'm sorry."

"Why? Why did he want to hurt Peyton?"

She swallowed and looked at her feet. When her eyes raised to meet mine, her voice was small. "He was in love with her. Apparently, when he saw that she'd gotten engaged, it set him off. He's not stable."

"Is he even fit to stand trial?"

"We've had two psychiatrists evaluate him. Both say he's capable of knowing right from wrong. He has obvious mental health issues, but he meets the standard of fit for trial."

"He confessed?"

"Yes. It's not perfect—we need to piece together twelve hours of interrogation with one- and two-word answers. But it should stick."

"And if it doesn't?"

"With the victim's testimony, he's going down for first-degree assault or attempted murder on the waitress. For Ms.

Morris's case, the DA says there's enough physical evidence to put him away without the confession. He was found with the knife on his person, and we interviewed the workers at the shelter. A few had seen him using the pocketknife to cut his food and remembered it. Apparently, it was an antique—a rare officer's edition made of walnut."

Walnut.

I froze. "Did it have initials on it?"

"Why, yes. It did. How did you know?"

I ignored her question, needing my own answered immediately. My heart was beating a thousand miles an hour. It felt like my ribcage was going to crack and explode from the pressure.

Detective Balsamo stared at me, her brows drawn. She'd get her explanation after I got my answer. I *needed* an answer.

"What initials were on it?" I asked.

Seeming to sense my urgency, she reached into her pocket and pulled out her notepad. She flipped through the pages for a while, and I stood completely still. Every muscle in my body had locked.

Eventually, she stopped and pointed to her pad. "The initials were S.E."

CHAPTER
31

Chase – Seven years ago

Twenty-seven stitches in his head. Peyton held Eddie's hand the entire time, even though I wasn't allowed within two feet. Somehow she'd managed to gain access to the no-people zone Eddie surrounded himself with like an invisible shield.

Looking over at her, I guess I shouldn't have been surprised. She was beautiful and soft, sweet and inviting. What man in his right mind would reject her touch?

The ER doc who'd sewed up Eddie's head asked to speak to me outside the exam room.

"He's got a collection of fresh scars on his face and head," he told me as we stepped into the hall. "This one was definitely made with a blade. The jagged skin slice is from a serrated edge. Probably a kitchen knife, if I had to guess. If the slash had been a quarter-inch to the right, he wouldn't have an eye right now."

I looked back into the room. Eddie's stitches ran from his forehead down to his chin. His right eye was swollen shut from the beating he'd taken again last night.

"Eddie doesn't talk much," I explained. "But we think it's a group of teenagers. Apparently it's a game they play. They earn points for damage they cause to homeless people."

"I heard about that on the news. Makes me scared for the future of our society." The doctor shook his head. "Has he gone to the police?"

"Peyton's tried to get him to. And she's gone herself a few times—tried to file reports on his behalf. They don't seem to care."

"Can you get him into a shelter?"

"He goes for meals. That's how Peyton met him. She volunteers at the place he usually eats. But he won't stay the night. When the tables for dinner are all full, he takes his food and eats sitting in the corner, away from the people. Beds in the shelter are too close together for him to handle. Doesn't like people too close."

"He's going to get killed out there if this keeps up. He needs to protect himself at least. He doesn't have any defensive wounds on his hands and arms."

"He's not protecting himself?"

"Doesn't look that way. He's either the aggressor, or he's cowering in the corner while someone kicks him in the head repeatedly."

"He's definitely not the aggressor."

"Then you might want to try to talk to him about defending himself. Or he'll wind up with a cracked skull."

I felt bad for Eddie—I did. But if I was being honest, that wasn't the reason I went down to the shelter the next afternoon. I went for Peyton. Okay, and also for myself. I needed this situation to get better.

There was a construction crew opening up walls to expand my new office space, a photo shoot going on in a makeshift studio in the research lab, and I'd just hired two new employees this morning. Interest in my new products kept the receptionist busy all day long. I was drowning in work, yet here I was—going to talk to a homeless guy about self-defense.

I knew Peyton had an audition and wouldn't be at the shelter. Figuring Eddie would pay better attention to what I had to say without any distractions, I arrived shortly before dinner service started and waited outside. He limped down the block, right on schedule.

"Hey, Eddie. Think we can talk a minute?"

He looked at me but said nothing. This was going to be a real quick conversation with only one of us speaking.

"Come on. Let's grab something to eat before it gets busy inside, and we can talk over dinner."

I let Eddie lead the way to where he wanted to sit. Following dutifully, with my tray in hand, I walked to the far corner of the cafeteria-style dining room. I didn't sit directly across from him, unsure of the proximity he would be comfortable with. Instead, I sat diagonally across, even though there was no one else anywhere in the vicinity.

"Peyton really cares about you," I told him.

Turned out that was a good way to lead in. Eddie made eye contact, something he rarely seemed to do. Since I had his attention, I got down to it.

"She gets really upset when you get hurt. How come you don't protect yourself, Eddie? You can't let these kids keep kicking you and hurting you."

He dug into his food. Apparently, only the mention of Peyton was worthy of his full attention. So I used it.

"Peyton wants you to protect yourself."

Again, that helped him focus on me.

"She wants you to cover your head when they hit you. Or get out of there when they come. Can you do that for her, Eddie?"

He stared at me.

"Do you have anything to protect yourself? You're a big guy. Maybe a piece of metal? A pipe? Something you can keep in your bag to try to scare them away?"

I was caught off guard when he spoke. "Knife."

"Yeah." Eyeing his fresh stitches, I nodded. "They got you good, didn't they?"

"Knife," he repeated.

"That's why you need to protect yourself. The doc said you're not even putting your hands up. Not shielding yourself from a knife."

He repeated himself again. "Knife."

It dawned on me then that he wasn't telling me what happened—he was asking me for help. "You want a knife? Is that what you're telling me?"

Shocked the shit out of me when he laid his arm across the table, palm up. "Knife."

"I don't have a knife for you." I looked down at his hands. They were dirty and scarred. Even they had taken abuse. "Wait. Actually, I do."

Reaching into my front pocket, I took out the small pocketknife I'd been carrying for as long as I could remember. It was an old, walnut-handled Swiss Army knife. I'd bought it at a garage sale when I was about twelve. Etched into the wood were the initials S.E., and there was a small stress crack next to the E that made a perfect X the same size as the initials. The thing was old, and the blade had a chip. Basically, I'd bought it because it said SEX on it...and I was twelve.

Over the years, I'd mostly used it for the bottle opener. I looked at Eddie and then at my knife, hesitating. Something about offering it to him didn't sit right. But it was the least I could do.

He let me place it in the palm of his hand and close it into his fist.

"Be careful. Don't use it for anything but protection. Okay, Eddie?"

He never agreed.

CHAPTER
32

Chase – Now (Two weeks post-Reese)

I'd become Barney.

Remember him? The guy at the bar the morning of Peyton's funeral who was too drunk to raise his head? *"That's Barney,"* the bartender had said when I'd asked about him.

That's Chase.

Me, the sole patron at the bar at ten-fifteen in the morning. Nursing the end of my first Jack and Coke, the hair of the dog that bit me. The bartender was too busy taking in a keg delivery to notice I needed a refill. The Budweiser driver looked around as the bartender signed the invoice. His eyes landing on me, he frowned and then forced a sad smile.

Yeah, that's right. I'm Barney. Fuck you, buddy.

Around four, I was again all by my lonesome. A few old timers had straggled in and staggered out throughout the day. But the day crowd was slim to none. Which suited me fine. Jack was my only choice for company the last two weeks anyway.

Carl, the bartender, attempted to strike up a conversation after returning to the bar with a crate filled with wet glasses from the back. For the past few weeks, all my answers had been curt. I'd thought he would have stopped trying by now.

"Not many early morning folks pay with hundred-dollar bills every day." He dried glasses with a hand towel and stacked them away under the bar.

"I'll bring my piggy bank tomorrow. Pay with change so I fit the part better."

He squinted, looking me over. "You could use a shave and a haircut, if you ask me, but your clothes are pretty nice, too."

"Glad I meet the dress code." I looked around the empty bar. "You should think about getting rid of it. Might drum up some business." I sipped my drink.

Carl shook his head. "Got a good job?"

"Own my own company."

"What are you, some sort of high-falutin, stock-trading-type guy?"

"Not exactly."

"Lawyer?"

"Nope. Got a wife?" I asked.

"Yeah. Mildred. Old bird, but keeps herself in good shape still."

"My company makes pain-free ladies' grooming wax. And some other stuff. Mildred is more my customer than you."

His face scrunched up. "Grooming wax? What the hell is that?"

"Removes hair in places women don't want it. Bikini line, legs..." I took out a wad of cash from my pocket and tossed a hundred on the bar. "Some women like to be bald down below, if you know what I mean."

"Are you pulling my leg?"

For some reason, that question reminded me of Reese and the first night we met, how she'd gone along with my bullshit stories. Suddenly I couldn't sit on this barstool any more.

"Nope." I knocked twice on the bar. "Same time tomorrow?"

"I'll be here."

At home, I was out of Coke, so I reached for a glass, intent on pouring just straight Jack. Then it dawned on me—what the hell do I need the glass for if I'm not mixing shit? I took a healthy swig from the bottle and dropped down on my couch.

The ache in my chest that I could usually dull at the bar returned when my eyes landed on Peyton's guitar. So I took another swig. And stared at the guitar some more.

That...led to another swig.

Maybe two.

Since my eyes were apparently unable to see anything else, I shut them, letting my head loll back on the top of the couch. An image of Reese filled the darkness. She looked so beautiful beneath me, smiling with her big blue irises. So I opened my eyes again and took another gulp from my bottle while staring at the guitar.

As I swallowed, my lids drifted closed again. Reese bending over my desk, looking back at me while she bit her lip nervously and waited for me to take her.

Another swig.

Eventually, I must have passed out. Because I woke to daylight streaming in the window and the sound of my doorbell being pressed over and over again.

The only thing that could have been worse than the two women I found standing on the other side of the door at six a.m. was if my mother had also been with them.

I hesitated, and my sister Anna yelled. "I saw you look through the top of the door, jackass! Open up."

Groaning, I begrudgingly unlocked the door. I attempted to impede their entry after I opened it, but the two of them walked right past me.

"Come on in," I grumbled sarcastically.

Sam's hands were on her hips. Anna handed me a giant cup of coffee.

"Here. You're going to need this."

"Can we do this later in the day?"

"We didn't want to chance you being drunk." Anna leaned in, took a sniff of me, and scrunched up her nose. Waving her hand in front of her face, she said, "Are you still drunk from last night?"

I shook my head, walked back to the living room, and slouched into my couch. My head was pounding, and the last thing I needed to hear was whatever these two had come to say.

They followed me. It was a mistake to sit in the middle. At least if I'd sat near one armrest, I couldn't be the middle of an estrogen sandwich.

Sam started in first. "This crap needs to stop."

"You're fired."

"You'd have to *be* a boss to fire me. Right now you're acting more like a little boy."

"Screw you, Sam."

"Screw you, too."

Anna joined in. "We gave you two weeks. That's all you're getting."

"How are you going to stop me from taking more time off if I want?"

Sam crossed her arms. "We've made a schedule."

"For what?"

"To babysit you. Until you come back to work and rejoin the land of the living, one of us will be following you around."

"I need Motrin." I stood and walked into the kitchen. To my surprise, my shadows didn't follow. Since the kitchen was empty and didn't have two women in it, I drank a few glasses of water and quietly attempted to get my thoughts in order.

My peace didn't last for long. They took seats at the table and stared at me.

Anna started the lecture. "We left things too long when Peyton died. You lost years that you can't get back doing shit like this. We gave you two weeks to grieve your loss again, but that's it. Time's up."

"I'm a grown man."

"So act like one."

"Don't you have a child to take care of?"

"Apparently I have two." Anna stood and walked over to me. My arms were folded across my chest, but she reached out and touched my shoulder. Her voice was quiet. "It's a good thing. They caught the guy. I know you feel betrayed all over again, finding out it was a man she trusted and was trying to help, but it's the closure you needed, Chase. It really is."

If only that were the truth. If they'd caught the teens we'd all thought did it, maybe it would have been. Hell, even finding out it was Eddie—it would have been tough, but I think I could have eventually accepted it.

But discovering that what happened to Peyton was my fault? That I literally gave the killer the knife he used to kill my fiancée? I doubted I would ever get past that.

"I didn't get closure, Anna. You don't know what you're talking about. If you did, you'd leave me alone."

267

"So tell me, then. Tell me what it is that's sending you off the deep end when I thought you were finally happy for the first time in years."

I looked into my sister's eyes. All I saw was raw determination. There was only one way to break it.

"You really want to know?"

"Of course I do. It's why I'm here. I want to help."

I turned around, opened the cabinet where I keep the liquor, and pulled out the first bottle my hand reached. Grabbing three glasses from another cabinet, I lifted my chin toward the kitchen table. "Sit."

Eight hours later, I called a car service to take Anna and Sam home. Neither was functional enough for public transportation. We'd spent the day mourning Peyton all over again, and after they found out about the knife, I believed they finally understood why I needed more time.

"I love you, little bro." My sister wrapped her arms around my waist and squeezed tight.

"Love you, too, you pain in the ass." I kissed the top of her head.

Sam waited on the front steps while Anna clung to me. The last time we'd really hugged like this was before the wake. I made sure the two of them got into the town car and watched it pull away.

Even though I'd been drinking all day, I wasn't really feeling drunk. For a change, I went into the kitchen and started to straighten up after myself. When my bell rang again five minutes later, I was surprised to find Anna and Sam back at my door.

"What did you forget?"

Their arms were hooked, and they didn't attempt to come in.

"Nothing," Sam said. "We just wanted to remind you that we love you and tell you we'll see you tomorrow."

"Tomorrow?"

"What you shared today was horrible. But it didn't change anything. We're not letting you disappear off the grid again and drink yourself into a coma."

My jaw clenched. I knew they meant well, but I really just needed time. "Don't do this to me."

"We're not," Anna said. "We're doing it *for* you. Because we love you."

I stared at them until they said goodbye and started back down the steps.

Sam turned as she reached the bottom. "Oh, and Reese's last day is Friday. She quit. So whatever you screwed up there, fix that shit, too."

CHAPTER
33

Reese

I stared at my screen. It was the first time in more than two weeks that I'd seen or heard a word from Chase, and he'd picked my last day at work to reappear.

Can you come by my office around noon, please?

I read that one stupid line over and over. Each time, I became more and more irate. I'd started my ridiculous mourning over the loss of Chase as soon as he dumped me. Lucky for him, I was stuck at stage two: angry.

Today was my last day. I had nothing left to lose. So I typed back.

Screw you.

It made me feel a lot better. It also made me want to eat. Grabbing my bag from the desk drawer, I slammed it shut and headed to Travis's office. "Still want to take me out to lunch for my last day?"

"Fuck, yeah."

"We're taking Lindsey, too. It's not a date."

He stood. "It's a pre-date. As soon as you see how charming I am outside of the office, you'll give in."

I pretended to want to invite Abbey, Chase's secretary, just so I had an excuse to strut past the boss's office, even though I already knew she wasn't in today. The blinds were wide open as we passed. I was dying to look inside, but I wouldn't give Chase the satisfaction. I wasn't even sure he was in there until Travis and I were almost at Abbey's empty desk, and the bossman's deep voice stopped me in my tracks.

"Reese."

I closed my eyes, dreading turning around. But there was no way I was making a scene. I wouldn't stoop to that level. I'd made my mistake of getting involved with someone from my job *again*, but I'd at least go out with my head held high in front of my peers.

Mustering up all the professionalism I could, I turned. "Yes?"

What I found broke down the wall I'd built around my heart. Chase looked absolutely terrible. His normally tanned skin was sallow, and his face was sunken. He had dark circles under his eyes, and he looked…sad. I had to stop myself from walking back to him—my immediate reaction was to want to offer him comfort. Then I remembered. Where had *he* been to offer me comfort the last few weeks when I was hurting? Still, it went against my nature to kick someone when he was down.

"Can we speak a moment?" He tilted his head toward his office door.

I looked at Travis standing next to me and then back at Chase. "We have plans for lunch. Can it wait until I get back?"

He nodded, looking forlorn. "Sure."

Our eyes locked for a few seconds, and I forced myself to look away. "Ready, Trav?"

Over lunch, the boss's return was the topic of conversation.

Lindsey started with the gossip. "Did you see Chase is back? He looks like he got run over by a freight train."

Travis responded. "He looks like he's sick or something."

I'd told Travis that Chase was just kidding around when he'd kissed me that day in the break room, and we were actually just old friends. He seemed to believe it.

Two weeks ago, an office memo had come out saying Chase would be traveling on unexpected business for an unknown amount of time. He could have just been exhausted from travel, but it looked like more than that to me. Maybe he *was* sick. *Oh God.* The thought made me feel ill.

Throughout the rest of lunch, Travis and Lindsey chatted away, but I couldn't get the picture of Chase out of my head enough to enjoy myself. What if he was sick? Maybe he'd broken things off to spare my feelings. What was it exactly he'd said to me?

"I'm not the right man for you."

It was so vague and detached. Thinking back, it was the ambiguous blow-off that really made our breakup hurt. While I'd fallen hard for him, he hadn't even given me enough consideration to fully explain what had changed. *Because we work together* had seemed like a cop-out right from the start. He'd certainly never accepted it from me.

It had been more than two weeks, but the pain in my chest was back with a vengeance. I tried to shake it off on the way back to the office after lunch, but it was no use. Knowing how I was, how obsessive I could be, I decided I needed to see Chase one last time before I left today. Maybe he'd have the answers I'd been searching for.

The blinds were drawn on his office as I approached. Remembering what had happened the last time I was inside with the blinds concealing us, I considered turning around rather than facing him again. Unfortunately, Chase walked out and caught me in the hall before I could change my path.

Again, I froze.

He stared at me and seemed to know I was struggling. "Please. Just give me a few minutes."

Giving in, I walked past him and into his office. He shut the door behind me and locked it.

"I don't think it's necessary to lock it. *Anymore*."

Chase's voice was quiet. "That's not what I was doing. I just wanted some privacy so we could talk. Sam tends to barge in."

I stood in the middle of his office awkwardly. The thought of settling in and making myself comfortable was terribly distressing. Chase walked to the seating area, rather than to his desk.

When he turned around and realized I was just standing in the middle of his large office, he called to me. "Reese."

"Don't say my name." I have no idea why, but it bugged me. Probably because I liked the way it sounded coming from his mouth, and I didn't want to like anything about him.

He stared at me. "Okay. Would you please come sit for a few minutes? I won't say your name."

Begrudgingly, I sat. It was childish, but I wouldn't look at him. Even when he cleared his throat, I stared at my nails, pretending I was interested in them.

"I don't want you to leave. You're good at your job, and you were happy here."

"*Were* being the key word in that statement. Notice the tense there. It makes all the difference."

"I can't take back what happened between us. I wish I could so I wouldn't have hurt you."

It felt like he'd slapped me. *He wished we'd never happened?*

"Screw you."

273

"What did I say? I was just trying to apologize."

"I don't want your apology. Nor do I want to hear about your *regret* over me."

"I didn't mean it like that."

"Whatever." I waved my hand. "Are we done?"

"I meant I regret hurting you. Not that I regret us being together."

"Are you done?"

He sighed. "Can you look at me? Just for a minute."

I pulled together every ounce of my anger and stared daggers at him. But seeing him look the way he did, I broke within five seconds.

My eyes softened, along with my voice. "Are you sick?"

He shook his head and whispered, "No."

"Then what is it?" I hated the desperation in my voice. Hated that all it took was one pitiful look from him, and I turned soft.

He stared into my eyes for the longest time. There was so much emotion swirling around in his, so much heartbreak and pain. Yet I could have sworn there was something more... the same something I felt for him deep down inside. The man still had my heart, even though it now lay in his hands, broken.

The more he stared, the more I saw inside of him, and the more it grew inside me again.

Hope.

I'd given it up. Yet somehow it found its way back.

Talk to me, Chase. Tell me what's going on.

Hope. It's an amazing thing. It grows inside of you like a vine and wraps around your heart, making it warm.

Until someone stomps on it. Then that vine tightens its hold until the blood can no longer pump through, and your heart quickly dies.

Chase looked away when he finally spoke. "I'm not the man for you." Abruptly, he stood. His voice changed to cold and distant. "But you should stay. I know your job means a lot to you."

Tears were starting to build, and I felt the burn of salt down my nasal passages as I swallowed them back down. I needed to get out of there.

"Go screw yourself." His office door slammed back against the wall in my wake.

Packing up an office I'd settled in to less than two months ago wasn't hard. All of my personal belongings fit in my purse. I made my rounds, saying goodbye to the people I'd become friends with. I'd told everyone another opportunity had come along that I couldn't pass up. Josh had asked questions, and I'd told him I was going to start my own business with someone I used to work with. It was easier to explain than why I was leaving with no job lined up.

I'd almost made it to the lobby door when Sam caught me. "Reese? You have a minute?"

"Ummm...sure."

She motioned for me to step into a conference room and shut the door behind us. "I have a lot of connections. If there's anything I can do to help you find something new..."

I hadn't told her anything different than I'd told everyone else. Yet she seemed to know I wasn't leaving to start my own business. I assumed Chase had said something to her.

"Thank you."

She hesitated, then looked me in the eye. "He cares about you. I know he does."

"He has a funny way of showing it."

"I know. He's just hurting right now."

"Why?"

Sam looked sad. "It's not my place to share. But I thought it was important to let you know. Being with you was the first time I've seen him happy in years. I had hope."

So did I.

"You're a good friend to him," I said. "I know that. And I'm glad he has you if he's hurting. But if he can't even share why he's hurting with me, I can't stick around."

Sam nodded, understanding. She pulled me in for a hug. "I mean it. If you need anything at all, you have my number."

"Thanks, Sam." I swallowed. "Take good care of Chase."

CHAPTER
34

Reese

I finally had a hot date.

At least I thought my brother was handsome. After a week of self-pity for all of my stupid man mistakes, I decided to take the one man I trusted with my love up on his dinner invitation.

We ate in the Village and rode the subway back to my stop. Even though I told him it was completely unnecessary to see me home, he always insisted.

When we came up the stairs from the subway, my phone buzzed in my purse. There were five missed calls, all from an out-of-state number I didn't recognize. Figuring it was a spammy sales solicitation, I ignored it. Until it rang again as we turned the corner onto my block.

My heart began to race as soon as the caller said he was from my security company, and my alarm had been tripped. It was then I noticed a police car parked outside of my building. The alarm company put me on hold and checked in with the police, who said they were upstairs, and it was safe to come up.

Two uniformed officers were talking to my neighbor in the hallway when I stepped out of the elevator.

They turned toward me. "Ms. Annesley?"

"Yes."

"I'm Officer Caruso, and this is Officer Henner. We responded at your alarm company's request since we weren't able to reach you to determine whether things were okay."

"What happened?"

"Seems like it was a false alarm. Your building lost power for a few minutes, and the surge when the backup generator kicked in might have sent a false signal. It's not uncommon. Your apartment is still locked, and there's no sign of breaking and entering."

I felt Owen stiffen next to me when the policeman said *breaking and entering*. His arm had been on my shoulder as the officer spoke, and he pulled me to him, protectively.

I turned to him. "Did you get all that?"

The officer's brow furrowed.

"My brother is deaf," I explained. "He was reading your lips."

Officer Caruso nodded. "If it's all right with you, we'd like to take a look inside and just make sure everything is okay."

They had no idea how all right that was with me. The officer took my keys and asked us to wait outside while they did a search. A few minutes later, they opened the door.

"It's all clear in here. Like we said, it's pretty common for power surges to trip these alarms. We just need to fill out a report and get you to sign it, and we'll be on our way."

"Thank you."

Inside, even though the officers had inspected the place, I still needed to do my own search. While they sat in the kitchen and filled out the report, I discreetly did my usual routine. I was good at concealing it, having concealed it from every date I'd ever brought home. Except for Chase.

I took off my shoes as an excuse to open the hallway closet, then shut myself in the bathroom and ran the water to cover my shower curtain check. Finding all clear in the bedroom, I returned to the living room just as Owen opened the front door.

Chase stood in the hallway, bracing himself against the wall as his chest heaved. He looked at Owen and then found me over his shoulder.

"Chase. What are you doing here?" I asked.

"Is everything okay?" He was really winded.

"Yes. Why? What's going on?"

"The alarm company called. They weren't able to reach you, and I'm listed as your backup contact. I told them to call the police and came as soon as I could get here. Are you sure everything is okay?"

I opened the door wider so he could see the police in the kitchen behind me. "The police inspected, and they think it was a false alarm from a power surge. The building is old and loses power occasionally. There's a backup generator, but it takes a few minutes to kick on, and apparently that can cause a surge and a false alarm."

"Do you want me to double check for you?"

I gave him a reassuring smile, even though I didn't feel very sure of myself at the moment. His presence was making my already racing heart palpitate. "I'm good."

Chase looked at Owen, then back to me. His jaw was rigid. "If you need me, just call."

It would do him good to wonder, so I didn't mention that the man he was eyeing was my brother.

Instead, I said, "We'll be fine. But thank you for coming. I appreciate it."

And just like that, he was gone.

After Owen and the police left, I spent the night tossing and turning, trying to figure out what Chase's appearance tonight had meant. It was nothing. He probably had a sense of obligation because he was listed with the alarm company. He would have done that for anyone, I was sure. Yet...there was no mistaking the jealousy in his eyes when he'd looked at Owen.

He'd wanted an explanation.

I didn't think he deserved one.

Since my mind was whirling and not going to let me go back to sleep, I decided to get my lazy ass out of bed. I hadn't been to the gym in weeks, and the sun was already up anyway.

After a quick cup of coffee, I pulled my hair into a ponytail and threw on some yoga pants and a cropped workout shirt. I grabbed a zip-up sweatshirt from the hall closet before walking out my door.

My eyes darted all over the street before I exited my building. Last night had made me hyperaware of my surroundings. Otherwise I might not have spotted it.

Spotted him.

Sitting on the steps three buildings to my left and across the street was none other than Chase Parker.

He turned his head when he realized I saw him, but I'd know that face anywhere. As soon I started walking toward him, he stood. The air was cold, so I slipped on my sweatshirt as I crossed.

"Chase, what are you doing here?"

"I just wanted to make sure you were okay. I didn't expect you to come out so early."

Noticing his clothes were familiar, I was confused. "Have you...been here all night?"

The look on his face answered for him.

"Why?"

"I figured you'd be nervous. Wanted to make sure you didn't need anything."

My gut reaction was to snap *I'm fine*. But he wasn't wrong, and his actions—no matter how much I disliked him for the way things had ended—were very thoughtful.

So I held back my snark and instead said, "Thank you."

He nodded, and his eyes dropped to my exposed stomach beneath my unzipped sweatshirt. It was brief, but I caught it, and he knew I'd caught him checking me out.

"Your date left right after the cops."

"Is that what you were doing? Spying on me? Because you have no right to—"

"That's not what I was doing. I didn't want you to be alone. I wanted to be close in case you needed someone."

I narrowed my eyes at him and was met with sincerity. "Well, again, thank you."

As much as I wanted to stay, wanted to tell him I *didn't* want to be alone, I wanted him to be with me, I knew I needed to go. I looked down at my feet, trying to think of one reason I should stay. Then I made a last ditch effort.

"Why aren't you the man for me?"

He stared at me and then did what he'd done every time I tried to get the truth. He looked away.

"Have a good day, Chase." I smiled sadly and walked away from him. Yet again.

That night, I was exhausted but still had trouble sleeping. My anxiousness and constant movement had even sent Tallulah off the bed to find elsewhere to sleep. At one point, around two in the morning, I went to make some Chamomile tea and found Ugly Kitty curled up on the windowsill in the kitchen. I lifted her and started to pet her mindlessly while looking outside. I almost dropped her when I saw him. *Same spot.* He hadn't been there earlier when I came in from the grocery store. What the hell was he doing?

I turned off the kitchen light and went to grab my phone. Texting in the dark, I watched to see if he would respond.

Reese: *What are you doing out there?*

Chase reached into his pocket and pulled out his phone. He looked up, right at my window, and I jumped to the side out of view, sucking in a deep breath as if that would keep him from seeing me. I leaned enough so that one eye could see what he was doing. After a minute, his head bowed, and I looked at my phone to find the little dots jumping around.

Chase: *Just keeping my eyes on the place.*

Why does he care? One night after a call from the alarm company and knowing my fear, I could understand. But again? It made no sense.

Reese: *Why?*

I watched as he stared up at the window for a long time before dropping his head down to text.

Chase: *Get some sleep. I'll be here until the sun comes up.*

I went back to my room with my ugly cat and slipped under the covers. I plugged in my phone and turned off the light. After a minute, I flicked the light back on and reached for my phone.

Reese: *Why aren't you the man for me?*

A minute later my phone pinged.

Chase: *Good night, Buttercup.*

I slept like a baby after that. It was after eight the next morning by the time my eyes opened. The first thing I did was go to my window. There was an emptiness in my chest when I found the stairs across the street empty.

But I wouldn't have to wait long for my bodyguard to reappear. He was there the next night when the sun went down. And the night after that, and the night after that, and the night after that.

Each night we'd exchange a text or two. They were even growing friendlier as the days passed. But it always ended the same way...me asking why he wasn't the man for me. And him not giving me an answer.

After a week, I finally decided I needed answers, and if he wasn't going to give them to me, I'd get them somewhere else.

CHAPTER
35

Reese

He cooed up at me with those big chocolaty eyes that both made me melt and broke my heart. Sawyer looked just like his uncle. Well, technically, he looked like his mother. Only his mother was the spitting image of her brother. Needless to say, all three had been blessed by their gene pool.

"He's absolutely gorgeous, Anna."

She scooped baby Sawyer from my arms and positioned him to take a bottle. "He looks just like Chase. Let's hope he gets his uncle's brains and not his attitude."

We'd met at a small Greek restaurant within walking distance from Anna and Evan's apartment. They must have been regulars because the owner took Sawyer from Anna's arms the minute she walked in and smothered him with kisses. The restaurant also sent over a half-dozen plates of food without our even ordering.

I'd debated whether to reach out to Sam or Anna but ultimately decided on Anna. Sam was locked up like a bank vault when it came to Chase. Between working for him and being Peyton's best friend, her loyalty ran deep. That's not to say Anna wasn't extremely loyal to Chase. However, I had a feeling she'd do what she thought was best for him, no matter what—even if it meant telling a story he might not have wanted to be told.

"I hope you don't mind my looking you up and calling."

"Mind? Call me every day. I love this little guy, but I'm starting to talk in baby talk even to adults. I could use an excuse to get out more often, to make me get out of my sweats and wash my hair before eight at night."

We made small talk for a while, about the baby, plans for the fall, and even some of the products Parker Industries was working on. I thought I'd have to uncomfortably bring up what I wanted to ask, but Anna beat me to it.

"Can I ask you something personal?" she said.

"Of course."

"Did my brother do something to upset you? That's why you're not together anymore?"

"Yes, actually."

"I figured. What did the idiot do?"

I deadpanned, "He broke up with me."

She seemed genuinely shocked. "Why?"

"I have no idea. That's part of the reason I wanted to talk to you. He broke up with me, and yet he's sitting and guarding my apartment every night."

Anna scrunched up her face. "What is he doing?"

I gave her the full story, although even as I told it aloud for the first time, it sounded like parts were missing. Which made me even more certain several parts were... Big parts.

When I finished, the baby had just fallen asleep, and Anna gently set him down in the stroller. I was surprised to see tears in her eyes when she sat back down in her seat.

"It all makes sense now."

"What does?"

Big drops slid down her cheeks, staining her face. "He

feels like he failed to keep Peyton safe, and your biggest concern is safety. He doesn't feel worthy, but can't let go."

The gates opened wide after that. Anna filled me in on everything I'd been missing, from Detective Balsamo to Chase's walnut knife, and all about Eddie in between. By the time she was done, we were both full-on crying. My heart broke for Chase. It was bad enough to have lost someone he loved, but to find out it was his knife—a knife he'd voluntarily given the man who killed her—made him feel like he'd been the cause of Peyton's death. Like he hadn't protected her. *Oh God*.

Anna and I walked with our arms linked as she pushed the carriage back to her apartment.

"Do you want to come in? Have a glass of wine?" she asked.

"I'd love to. But another day, maybe?"

She nodded. "I'm going to hold you to that."

"You won't have to. I'm going to keep in touch whatever happens."

We hugged each other like long-lost friends.

"What are you going to do?" she asked.

"I don't know. I need to give it some thought. It's so much to take in right now."

"I understand."

"Could you...do me a favor? When you talk to your brother, don't let him know you told me? I'm still holding out hope that he'll tell me himself. I think I've just been going about it the wrong way to get him to open up."

"Of course. I hope everything works out for you two. I really do."

"Thank you, Anna. For everything."

I walked away finally understanding why Chase *thought*

he wasn't the man for me. Now I just needed him to realize *he was.*

Chase arrived at nine that night. I wondered if he was even going to work anymore. He was spending all night guarding my apartment building. He couldn't possibly be working all day.

I left him out there for an hour while I got things ready and then went downstairs without warning.

When I approached him, he stood. "Everything okay?"

"I...just wasn't having a good night. Mind if I join you for a while?" I held up the plate I carried. "I made cookies."

He searched my face, clearly unsure what I was up to. Finding sincerity—I *was* having a bad night—he nodded. "Of course."

Our conversation was slow at first, neither of us knowing what to say. I asked him about work, and he asked me about job prospects. I gave some vague responses about considering my options, and eventually, I brought the subject around to what I'd come out to share. There was a lull in the conversation, and I took a deep breath and exhaled audibly.

"I don't know if I locked the door."

"Tonight?"

I shook my head. "No. When our apartment was broken into. The key was on a long, red ribbon I liked to wear around my neck. I was the last one out, and I was supposed to lock the door. But I can't remember if I did. That's why I always check it three times before I leave."

"You were a kid."

"I know. And the neighborhood had a dozen break-ins in the weeks leading up to ours. Some had no signs of forced entry. Others had windows and doors broken. It probably wouldn't have mattered either way. They still would've been inside when we came home. The police said if they wanted to get in, they'd have gotten in one way or another." I shrugged. "But tonight I was trying to remember if I'd locked it again. I used to replay that day over and over in my head, trying to remember."

Chase put his arm around me and squeezed. "What can I do?"

"Nothing. Just talking to you made me feel better, actually."

His grip around me tightened. "Come on down anytime. I'm here between sundown and sunup."

I heard the smile in his voice, and I turned, wanting to see it. I'd missed it so much. For a brief second, the way he looked at me, I could see that everything he felt for me was still there. He'd just buried it so damn deep, I could only catch distant glimpses of it before it was out of reach again.

Figuring I'd pushed as much for one night as I probably should, I forced myself to get up. "I'm going to head to bed. Thanks for listening, Chase."

"Anytime."

"I'll leave you the plate. I figure cops get free donuts, the least I could do was give my bodyguard some cookies."

I started on my way and then turned back. I was so thrilled to catch his eyes on my ass, I almost forgot what I wanted to say.

"Why aren't you the man for me, Chase?"

Some day, I'd get him to tell me. Today just wasn't that day.

We went on that way for another week. I'd bring him a snack, and we'd sit and talk for an hour or two on the steps of some random apartment building across the street from my place. Each morning when I woke, the plate I'd left behind was sitting outside my apartment door.

While it was great for my sleep—I'd never slept better, knowing someone was watching over me like a hawk—I began to think he'd never come around. Chase seemed content with our newfound friendship. Me, not so much. So I decided to push a little harder.

It was a misty night, and I'd made him cupcakes. I went outside to offer him his daily snack. He was wearing a windbreaker with a hood, and the craziness of him sitting outside in the rain provided the perfect opportunity.

I opened my golf-sized umbrella and held it over us as I sat on the wet steps.

"Hey."

"It's gross out here tonight," I said.

"Had to happen eventually. We've had good weather the last few weeks."

An unseasonably warm breeze caught the smell of his cologne and reminded me of our nights together. His chest would glisten with sweat, and the cologne he'd put on that morning would rise to the surface. I wanted to lean in and take a deep breath. But I couldn't. It was frustrating as hell.

Losing my patience, my invitation came out differently than I'd planned. "Just come inside," I blurted. "You don't need to sit out here all night."

It seemed like my suggestion was completely unexpected. Chase just stared at me. Could he really be that blind? Did he think we would just go on forever with him sitting across from my apartment all night and me delivering baked goods?

When he still hadn't answered, I repeated myself. "Come inside. This is silly. It's raining out, and I have a perfectly dry apartment just footsteps away. You can stand guard from the couch all night, if you want. Just come inside."

The nice, friendly face I'd come to expect for my nightly visits transformed, replaced by the stony and distant face he'd used when he dumped me. I knew what was coming next, and I wasn't accepting it anymore.

"I don't think that's a good idea, Reese."

I stood. "Well, I do."

"Things between us are good. I don't want to give you the wrong idea."

He couldn't really believe that crap, could he?

"Things between us are good? What are we even, Chase? Tell me."

His jaw flexed. "We're friends."

I could see him shutting down, and I didn't care. My emotions had been all over the place lately, and I needed an outlet. Unfortunately, the outlet was going to be Chase tonight.

"I don't want to be friends!" I yelled. "We were never friends."

I hadn't come out planning to give him an ultimatum tonight, but somehow I was there.

It was time.

"I can't give you anything more, Reese. I told you that."

"Maybe. But your words and actions vastly contradict each other, and I've always been taught to believe what people show you, not what they tell you."

Chase raked his fingers through his wet hair. "You want something I can't give you."

"What I want is *you*. That's it. I don't need someone outside to guard me and be my friend. I need someone to *be* with me."

"I can't."

"Can't or won't?"

"Is there a difference? They both wind up with the same result."

"Is this really what you want? You're going to sit out here night after night? What happens when I start bringing home men I plan to fuck?" I could see the anger brewing in his eyes, and I thought maybe it would break him. "How will that work, exactly? Will you shake hands and ask him what time he'll be done with me so you can take a break from your post?"

"Stop it, Reese."

I was beyond frustrated that I couldn't get through to him.

"You know what? I will stop it. Because I'm done. You don't want me, that's fine. But don't say I didn't warn you. Stick around here much longer, and I'll be bringing home a man to stay for the night." I leaned in closer and nailed my point home. "I'll leave the window open so you can listen."

CHAPTER
36

Chase

Even stalkers eventually settled into a routine.

After Reese left her apartment in the mornings, I'd go for a run. It was four miles back to my place, and I usually sprinted half of it, fueled by the frustration of watching her walk away each morning.

The late-night snacks had stopped a week ago. She didn't even look in my direction anymore. I suppose I should have been grateful she was *only* giving me the cold shoulder. Her threat had been all I could think about lately. What the hell would I do if I watched her walk into her building with another man, and he didn't come back out? The thought made me run faster.

How long would it take?

Fuck.

It wouldn't take long.

Even though I normally ran the same route across town, today I didn't. It wasn't a conscious choice; my feet just led the way while my mind was busy with thoughts of Reese.

When I hit Amsterdam Avenue, I realized how far off course I was. And where my subconscious had taken me. *Little East Open Kitchen.*

The shelter where Peyton had volunteered.

Where Eddie had eaten every day.

I hadn't been down this block in almost seven years.

I stared at the window for a long time, my eyes dropping below it to the empty spot where we'd frequently found Eddie sitting. The place had aged, but not much had changed.

I hated the sight of it. It made me angry and brought back that feeling of helplessness I'd had when I'd gotten that last phone call from Peyton. Powerless and weak. It made *me* feel like a victim.

Yet I wandered inside, unsure what I was looking for. It was early, and the place was practically empty. Only a couple and their two children were eating breakfast. A few volunteers kept busy going back and forth, carrying metal trays of food out from the kitchen and dropping them into their spots on the assembly line.

Looking around, I had no clue what the hell I was doing inside. Then the framed pictures on the wall caught my eye. When the interior was redecorated all those years ago, each volunteer had donated a poster of an inspirational quote. Peyton never did get to show me hers. I walked around the room, reading some of them.

You don't need to climb the whole staircase. Just take the first step.

You have two hands—one to help yourself and one to help others.

The next one got me thinking.

If you don't change direction, you may end up where you're heading.

Where the hell *was* I heading? Thanks to Frick and Frack, I wasn't sitting in a bar anymore from dawn to dusk. Instead I was sitting outside a woman's apartment from dusk to dawn. I owned a successful company that I hadn't been to in weeks, and I'd lost a woman who was the best thing that had happened to me in years. Maybe *lost* wasn't exactly the right word. *Given up,* unfortunately, was more like it.

My anger was heavily laced with regret. I hated that I felt so undeserving of everything I had, and that because of it I'd sabotaged the things that meant the most to me. But I had no idea how to change what I felt. Right or wrong, the emotions were real.

"I stare at that one every morning when I get in." Nelson, the shelter manager, slapped me on the back as he came to stand next to me. "How you been, Chase?"

"Hanging in there." *By a thread.* "You?"

"Not too bad. Not too bad. I'm so sorry, man. Some crazy shit, cops finding out after all this time that it was Eddie, huh?"

I tensed but somehow managed to nod.

"Unfortunately, a lot of our patrons have mental health issues." He pointed his chin toward the family finishing off their breakfast. "Families down on their luck because someone lost a job are a small part of our service these days. Every day we see more and more people who should be getting mental health treatment. But even when they do, they get spit out after a few days of observation because insurance won't pay for more or they don't have insurance in the first place."

"How's anyone supposed to feel safe in here?"

"In here is where it *is* safe. It's when they walk outside these walls that they can't manage the things going on in their head. We lose a dozen knives and a half-dozen forks every week. Makes me wonder what they're doing with them on the street."

I stared at him. He couldn't possibly know the knife Eddie used had come from me. Detective Balsamo came to me *after* she'd interviewed the shelter workers. Plus, if there was one thing I knew about her, she didn't give out anything that wasn't necessary for people to know.

"Nelson!" a man called from the kitchen.

"Gotta finish up breakfast. Good to see you, Chase. Don't be a stranger."

He slapped me on the back and began to walk away. Turning back, he called to me. "Have a framed picture of Peyton in the back. Think I'm going to hang it there next to her quote."

He lifted his chin in the direction of the framed poster in front of me. Peyton's was the last in the line of inspirational quotes, the only one I hadn't read.

Don't focus on the what ifs. Focus on what is.

That afternoon, I felt like a stranger showing up at my own office—like I should've called ahead to let people know I was coming, even though I own the company and have no one but myself to answer to. At first, people were hesitant to approach me, which worked to my benefit since I really had no desire to make idle small talk.

The pile of messages and emails I found would take a week to return. I specifically left the blinds drawn to attract as little attention as possible while I worked, but, of course, that didn't stop Sam. The woman was a bloodhound with my scent in her nose.

"You look like shit."

She should have seen me before I showered and shaved a little while ago.

"Nice to see you, Sam."

"Are you back for good?"

"I'm working on something at night. I'm not sure how much I'll be in."

"Oh? A new product?"

Years of dating had taught me the art of avoidance when being pinned down. "Have you found someone for the vacant IT director position yet?"

"I have a few candidates. But I've been busy…trying to fill an open *marketing position*."

She could open the door all she wanted. I wasn't walking in. Not today.

"Good. Glad to hear it. Not paying you to sit on your ass all day."

"I can't believe I'm going to say this, but I like obnoxious, sober Chase better than drunk, nice Chase."

We talked for another ten minutes. Sam filled me in on some personnel stuff and rates she was negotiating with a new insurance carrier. When my phone buzzed on my desk, I caught the time. I was going to be late to Reese's if I didn't get moving. Surprising me, Sam took the hint when I started to shut down my computer and pack up some files. I'd assumed she was going to take another run at my personal life.

"Well, I'll let you go."

"Thanks, Sam. I'm kind of in a rush to get out of here."

She took a few steps toward the door and then turned back. "Oh. One other thing."

Here it comes. "What's that?"

"Pink Cosmetics wants a reference on a former employee. They asked to speak to you personally. John Boothe from Canning and Canning is the VP now. Remember him?"

"I do. Good guy. Sure, I'll give him a call."

"I'll text you the number."

"Thanks. They're in Chicago, right?"

"Yes. Downtown."

"Who left New York and relocated to Chicago?"

"No one...*yet*."

We locked eyes. Mine asked the question, even though I already knew the answer.

That night, I sat on the steps across the street from Reese's apartment. The warm sun from a late Indian summer day was gone, but the heat was still oppressive. It was humid, hot as hell, and my heart was beating rapidly. Before today, I'd been wallowing in self-pity and guilt, but ever since Sam told me Reese was considering leaving New York for a job, a new emotion had taken over: *fear*.

I hated it. I'd considered stopping at the liquor store on the way here to soothe my anxiety. But there was no way I was drinking on the job. Even if it was my own insane mission I'd created, and Reese didn't want me here anymore.

It was about an hour into my shift when a man who looked familiar approached her building and went inside. It took a minute for me to place where I knew him from. My fists balled when I remembered he was the guy who'd been in her apartment the night the alarm went off.

A second date.

I knew how my second dates always ended.

Fuck.

Fuck.

Fuck.

Fifteen minutes later, the two of them emerged from the building. Reese wore a halter-top dress with a little sweater over it and high-heeled sandals. Her hair was down, and the humidity made it fuller and sexier. She'd never looked more beautiful. Stopping as they reached the sidewalk, Reese lifted her hand and fanned her face. It was hot as hell. The ache in my chest grew almost unbearable when she slipped the tiny sweater off, revealing a healthy amount of cleavage and an almost completely open back.

Beads of sweat dripped from my brow as I watched it all play out in front of me. I was in my own private hell. He stood behind her and took the sweater from her arms. My heart thudded away, and it was all I could do to not run over and tell him to get his fucking hands off of her. Yet I sat and did nothing but grind a layer of enamel off my teeth.

I have no right to stop her from doing anything anymore. Although it felt like he was touching something of mine. Something I very much had rights to.

Watching them walk down the street, I stayed frozen on the step until they reached the corner. Then I grumbled a string of curses and got up to follow them. *New duties added to my security detail.* Apparently I was taking this stalking shit pretty damn seriously.

I walked on the other side of the street for four blocks, keeping a safe distance behind them as I focused on their body language. They walked closely, like two people who had a certain comfort level with each other, yet they didn't hold hands or touch. When they strolled into a small Italian restaurant, I thought I'd have to wait around for an hour or two before the continuation of the show. Lucky for me, the hostess sat them right in front of the picture window.

After a few minutes, I wasn't sure if it was a blessing or a curse that I would have to watch them all night. Regardless, I found myself a doorway diagonally across the street. It concealed me but still allowed for comfortable viewing.

They ordered wine and appetizers, and it looked like there was no shortage of conversation. Each time Reese laughed, I felt happy seeing her beautiful smile. Then a crushing feeling would slam down on that momentary joy when I remembered it wasn't me who'd put that smile on her face.

At one point, I watched in slow motion as her date reached out and touched her face. His hand cupped her cheek in an intimate gesture, and for a second, I thought he might lean across the table and kiss her.

Fuck, I can't take it anymore.

I had to look away.

My head fell into my hands, and I struggled to figure out how I was going to move on from this. How could I let her walk out of my life? I needed to break free from her.

I'd been trying for weeks, yet something kept holding me back.

Suddenly it hit me.

It was my heart.

She was already inside my damn heart.

I could physically walk away from her, but she was already inside of me. Distance wouldn't change that. She'd be in my heart, even if she wasn't in my life.

How could it all be so clear when five minutes ago I couldn't see any of it?

It had to be the threat of losing her. Up until now, I hadn't actually believed she would move on. But seeing it with my own eyes was a wake-up call.

Now it was a matter of what I was going to do about it.

What if we were together and something happened to her? What if *I* wasn't there to protect her? What if I failed her? Failed us? What if...she left me someday like Peyton had?

I wished I had the answers. Wished I knew how things would turn out.

My mind raced for the longest time, going back and forth between all the reasons I should beg her to take me back to all the reasons I should let her go.

What if I failed her?

What if she needed someone stronger than me?

What if...she was already starting to move on?

I looked up just as Reese threw her head back in laughter at something the asshole sitting across from her had said. As I closed my eyes in physical pain, something from earlier in the day flashed in my memory—the framed quote Peyton had chosen to hang up at the shelter. For seven years I hadn't been inside Little East Open Kitchen. Why today, of all days, did I decide to wander in there? It had to be a sign.

Well, it *was* a sign in the literal sense. Now I just had to understand its figurative meaning.

Don't focus on the what ifs. Focus on what is.

CHAPTER
37

I'd pushed him too far.

Seeing the empty steps across the street when I turned the corner, sadness washed over me. My heart lumped in my throat, leaving my chest to feel hollow. Last week I'd given Chase an ultimatum and threatened to move on without him. I'd hoped planting the visual of my sleeping with another man might jolt him. If he really cared about me, felt a fraction of what I felt for him, there's no way that wouldn't affect him.

When another week went by and he still sat across the street with no sign of coming back to me, I thought perhaps reality might set in if he saw me go out on a date in person. Which is why when Owen asked me out to dinner and a movie again tonight, I saw it as the perfect opportunity. Chase had no idea the tall, handsome thirty year old was my brother.

Unfortunately, my plan seemed to have backfired. My guard was gone.

For the entire walk down my street, I couldn't stop staring at the steps. When he was there, I had hope. Now vacant, that light of hope had been extinguished. The stairs were a metaphor for how I felt—empty.

The thought of going back to my apartment, sleeping in

the bed where we'd spent nights making love, made me dread going home.

I looped my arm through my brother's as we walked the rest of the way. He was still wearing his Access glasses from the movie we'd gone to after dinner. When the IMAX theater started to show movies that could be enjoyed by the deaf with special closed-captioned glasses that projected the dialogue from the movie ten feet in front of the wearer, I had to buy him his own pair. The spectacles looked like a cross between typical plastic 3-D movie glasses and old-school BluBlockers. Yet no one looked twice as we walked down the street at midnight in New York.

I didn't bother to tell Owen it wasn't necessary to walk me up. He'd always done it, and he'd cover the interior inspection for me, too. Chase was the only other person who'd figured out it was so important to me and insisted on handling it. I sighed audibly in the elevator at the thought. Tonight was not going to be easy. It felt like losing Chase all over again now that he was gone.

I exited the elevator with heavy footsteps and Owen close behind me. But I froze as soon as I turned toward my door, leaving my brother to walk right into me.

The heart that was stuck in my throat slid down to my chest and started beating again. And it seemed to be making up for lost time because it was hammering away.

"Chase?"

He was leaning against the wall next to my apartment door, looking down. When he looked up, I had to take a deep breath to steady myself. Even worn and tired, he was still the most beautiful man I'd ever seen. His eyes were glassy, and I wondered if he was drunk. *Is that what he's here for? Showing up at my apartment only because he's been drinking?*

I'd forgotten Owen was behind me until I felt the hand on my shoulder squeeze. Apparently Chase noticed the man behind me for the first time because I watched his eyes rise over my shoulder and his jaw clench.

"What are you doing here?" I asked. I still hadn't moved, leaving an awkward fifteen feet between us.

"Can we talk?" Chase asked.

"Umm...sure." It took another few seconds before I could figure out how to make my feet move. Then, hesitantly, I took a few steps.

When I reached the door, Chase caught my eye.

"Alone," he clarified.

Reaching into my purse, I took out my keys and offered them to him, tilting my head toward the door. "Go ahead in. Give me a few minutes."

For a second, he glared at Owen, and I thought something ugly was going to happen. But eventually he nodded, unlocked the door, and went inside.

It took a few minutes to assure my big brother that I would be fine. I'd already told him about Chase, but being overprotective, he found it difficult to walk away. I kissed him on the cheek and promised to text him within an hour. Otherwise, he assured me, he'd be back at my door.

When I was finally alone in the hallway, I took some time to gather myself. Eventually, I smoothed my dress, summoned my courage, and walked into my apartment.

Chase was sitting on the couch when I walked in. A creature of habit, I immediately turned to the coat closet and slipped off my sweater, even though I didn't keep it there.

"I already did it. Twice." He offered a smile, but I could see the sadness looming behind it.

God, please don't break my heart. Again.

"Would you like a glass of wine?" I walked to the kitchen to pour myself some. *To the brim. Maybe even drink from the bottle.*

"No, thanks."

I felt his eyes on me as I maneuvered my way through the kitchen. When I was done, I stuttered before choosing a seat. Deciding on the chair, rather than the couch next to Chase, I sat and sipped my wine.

He waited patiently until I gave him my attention. "Come here."

I closed my eyes. There was nowhere I'd rather be than right next to him, but I needed to know what he was here for. What this was.

"Why?" I sipped my wine again so I had an excuse to look away.

"Because I need you near me."

I looked at him. Still debating, still unsure.

"Because I *miss* you. I miss you so goddamn much, Reese."

I had to swallow because tears of happiness were starting to threaten. Yet I was still afraid. There was something he still needed to do. I couldn't allow myself to get sucked back in unless he gave me everything. He was an all-or-nothing for me.

I moved to the couch, and Chase took the wine from my hand, setting it on the table. He wrapped his arms around me and pulled my body close against his. I could barely breathe, he held me so tight. Yet it felt so good to be back in his arms. So right.

"I'm so sorry, Reese. So sorry I hurt you," he mumbled into my hair.

After a long time, he pulled back so we could face each

other. His eyes searched mine, looking for something. Assurance, maybe?

Finding whatever he needed, he cleared his throat and spoke softly. "When I was twelve, I bought an old Swiss Army knife at a garage sale. Carried the thing with me for years." He paused and looked down. Taking my right hand in his, he ran his thumb over my scar repeatedly. When he looked back up at me, there were tears in his eyes. "I gave it to Eddie. The homeless guy Peyton was trying to help." His voice broke. "I thought he could use it to defend himself in an emergency."

The pain in his voice was unbearable. I wanted to do something to soothe him, bring him comfort. But I knew he needed to get it out. It wasn't just a hurdle for *our* relationship; it was a monumental step for *his* healing. And I wanted that more than anything. I squeezed his hand and gave him a small nod.

"All these years, we thought it was a group of teenagers beating up on homeless people who killed Peyton, that she was caught in the crossfire of an attack on Eddie." He took a deep breath in and released it with a whoosh. "It wasn't. It was Eddie who killed her." He looked down and squeezed my hand, then his eyes came back to mine. "With the knife I gave him. It was my knife that killed her."

I might not have been the one cut, but I felt gutted nonetheless. Tears streamed down my face. "I left the door open, and my brother can't hear."

Chase wiped my tears with his thumbs as he took my face in his hands. "It's not your fault."

I looked into his eyes. "It's not yours either."

Hours later, I was physically and emotionally exhausted. Once the cork had come out of the bottle, Chase completely opened up. We talked more about Peyton and Eddie, and I told him details of the night Owen and I had walked in on our home being robbed. I admitted things to him that I'd barely even admitted to myself—how the guilt had affected me, and how I'd gone through bouts of depression growing up. It was important for him to know he wasn't alone, and I didn't expect him to heal overnight.

I'd just gone to the bathroom, answered a concerned FaceConnect video call from my brother—whom I'd forgotten to text—and come back to sit on the couch. Before my ass hit the pillow, Chase grabbed me and pulled me into his lap. The smile on his face was beautiful and real.

He pressed his lips together, then leaned his forehead against mine. "Would you really have gone to Chicago?"

"Chicago? For what?"

"Pink Cosmetics. The job you applied for?"

I furrowed my brow. "I have no idea what you're talking about. I didn't apply for a job with Pink. Actually, I haven't applied anywhere. I have money saved and decided to take a little time off before making any career decisions. I'm kicking around starting my own small marketing firm with my friend Jules, who you met. We talked about it last year before I left Fresh Look, and I wasn't ready. But it sort of feels right now." I paused. "What made you think I was going to move to Chicago?"

"They called for a reference."

"That's odd."

Chase closed his eyes and chuckled, shaking his head. "Sam."

"Sam?"

"I never actually spoke to them. Sam told me they'd called for a reference as I was getting ready to leave the other day."

"I don't understand."

"She was lighting a fire under my ass. Knew it would push me to get over my issues."

"Oooh...and here I thought it was my hot date that pushed you over the edge."

"I almost lost it at the Italian place, watching him put his hands all over your face."

My eyes widened. "You followed me?"

"Just tonight. I was going crazy watching you go out with that guy again. Do you remember what you told me last week before you stopped speaking to me?"

Of course I do. "What?"

"That you were going to bring some guy home and open the window so I could listen." He swatted my ass playfully. "You have a cruel streak in you, Buttercup."

I started to crack up and quickly found myself lifted into the air and then flat on my back. Chase hovered over me, grabbing my hands and pinning them above my head. "You think this is funny?"

"I do, actually."

He rubbed his nose against mine and whispered, "You wouldn't really have slept with him, would you?"

"Most definitely not. But that has nothing to do with you."

Chase pulled his head back and pouted. It was adorable. "It's not because you're so into me, you couldn't possibly touch another man?"

"Well, that's true in general. But my date tonight was my brother, Owen."

Chase dropped his head and laughed. "Are you serious?"

"I am. What you saw in the Italian restaurant? Him touching my face? I was humming a song to him."

"Well, then I guess I had nothing to worry about after all," Chase whispered against my lips. "Although you never know. You're about to get fucked by your favorite cousin."

"Oh, am I?"

Chase's normal cocky confidence had been back, but it suddenly faltered.

"Can you forgive me?" he asked. "I promise not to push you away again and to do everything in my power to protect you."

"There's only one thing I need you to guard for me."

"Name it."

"You have my heart. Promise me you'll keep it safe."

"Only if you promise never to give mine back."

My heart had been beating his name since that first night at the restaurant. He'd never have to worry about me giving his heart back, because I'd realized that somewhere down deep, it was mine to keep—even when he hadn't figured it out yet.

"Make love to me, Chase."

He reached back with one hand and tugged his shirt over his head. "I'm going to, but not now. I promise, slow and sweet making love to you later. Showing you how I feel with my body. But right now, all this talk about you leaving me and being with another man has me feeling territorial."

He raised up on his knees and looked down at me. The way his eyes raked over my body was really all the foreplay I needed.

"I want to come inside of you. Can I do that, Reese?"

I swallowed. "Yes, I'm on the pill."

"Good. I don't want anything between us anymore. Not our pasts, our secrets, or even a damn piece of latex."

"Okay."

He trailed his knuckles down the side of my body over my dress, following my curves languidly. "First I'm going to bury my face in that pussy that I've missed so much until you come all over my face."

He reached the bare skin of my thighs, and his hand disappeared under the skirt of my dress. I gasped when I felt him cup me between the legs.

"Then I'm going to fuck you hard and fast, bury myself so deep inside of you, that my come won't come out for days."

He lifted the skirt of my dress, pushed my panties to the side, and ran two fingers down the length of me. He groaned. "So wet."

I watched him as he stared, mesmerized as one finger slipped inside of me. After a few strokes, he added a second finger and pumped harder and faster. I nearly came when he licked his lips.

"I can't take it anymore."

When his fingers left me, and he brought them to his mouth, licking and sucking, my body began to hum. "Chase..."

Suddenly, he lowered himself, and his mouth was on me. Guiding my legs over his shoulders, he lifted my ass to position me where he wanted. I moaned when he flattened his tongue and licked his way up to my clit. When he sucked hard and nearly made me finish—even though we'd barely started—I wriggled around, trying to move him from that spot.

Chase gripped my thighs, holding me in place as he devoured me, taking me at his own pace, alternating between his tongue inside of me and sucking hard on my clit. My orgasm hit so hard, I saw nothing but black as it washed over me.

By the time my vision cleared, Chase was back on his knees as he undid his pants. His cock was so swollen, it bulged against the material, making it difficult to pull down the zipper. It was my turn to lick my lips.

He buried his head in my neck and began to suck hard on the sensitive skin below my ear, mimicking what he'd just done to my clit.

"I'm going to apologize now because this isn't going to be easy," he said. "I have no restraint left when it comes to you."

"Do it. I want it that way. All I've ever wanted was you. As is."

Chase didn't have to be asked twice. He aligned his incredibly swollen head with my opening and covered my mouth with his as he pushed himself inside. Kissing me like I was the air he needed to breathe, he seated himself deep inside of me. I could feel his body shake as he waited for my muscles to relax around him. Then he began to move. Really move—pulling almost all the way out and slamming back in, over and over again.

My nails dug into his back as my body greedily clenched down around him. Each time he withdrew made me want him more and more, until my body was begging for climax.

"Fuck, Reese." He pulled back enough to look at me. "I want to fill your body with my come. Every part of you. Your pussy, your mouth, your ass. I want to own it all."

I was helpless as pleasure crashed through me. I heard myself calling his name, but it was more like an out-of-body experience as I throbbed all around him. Distantly, I heard Chase grumble a string of curses as he sank into me deep. Then I felt his amazing body shudder as he released.

Later, my head rested on his chest while I listened to his heartbeat. He stroked my hair as we lay content and sated.

"I really am sorry for the last few weeks," he said. "I acted like a total asshole."

I looked up at him, resting my chin on my hand above his heart. "You did. But it's okay. I forgive you. Well, you'll be making it up to me for a long time. But my heart has already absolved your sins."

I was joking, of course, but Chase responded seriously. "Thank you."

I yawned. "So it was good, old-fashioned jealousy that made you come to your senses, huh? If I'd known that, I would've taken Owen out on a hot date weeks ago and saved us both a headache."

"Actually, seeing you with another man might have pushed me over the edge, but it was something else that made me realize what you meant to me."

"Oh? What was that?"

"It was a poster. It said *Don't focus on the what ifs. Focus on what is.*"

"Meaning focus on what you have and not what could have been?"

He nodded. "Exactly."

I dropped a kiss directly over his heart, nervous to ask the question, but needing to know the answer. "What *do* we have, Chase?"

He pulled me up so we were eye to eye. "Everything."

EPILOGUE

Reese – Nearly one year later

I wondered if he knew what today was.

Chase didn't see me immediately when he walked into the restaurant. I was seated in the corner of the bar, partially concealed by a couple sitting at a pub table. I stole the moment to appreciate the beauty of the man without him knowing I was looking. *My man.* I didn't think I'd ever get used to how incredibly handsome he was.

You know how after a while even the most amazing things become familiar and you start to forget that the sight once took your breath away? Shiny things lose their luster in our eyes even though they still sparkle? Yeah, well, that never happened to me with Chase Parker. Even after a year to the day, he still took my breath away and sparkled every moment.

I watched as his sharp eyes scanned the room. For a second, I considered shifting in my seat to hide, just so I could take more time to appreciate him properly. My soon-to-be-live-in boyfriend was the epitome of tall, dark, and handsome. He was well aware of it, too. His cocky, self-assured attitude only added to the list of things that made him attractive. Factor in wealthy, brilliant, and exceptional in bed (not to mention in his office, in the car, on the kitchen floor, on top of the washing machine, and most recently on the conference room table in my new office space), and it was no wonder the hostess was currently frothing at the mouth as she vied for his attention.

Finding me across the room, his gorgeous face softened, and he gave me the sexy, dimpled smile I knew was only for me. He strode across the restaurant, completely zoned in on his intended target. Goosebumps littered my arms as I watched his determined face. Reaching me, he said nothing, instead greeting me the way he frequently did when we went more than a day without seeing each other. Winding my hair around his hand, he gave it a soft tug and took my mouth in a deep kiss that wasn't really appropriate for a restaurant bar, although that would never stop him.

I was still lightheaded when he pulled away and spoke in a strained voice. "Next time, I'm going with you."

"You could have come this time. I told you that."

"You also told me you would be gone two days, not five."

I'd just returned from California this afternoon. Jules and I had expected to be in San Diego for two nights to pitch a new client. But after we signed that new account, the VP of marketing offered to get us an appointment with a sister company in Los Angeles, so our two-day trip wound up being a full five.

"I can't help it if people want us."

"People want you right here. The line forms behind me."

The bartender came by to take our drink order just as an older couple walked up next to us.

"Are these seats taken?" the man asked.

There were two seats open next to me at the bar.

Chase answered, "All yours. I'm going to stand so I keep close to her anyway."

The older woman gave him a smile that said he'd just melted her heart a little. I knew, because I wore the same one.

She took the seat to my left and her husband sat beside her. "I'm Opal, and this is my husband, Henry."

"Nice to meet you. I'm Reese. This is Chase."

"Today is our fortieth wedding anniversary."

"Wow. Congratulations. Forty years. That's pretty amazing," I said.

"How long have you two been married?"

"Oh, we're not—"

Chase interrupted. "Married anywhere as long as you. But today is our anniversary as well. Five years of wedded bliss."

I looked at him incredulously, although I'm not sure why I was surprised. I knew of his penchant for stories, and today *was* our anniversary of sorts. One year ago today we'd sat in this restaurant together. Only the last time, my date had been Martin Ward and Chase had been the date crasher. It seemed like a lifetime ago. Just as I'd done that fateful night, I propped my elbows, folded my hands, and rested my chin atop them.

"Yes. Five years ago today. You should tell them the story of how you proposed, sweetheart. It's a really good one." I smiled sweetly and batted my eyelashes.

Of course, Chase being Chase, he wasn't at all freaked out that I'd just put him in the hot seat. Instead, he looked pleased that I was playing along.

He stood behind me and squeezed my shoulders. "Mrs. Parker is sentimental, so I took her to the place we first met for dinner. I had been planning to propose to her for a while, but she was busy with her new company, so the right time never presented itself. We'd just found out that she was pregnant, and I decided right time or not, I was going to pop the question."

My mouth hung open. Not because he was weaving yet another crazy tall tale, but because he couldn't possibly know the irony of the story he was telling. The afternoon before I'd left for California, I *had* found out I was pregnant. I just hadn't had a chance to tell him yet, and here he was making it up as part of his crazy story. I decided I had to add to his tale. It would be fun later when he found out that *my* addition to his story wasn't fiction like his. Taking his hand, I brought it to my stomach. "We're actually expecting another child now."

Chase smiled, pleased I was playing along, and rubbed my tummy as he continued. "Anyway. When we first got together, she made us keep it a secret because I was her boss. I'm a little territorial when it comes to the Mrs., and that never sat right with me. But then she went and quit on me—that's a whole other story—and started her own successful company, so I figured it was okay to make a public statement. While she wasn't paying attention, I had all of our friends and family slip into the restaurant. You see, back then, before the first two kids came, she was still googly-eyed over me. People could come and go, and she didn't notice most of the time when we were together."

Opal smiled. "I don't think that's changed. I see the way she's looking at you right now. Your wife is still pretty smitten."

Chase looked at me. "I'm one hell of a lucky guy."

"So you proposed in front of all your friends and family in the restaurant where you had your first date? That's beautiful." Opal said. "Henry wasn't quite as romantic. He was about to get on the bus to go for his second tour in the army, and he asked me if I wanted to get hitched. Didn't even have a ring."

"Considering it's been forty years, I'm thinking it all worked out pretty well anyway." I looked up at Chase. "It's not the proposal that's important. It's the man you spend the next forty years with. I would've been happy with any proposal from this crazy man."

Chase grumbled, "Now you tell me."

The hostess came to tell Opal and Henry their table was ready and said ours would be just a few more minutes.

"It was nice meeting you, Opal, Henry," I told them. "I hope you have a great anniversary."

"You too, dear."

After they disappeared, Chase kissed me again.

"I missed you," he groaned into my mouth.

"I missed you, too."

"You should come back and work for me. I like having you in the office every day."

"You like having me on your desk, you mean."

"That, too. But the place isn't the same without you."

"I saw your new billboard on my way over. It came out great."

A week after we got back together, Chase had painted over the existing Parker Industries ad that had been on the building across the street from his office for years. We'd never spoken about him changing it, but I knew it was monumental that he'd gotten rid of an ad featuring Peyton. This week, while I was away, an image from his new ad campaign had finally been put up over it.

Although I wasn't the one who'd created the final ad, I'd been part of the ground-floor brainstorming on that campaign, and it warmed me to know a piece of me was up there now where he could see it from his office. He was truly moving on.

That's why when we were cleaning out his place to make room for some of my stuff, and I noticed Peyton's guitar had been packed away, I'd insisted he keep it out. She was part of his life, part of the man he was today. I didn't want to replace those memories. I wanted to make new ones with him, be part of the dreams that freed him from the nightmares.

Eventually, the hostess came and told us our table was ready, and we followed her back to the dining room.

"Is this the right table?" she asked as we arrived at the same spot where we'd been seated a year ago tonight.

Chase looked to me. "It is. Right, Buttercup?"

I was touched he actually remembered. "You know it was exactly a year ago we sat here, right?"

"I do."

He pulled out my chair before taking his seat. We both sat exactly where we had on that first night.

"Do you remember which table I was sitting at before I moved to yours?" Chase asked.

"I do." My eyes searched across the restaurant, and I pointed, remembering that night. "You and your *date* were sitting right over..." I squinted, sure my eyes were playing tricks on me. "Right over—wait...is that? Oh my God. Is that, is that *Owen*?"

My brother smiled, held up a champagne glass, and tilted it in my direction with a nod.

Chase didn't turn around. "It is."

There was no surprise at all in his voice. I looked to him, confused.

He smiled mischievously. "See anyone else you know?"

For the first time, I looked around the room, and it was as if all the faces suddenly came into focus. There were my parents to the left. Chase's sister, Anna, and her family to the right. In fact, the entire restaurant was filled with our family and friends.

My old boss, Josh, and his new wife, Elizabeth.

My best friend and business partner, Jules, and her boyfriend, Christian.

Travis, Lindsey, the entire Parker Industries marketing department.

Chase leaned in and whispered, "It really is my Aunt Opal and Uncle Henry's anniversary. That part was just a coincidence."

I was confused as hell.

Why was everyone here?

And why was everyone smiling and staring at me?

My mind was a muddled mess. I couldn't even add two plus two and see that everyone was there *four* me.

Until...

Chase stood.

The restaurant, which had been a loud rumble, suddenly quieted.

Everything after that happened in slow motion. All of our family and friends faded away as the man I love got down on one knee. I heard and saw nothing but him.

"I had this whole thing to say planned out in my head, but the minute I saw your face, I completely forgot every word. So I'm just going to wing it here. Reese Elizabeth Annesley, since the first time I laid eyes on you on that bus in middle school, I've been crazy about you."

I smiled and shook my head. "You got the crazy part right."

Chase took my hand, and it was then I noticed his was shaking. My cocky, always-confident bossman was nervous.

If it was possible, I fell a little more in love with him in that moment. I squeezed his hand, offering reassurance, and he steadied. That's what we did for each other. I was the balance to his unsteadiness. He was the courage to my fear.

He continued. "Maybe it wasn't a school bus or middle school, but I fell hard for you in the hall, that much I'm sure of. From the moment I saw your beautiful face light up that dark hallway a year ago, I was done. I didn't even care that we were both on dates with other people, I just needed to be closer to you any way I could. Since then, you've distracted me every day whether you're near me or not. You brought me back to life, and there's nothing I want to do more than build that life with you. I want to be the man to look under your bed every night and wake up next to you in it every morning. You've changed me. When I'm with you, I'm myself, only a better version, because you make want to be a better man. I want to spend the rest of my life with you, and I want it to start yesterday. So, please tell me you'll be my wife because I've already been waiting for you my entire life, and I don't want to wait any more."

I pressed my forehead to his as tears streamed down my face. "You know I'm going to be even crazier once we live together, and probably even worse when we have our own family. Three locks might turn to seven, and doing my check in that big house of yours is going to take a long time. It might get old and tiring. I don't know if I'll ever be able to change any of that."

Chase reached behind me and bunched my hair into his hand, cupping it along with the nape of my neck.

"I don't want you to change. Not any of it. I love everything about you. There's not a single thing I'd change if I could. Well, except your last name."

Dear Readers,

Want an exclusive sneak peek at my next release, co-written with the amazing Penelope Ward? Just click to sign up for our mailing list, and you'll receive back an EXCLUSIVE look at Playboy Pilot.

Read Chapter 1 of Playboy Pilot *right now!*

http://www.subscribepage.com/i1a4m5

ACKNOWLEDGEMENTS

The true list of people I should thank for helping to release this book might actually be longer than the book itself! First and foremost, thank you to the readers—your continued support and excitement for my books never ceases to amaze me. As an avid reader myself, I recognize there are many, many choices, and I'm flattered that you chose me amongst the sea of wonderful authors.

To Penelope – Even though we spend half of every day chatting away, I don't say thank you nearly enough. Thank you for...well...everything! You're my sounding board, advice columnist, grammar queen, human diary, business partner, and beautiful friend. Thank you a million times — I'm sure I owe you that many by now.

To Julie – Thank you for your friendship and support. Who else would I run crazy business ideas by?

To Luna – For keeping Vi's Violets active with your beautiful teasers and excitement. Your enthusiasm is contagious, and your friendship and loyalty are a gift.

To Sommer – You've absolutely outdone yourself with the *Bossman* cover. I love it and all the stunning teasers. I don't know how we will ever top this one!

To my agent, Kimberly Brower – For always thinking outside the box. You create new ways to help an author grow and are never afraid to challenge tradition and forge your own way.

To Lisa – For organizing the release tour and all of your support.

To Elaine and Jessica – For making my New York laden grammar appropriate for publishing.

To all of the incredible bloggers that help me every day – Thank you for taking time to read my books, write reviews, share teasers, and help spread your love of reading! I am humbled by all of your support. Thank you! Thank you! Thank you!

Much love
Vi